# THE BODY IN THE CATACOMBS

---

## A RITCHIE AND FITZ SCI-FI MURDER MYSTERY

### KATE MACLEOD

# 1

MURDINA RITCHIE RESISTED the urge to bounce on her toes like an eager child as she and her fellow cadet Antoinette Moreau waited in line to order what she knew was the finest beverage in the universe. The dark roasted, almost smoky aroma from whatever it was that wasn't quite coffee was thick in the air all around the little café tucked off the intersection of the two main concourses of Intergalactic Transport Depot Delta-Gamma-Delta. Now that they were closer to where the magic happened, the sugary smell of caramel was a more prominent undertone.

Her mouth was watering already.

Surely Moreau could smell it too, but to judge from her face all she felt was boredom. But Ritchie was no longer fooled by her buddy's seeming lack of interest in anything around her. She knew it was a just façade.

"We're next," Ritchie said, when the two of them took a step closer to the counter. Completely unnecessarily; it wasn't like Moreau's family were so wealthy she didn't know what queues were.

"I had no idea there were shchupals in this part of the Union of Free Worlds," Moreau said.

"Shchupals?" Ritchie repeated. She was pleased to note that while she had never heard the word before, her tongue didn't trip her up when she said it aloud.

"Those are shchupals," Moreau said, pointing discreetly with her chin to the two creatures behind the counter. Their large, round bodies brought to mind certain slow, ruminating species that subsisted on grasses, always ponderously chewing and not moving more than necessary. Their legs, too, were thick and sturdy, built to stand in one place all day without discomfort.

But coming out of those round bodies was an array of slender, boneless tentacles. It was with these tentacles that they carried out the elaborate preparations of mixing a variety of hot drinks, the most famous of which was colloquially known as the uber coffee bomb. Those tentacles turned handles on machines, poured foamy cream from cute little pitchers, and even dribbled elaborate shapes on the top of that cream by dripping streams of caramel from the ends of spoons.

And they did all that at great speed, so many tentacles waving through the air, never tangling, even reaching around the other large, never moving body on its trunk-like feet to grab this or that. The juxtaposition was so extreme Ritchie wondered if what she was looking at was really just one creature, or two creatures in a tightly interconnected symbiotic system.

"Well, this is one of the larger depots," Moreau went on. "I suppose you get all sorts here."

Then it was their turn. Ritchie carefully spoke the words "uber coffee bomb" and touched the picture on the display between her and the shchupal. The shchupal nodded and most of its tentacles got to work on her order, while the one closest to her gestured to the credit meter. Ritchie pressed her thumb against it and watched almost her entire savings disappear in an instant.

It was going to be so worth it, though.

"The same for me," Moreau said as Ritchie moved down to the end of the counter to take her already waiting drink. This time she had gotten the order right, not in a bulb for travel through freefall like last time but in a cup. A cup so large she would call it a bowl, except it was clearly resting on a matching saucer. She picked it up and carried it carefully to an open booth close to the flow of traffic up and down the concourse and sat down. She leaned over it, feeling the steam on her face and inhaling the scent deeply. But she didn't taste it yet. She wanted to see Moreau sample hers first.

Moreau sat down across from her with an entire tray. She had her own drink in its bowl-and-saucer, but also a couple of plates holding heaps of golden fried pastries. She leaned over her own drink and breathed in the aroma with the smallest of smiles. Then she said a word that Ritchie was positive she could never pronounce.

"What's that?" Ritchie asked.

"It's how you say this drink in the native language of the shchupals," she said. "I haven't had one in forever, though."

"Oh," Ritchie said, trying desperately not to let her disappointment show. "Of course you've had this before."

Moreau gave her a look. As usual, it was hard to tell what her look meant, and Ritchie couldn't work up the energy to try to figure it out. She just took a sip of her uber coffee bomb, or whatever Moreau had called it.

The rich creaminess melted over her tongue, and then the caffeine quickly followed. It was still the best thing she'd ever tasted. But of course she hadn't been to so very many places in the Union of Free Worlds.

"Wow," Moreau said appreciatively. "Who'd have thought? I've had this prepared for me by some of the finest shchupal baristas in the universe, but they had nothing on what these two running a café off a transport depot concourse have got going."

Ritchie took another sip without speaking. She wasn't sure if Moreau was messing with her or not.

Moreau watched her for a minute, then took another drink of her own. Then she pushed one of the plates of pastries towards Ritchie.

"What's this?" Ritchie asked, curious despite herself.

"It's traditional to dunk these," Moreau said, picking one up and demonstrating with her own drink. "There's a trick to timing it just right. You want to soak up as much as you can, but not so much that it just dissolves. They have a savory spiciness to them that really complements the rich sweetness of the uber coffee bomb. Try it."

Ritchie took one of the pastries and followed Moreau's example.

She must have timed it too short, since when she bit into hers it was still so brittle and crunchy that it shattered, raining bits down onto her cup and saucer. She tried to name what she was tasting, but just as what the shchupals brewed wasn't exactly coffee, what was in the pastries wasn't exactly cinnamon or cloves or ginger. Or... was that caraway?

"Good, right?" Moreau said as she took another bite of hers.

"Good," Ritchie agreed, and dunked her pastry again, letting it soak just a bit longer.

"Thanks, Ritchie. This was a great idea," Moreau said. "We're not going to get food like this on the train, let alone at the academy." She sighed dreamily, then took another bite.

Ritchie found the food at the academy quite a bit better than anything she ever got at home. But there were other things she would miss while at the academy.

"I'm going to miss being warm enough," Ritchie said, stretching out her arms as if she could soak up the atmosphere and bring it with her. "I always thought planets were supposed to be warmer and nicer than space stations."

"Most planets are," Moreau said. "Oymyakon is definitely an outlier. I've enjoyed two whole months of never getting wet."

"I know, right?" Ritchie agreed. "My feet in particular really appreciate staying dry when I run."

"Ugh, you've been *running*?" Moreau said. "I've enjoyed my vacation from that as well."

They lingered as long as they could over their pastries and coffee, but all too soon it was time to pick up their bags and continue on down the concourse to where their train was about to board.

Until the two of them had met an hour before, Ritchie had been the only person she'd seen in a cadet's uniform. Now, as they made their way through the foot traffic, she spied more and more cadet uniforms in the crowd around her. Most of them were in other school colors, but a few were in the earthy browns of the Oymyakon Foreign Service Academy.

Then they reached their boarding area and found themselves in a little sea of brown uniforms.

"I don't see Fitz," Ritchie said, rising up on tiptoe to scan the crowd. Moreau didn't bother doing the same. Even on tiptoes, she was too short to see over most people's shoulders.

"You thought he was going to be on time?" she said. But then someone else must have caught her eye, because the little groan of irritation couldn't have been at the sight of Fitz.

"What?" Ritchie asked, moving closer so that Moreau could speak without being overheard.

"Nothing. I just saw the Berweger twins."

"Who are the Berweger twins?" Ritchie asked, looking around. She guessed they must be tall, if Moreau had seen them in the crowd.

"Finn and Feena Berweger," Moreau said. "Their parents are admirals or something. Although to hear them talk, you'd think that made the two of them crown prince and crown princess."

"There are no monarchies in the Union of Free Worlds," Ritchie said with a frown.

"Maybe you can explain that to them," Moreau said.

"So, wait. You're telling me the two of them are insufferably elitist? When hanging out with you and your... non-cadet friends?" Ritchie said, searching for the most diplomatic way to put that she could.

"Exactly," Moreau said. "If you want to call the people I hung out with before I came to the academy 'friends', that is. They definitely thought of themselves as the crème de la crème, or whatever. But those two are something else. Well, it's what you said. *Insufferable.*"

"So why are they here?" Ritchie asked. "Are they catching some other train, do you think?"

"No, they're definitely transfers. They are wearing Oymyakon uniforms. I'm not going to point, but if you step up on the edge of the planter, you'll see them for sure. Tall, slender, dark blonde hair, blue eyes. They're obviously not identical twins, but they look like clones of each other."

Ritchie stepped up on the edge of the decorative planter. It was a low, wide ledge about the height of a bench and meant to serve as such. She only stayed up there long enough to get a good look around, then dropped back down to stand next to Moreau.

She had seen a blonde girl and a blonde boy standing and talking together just outside a pair of the train's still-closed doors. They had been engrossed only in each other, ignoring everyone around them. Their hair was already dressed according to regulations, and no adornments dangled from their ears or colored the skin of their faces.

Her first impression had been that no one should look so good in a school uniform. Especially not the exact same uniform she herself was wearing at that very moment.

Her second impression was that she was glad she wasn't seeing them actually dressed to impress. That effect must be almost lethal.

But those impressions were brief, just fleeting thoughts gone before she'd even settled back down on the ground.

Her third impression, however, lingered. She still felt it, like it was seared on her optical nerves. It wasn't a comfortable feeling, but she couldn't shake it.

"Wow," Ritchie said at last. "They don't look human."

"Yep, that's them," Moreau said. "I would say their parents must have tweaked their genetic codes at conception, except their parents are both super gorgeous as well."

"You think they're good looking?" Ritchie asked, hugging her arms as if warding off a sudden chill. "I meant more like inhuman. Like... not right."

Moreau gave her an assessing look. "Seriously?"

"Seriously. Neither of them even looked my way, but they both creeped me out." This time she really did shiver.

"Interesting. But you do have good instincts," Moreau said.

"What do you mean?" Ritchie asked.

Moreau sighed, and her cheeks turned ever so slightly pink. Then she gestured for Ritchie to bend forward so Moreau could speak close to her ear. "I'm not proud of it, but I had a bit of a crush on Finn there for years. You know, from afar. His parents and mine dragged us to the same parties when we were kids."

"All right," Ritchie said, not sure where this was going.

"I was never alone with Finn, and I'm kind of grateful for that now. But I was alone with Finn and Feena once. In a hallway, on my way to one of the bedrooms of a sprawling estate in the midst of an epic house party."

"What happened?" Ritchie asked.

Moreau gave a humorless laugh. "Really? Nothing much. He said something to me, something completely banal, like 'nice party' or 'like your outfit' or whatever. And she didn't say anything that I can remember. But they both looked at me, like really saw me, for just a fraction of a second."

"And then what?" Ritchie asked when Moreau trailed off.

"Then, nothing. But it was in that moment I felt what you just said. There is something not right about the two of them. Anyway, that was the end of my crush."

"I don't think you should read so much into my words," Ritchie said nervously. "I don't know them at all. I wouldn't assume anything much by my first impression based on a brief glimpse. That's just appearances, right?"

"No, I think your instincts are smarter than you are," Moreau said.

"Gee, thanks," Ritchie said.

"You know what I mean," Moreau said with a scoff. "Your instincts just screamed danger at you, but here you are talking yourself around to not listening to and trusting that impulse."

"I think I should at least talk to them first," Ritchie said.

"I'm sure that will come up sooner than either of us would like," Moreau said with a shrug.

"What do you mean?" Ritchie asked.

"There's only one reason I can think of that the highest ranked cadets in the finest academy in the Union of Free Worlds would transfer here," Moreau said.

"To be cadet captains?" Ritchie guessed. Moreau nodded. Ritchie's stomach sank, but a saving thought suddenly struck her. "No, I don't think so."

"Jeger transferred here to be cadet captain, remember?" Moreau said. "And her attitude of turning all of us cadets at the lesser school around? That's not unique to her, I'm sure."

"Jeger jumped at an opportunity she didn't have at the more competitive schools," Ritchie said. "But you just said they were the highest ranked at the very best school. So why wouldn't they be cadet captains there?"

Moreau opened and closed her mouth twice before finally saying, "okay, you might have a point there."

"See? No need to panic," Ritchie said. A bustle of motion moved like a wave through the crowd around them, and she guessed that the doors had finally opened. They were about to board the train.

And there was still no sign of Fitz.

"For the record, I was never panicking," Moreau said as she and Ritchie clutched their bags close and let the crowd jostle them ever closer to the train.

"No, that's not something I imagine you ever do," Ritchie said. She turned to look back, but none of the faces behind her were familiar.

"But I still want to know what they're doing here," Moreau said. "They are definitely in Oymyakon uniforms. But if either of them had done something to warrant such a huge demotion, let alone both of them, I would've definitely heard about it. So why are they here?"

Ritchie didn't answer, but she couldn't deny there was a real gnawing of anxiety starting in her gut. She didn't want to judge people based on their appearance, no matter how foul or how fine.

But she couldn't deny that Moreau had read her mind before. Her instincts had started screaming danger the minute she had seen the two of them standing there, waiting for the train. What had her subconscious mind noticed that the rest of her had not?

And who was likely to find themselves in danger?

2

SHACKLETON FITZ IV paced the center aisle of the seating area of his father's personal shuttle, shoving chip after chip into his mouth. As if eating faster would make the shuttle fly faster.

Well, they weren't so much chips as fritters, thick slices of the starchy root vegetable called kyaw that only grew on the planet Nisi. The vegetable itself had a certain sweetness to it that became more pronounced when fried and was complemented well by the generous coating of salt. He paused to fold down the top of the bag again and shake the contents to redistribute the seasoning before putting another slice in his mouth.

They were almost better cold than they were warm. Almost.

But eating them now, like this, just to pass the nervous time, was almost a crime. He wasn't savoring them at all, and he wouldn't have the like again until some point in his future too distant to be pinned down.

But he really hated that he was going to be late. He glanced at the chronometer in the corner of his vision and groaned aloud before stuffing another chip in his mouth. He was already too late to catch the train at the platform with the other cadets.

"Cadet Fitz?" the pilot called back from the cockpit.

"Yeah," he called back, and started to fold the bag closed before realizing it was empty. He tossed it into the replicator to be recycled, then headed down the narrow hallway past the galley and toilets to the cockpit, dusting the last of the salt from his hands as he walked. He leaned between the pilot and copilot seats and looked out the front window.

The Intergalactic Transport Depot Delta-Gamma-Delta was a main hub, not just in this quadrant of the Union of Free Worlds, but hosting a lot of traffic to and from the other quadrants. It looked a lot like an orrery, like the one his grandfather had in his library, with bulbous globes of various sizes protruding off the main cylinder, spinning around it on the ends of delicate limbs. It even looked a little like brass, especially the central body, which had no external illumination and only glowed softly as it reflected the lights around it.

The globes on their attachments moved at a slow but steady pace, but the lights that shimmered around them were in frantic motion, slowing to match the velocity of one of those globes or accelerating to peel away into the black.

And they were a part of that sea of twinkling lights. Only they didn't seem to be moving closer to any of the globes.

"What's the matter?" Fitz asked. "Aren't we clear to land?"

"We are," the pilot said. He was new, and Fitz had only met him briefly when he had boarded the shuttle. Fitz tried to remember his name. Had it been Riley?

"So?" Fitz asked, making a rolling gesture with his hand.

"The train has already left the depot, cadet," Riley said. "It's on its way to dock with the jump drive ring."

"So we have time," Fitz said, scanning the field of view outside the window for any sign of the jump drive ring. He didn't see it.

"We can take you there directly, you know," Riley said with a glance at his copilot. She said nothing, just sat back in her seat with arms folded, waiting for orders.

"I know you can," Fitz sighed, rubbing at the bridge of his nose tiredly. "Are we late because of my father?"

"He didn't delay us at departure. We left right on time," Riley said, but he sounded like he hadn't gotten Fitz's point.

"I'm saying did he tell you to fly slow?" Fitz asked. Riley opened his mouth to answer, but Fitz held up a hand. "Never mind. Forget I said that. Just... I don't want you to land this thing at the school. I'm not interested in being a spectacle."

*Again*, he added, but only to himself.

"We'd get you there before the train even reached the planet," Riley said.

"I'm sure you would," Fitz said. "But can't you just catch up with the train? I mean, we're here already."

"You want me to dock the shuttle with the train itself?" Riley asked. The copilot put a hand over her mouth to hide her sudden smile.

"It has to slow down to dock with the jump drive ring. We have plenty of time. Assuming you can do it?" Fitz asked. He tried to keep a taunting tone out of his voice, but didn't really succeed.

"We'd need clearance—" Riley started to say.

"You tell them who owns this shuttle and you'll get it," Fitz said. The copilot chuckled. Riley shot her a glare, but she just shrugged.

"Orders are orders," she said. "Besides, you know you want to. I'll plot the course, you call the tower."

Riley bit his lip in indecision, then started speaking low into his headset. Fitz stayed where he was, standing between the two seats, his hands braced on the back of each of them. The shuttle accelerated gently beneath him and a different section of space came into view.

Now he could see the cluster of jump drive rings waiting in an orderly array some distance from the orbiting arms of the transport depot. A single intergalactic train was snaking its way over to one of them.

There were quite a few more cars on there than there had been the last time he had nearly missed this train. But that made sense. Last time he had taken the train to Oymyakon, there had only been three other cadets with him. This time, it was nearly the entire student body, plus whatever few other random people were heading that way.

But there couldn't be many of those. There was nothing whatsoever to recommend Oymyakon, with its near-constant state of hurricanes and storms. Very little grew there. The mountains were neither gentle enough for casual hikers nor challenging enough for sport climbers. The only reason anyone chose to live there was because they were in exile from some other at least modestly better place.

Why anyone had decided to build a foreign service academy there, he still had no idea. Sadism, probably.

Fitz was pretty sure that sadism had been part of his father's decision to bring the family to Nisi for his break between school years. Nisi was a newly discovered world, all beaches of sparkling white sand, indigo skies only occasionally dotted with puffy white clouds, and oceans of vibrant green water. He had spent weeks basking in the hot sun, bathing in the warm waves, and stuffing himself on a variety of culinary items unique to Nisi, of which kyaw had been his far and away favorite.

It was the opposite of Oymyakon in every way possible. Fitz had seen the gleam in his father's eyes when he had said goodbye to his parents and gotten aboard this shuttle back to the academy. His father knew that Fitz was going to find Oymyakon even colder and damper and more miserable than he had before.

But Fitz wasn't bothered. What did the weather matter? Oymyakon was where his friends were. Nisi wasn't.

"We're going to match the train's velocity in twenty seconds," Riley told him. "I'll be docking just aft of the bridge car. You'll have a matter of seconds to make the transfer before they fully engage with the jump drive ring. They won't wait, even for a Shackleton Fitz."

"I'll be ready," Fitz said, and hustled to the back of the shuttle. He seized his bag and slung the strap across his body, then stood by the airlock door that was set in the floor just off the aisle. He got there just in time to grasp the safety bar in the wall and brace himself as the shuttle's directional rockets fired with a bang. There was a jostle, then they were gliding smoothly once more. Another bang sounded as the fore rockets fired, slowing them to match the velocity of the train.

He heard a clang beneath his feet as the shuttle settled onto the roof of the train. By the time Riley shouted back that they had docked, Fitz already had the airlock halfway open, spinning the wheel built into the door with both hands. The copilot jogged back to him in time to hold the door open for him.

"Thanks for the ride," he said to her, then jumped down into the train below.

He landed in the familiar-looking corridor to find two crew members standing on either side of him, just out of the landing zone.

"Five seconds!" one of them called up, but the copilot had already dropped the door closed with a clang.

"Sealed," the other side, consulting a screen on the wall. "And... they're gone."

The first one looked Fitz over, taking in the details of his uniform. His eyes lingered over the top of Fitz's head, and he suspected his dark hair was all disheveled, but resisted the urge to finger-comb it into place.

"Was that really necessary?" he asked Fitz.

"Of course it was," Fitz said. "My father doesn't arrange for such things if they aren't absolutely necessary."

Never mind that his father hadn't actually been on that shuttle.

"All the cabins are aft," the crew member said, pointing out the direction. Completely unnecessarily; the only thing fore of where they were standing was the bridge car, and that was impossible to mistake given the array of instrument panels and screens and the bustle of crew negotiating the docking with the jump ring. "Find where you're supposed to be before we jump."

"Of course. Thanks," Fitz said, then headed aft through the airlock between the bridge car and the first of the VIP cars.

And nearly collided with the steward standing in the corridor of the VIP car, arms filled with fresh linens.

"How did you get up there?" the steward demanded. "All cadets are in traveller class rooms."

"Tell me about it. It's not like I can't afford a VIP sleeper. They just won't let me do it," Fitz said affably. But the steward was clearly not amused. "Say, do you know Tassa Sokolov?"

"I've worked with her before," he said slowly, as if unsure if this was a trick question.

"Is she working this train?"

"No, I'm the only one on VIP duty on this train flight," he said.

"Oh. I was really hoping to see her," Fitz said. He still hadn't thanked her properly for saving his best friend's life.

"You need to move aft," the steward said.

"Of course," Fitz said, and hurried down the corridor and through the next set of airlock doors.

The next car was also a sleeper car. It was not so fancy as the one he had just left, but was nearly as quiet. The doors all stood open, and he could see cadet-issue bags dumped unceremoniously on the floors of all of them, but there was no sign of any cadets.

Fitz retrieved his room number from his implant data and moved through two more uninhabited cars before finding it. Three bags were already in the room, one resting on the top of the folded-down table, one sitting on one of the seats by the window, and a third on the floor but set carefully to one side where it wouldn't be tripped over. Fitz slung his into one of the empty seats. Only then did he finger-comb his hair and tug down his tunic before continuing aft down the train.

The very next car was the café car. The smell of French fries and chocolate sundaes washed over him, as did the excited babble of the dozens of cadets that pressed tightly together in that space. Cadets were packed together in every booth, with more standing in the spaces between.

A head of brown hair arranged in a thick crown braid caught the corner of his eye, but when he turned to look, it was gone, swallowed up in the crowd. But it couldn't have been Tassa. She wasn't working this flight. And even if she were, this room filled with noisy cadets would be the last place she would be.

"Fitz!" someone called. He suspected by the tone in Ritchie's voice that this hadn't been the first time she had said his name. Even then, she had to say it one more time before he finally spotted her and Moreau in a booth together halfway down the train car.

He pushed his way through the crowd that at first hindered him and then spat him out, sending him sprawling onto the bench seat next to Ritchie.

"I thought you'd missed the train," she said as she helped him to sit up and made more room for him beside her.

"Or decided to fly yourself there again," Moreau added.

Fitz held up a single finger. "Hey, now. I didn't decide that the first time."

"Hold that thought," Moreau said, and covered her face with her hands. At first, he was confused. Then he felt the train around them lurch.

They were in jump space.

"Why is she covering her eyes? We can't even see anything from here," Fitz said, looking around to confirm that was true. He could see no windows, shuttered or otherwise.

"Be nice," Ritchie commanded him. "You know she hates this."

"Oh. Crap," Fitz said. Ritchie's brow furrowed in a puzzled look, but he waved her concern away. "It's nothing. It's just that I was bringing something for you, both of you, but I just realized I ate all of it on the shuttle. Sorry."

"That's all right?" Ritchie said, but with an upward inflection, since she clearly had no clue what he was talking about.

"I spent the break on Nisi," he started to explain when Moreau interrupted him with a groan. But at least she took her hands away from her face to look at him. "What?" he asked.

"You were on Nisi?" she asked. "Did you see the Berwegers there, perchance?"

"No," Fitz said. "Why would I see the Berwegers there? Or anywhere else, for that matter."

"They're here," Ritchie said, pitching her voice low. He looked around but saw no sight of them. They would be hard to miss, both because of their golden hair and statuesque height and because they always, always drew a crowd.

"You're serious?" Fitz asked, but didn't need an answer. Ritchie was always serious. And the only reason she would even know who the Berwegers were would be because they were there, on the train with the rest of the cadets. "Wait a minute. Why?"

"That was my question," Moreau said.

"I had others," Ritchie said. He glanced over to her to see she was studying his face. He had the sudden urge to cover his face like Moreau just had. Not that he had anything to hide about the

Berwegers. But as usual, when she looked at him like that, he was sure she could read all his secrets if she just looked deeply enough.

And that was the very last thing he wanted.

"What are we talking about?" a familiar voice said.

Fitz looked up to see his two roommates from the year before standing over their table. Stucki, the friendlier of the two, had spoken, and was even now squeezing in beside Moreau. She scooted around the bend in the booth until she was elbow to elbow with Ritchie, so that both Stucki and the ever-scowling Imhof could fit in the booth.

"The Berwegers, apparently," Fitz said. His feeling like he was behind in the news grew when Imhof rolled his eyes.

"You too? Everyone is talking about them," he said, then took a long pull from the bottle of root beer in his hands.

"I feel like I'm missing all the context," Ritchie said. "Does everyone but me know who these people are?"

"Probably," Stucki said, but not unkindly.

"Fitz?" Ritchie asked, putting her hand on his arm to be sure she had his attention.

A million visions flitted through his mind. Parties he had gone to, some willingly, some less so. Parties where the Berwegers had been there.

Holding court. That was the only way to describe how they behaved at parties. And the court was always slavishly adoring. Like their sweat glands exuded pure pheromones. Even when they were just kids, they had been the center of attention in absolutely every room they entered.

"Fitz?" Ritchie said again.

He really didn't want to tell her about any of that. He didn't actually know what her life had been like on whatever space station her mother had taken her to, but he knew it hadn't been remotely like his life on his parents' palatial estate, on their home world of Buennagel. And he hated anything that exposed that gap between them.

"I suppose they're here to be the new cadet captains," he said lamely.

"Now that I know isn't true," Stucki said. "Blaser and Wyder are the cadet captains. Oymyakon through-and-through, not transfers from another academy. That's confirmed."

"Vilem Blaser?" Ritchie said, clearly remembering when she and Fitz had questioned him the year before, when he had led them down to the catacombs under the school, where his buddy Leodegrance Kung had been hiding while nursing a heartache.

"Yeah, he's a good guy," Imhof said and took another sip of root beer.

"And Milla Wyder," Stucki said. "Don't you know her?"

Ritchie exchanged glances with Moreau, then shook her head.

"Well, she's cool, too," he assured them both. "Her buddy Joosten is a bit intense for my tastes, but Wyder is cool."

"So why are the Berwegers here?" Fitz asked, feeling like he'd missed something somewhere. "If they were being punished for something, I think I'd have heard about that."

"Definitely," Moreau agreed.

But Stucki just shrugged. "What does it matter? They're here now. Among us."

"You say that like you think that's a good thing," Moreau said, her voice as deadpan as ever.

"Isn't it?" he asked, quite sincerely. "I mean, I've never met them. But I've certainly heard of them. And I saw them when they were standing with the rest of us on the platform."

"Most of the rest of us," Imhof said.

But Stucki pressed on as if he hadn't heard. "I would love to get to know her better."

"Not allowed," Moreau said, shaking an admonishing finger at him.

"I didn't mean—" he started to say.

"Yes, you did," she said. He just grinned and shrugged.

They all sat quietly together for a moment, none of them bothered by the lull in the conversation.

Then Stucki reached across the table to punch Fitz in the arm. "You weren't on the platform, roomie."

"No," Fitz admitted, sitting back to move his arms out of reach.

"You're why there was a momentary lag in docking with the jump ring," Imhof guessed.

"Yeah," Fitz admitted, more slowly this time. Leave it to Imhof to notice the train dock a second or two late.

"What happened?" Ritchie asked him.

"I was late," he said, hoping she'd let it go at that.

She might have, but Stucki wasn't about to. "You were late, so what laws of physics were bent to your will to get you here on time?" he asked.

"Don't be stupid," Fitz said, but they were all watching him intently now. He wasn't going to get away with not explaining. "Okay, so our shuttle docked with the train. That's it."

"Man, I wished I could've seen that," Stucki said.

"Yeah," Fitz said, with far less enthusiasm than his roommate.

Wait, were they still roommates?

"So we're bunking together again this year?" he asked.

"Of course," Imhof said. Clearly, he didn't relish the thought. At all.

"You didn't see our stuff in the sleeper?" Stucki asked. "Man, I *know* we were on board before you."

"There were three bags," Fitz said.

"Wait, you mean no one told you?" Stucki asked with undisguised delight.

"Told me what?" Fitz asked, and braced himself for the answer.

"You have a buddy," Imhof said before Stucki could speak. "A second-year."

"You make that sound like a bad thing," Stucki said, but there was a gleam in his eye.

*Of course* it was a bad thing. To have a buddy who was a year behind you? If he had had any hope of building his credibility with the other cadets, that had just killed it.

But did he care about what the other cadets thought of him?

Fitz realized he didn't. He never had before, but until that moment he had thought that might have changed. He cared about his academic career now, and that was new.

But social cred? Still not in the realm of things that concerned him. Still...

"Who is it? Do you know?" he asked as casually as he could.

"You know him," Stucki said. "It's that kid you were hanging out with all the time last year."

"Kristof Wyss?" he guessed.

"That's him," Stucki said.

Fitz reached across the table to take the bottle out of Imhof's hands and drink the last of his root beer.

He had had worse news in his life.

3

OYMYAKON WAS one of the few worlds that had to be serviced by intergalactic railway because of the persistent storms that made shuttle landings too dangerous in most conditions. The first time Ritchie had flown to the Oymyakon Foreign Service Academy, the railway had descended through the atmosphere on the far side of the continent then snaked its way through mountains and over barren terrain, circling the worst of the hurricanes in a meandering journey that had taken days.

So she was more than a bit surprised when she woke early the next morning to find not only had they arrived at the planet, they were nearly at their destination. No long days of hanging out with her friends on the train, eating food they weren't going to be getting at the academy and catching up after the long break.

Moreau seemed even grumpier about it than Ritchie felt, sullenly packing her bag back up again. They were barely ready in time to dash off the train before it departed for other parts of the planet.

Ritchie stopped while still on the platform, partly to adjust her bag over her shoulder, but mostly to watch the train as it pulled away. There was no such thing as a clear day on Oymyakon, but today was as close as it got. The cloud cover was far overhead, and thin enough to let actual beams of sunlight pierce through to reflect off the gleaming lines that ran down the sides of the flying train. She stepped out to the very edge of the platform to peer down into the bottom of the chasm below. She saw the guidance pods that ran like the tracks under a normal train, buoying it up to hover at platform level. As she watched, the last pod in line lifted up off the ground and sped to the front of the train to settle back down in a new position, first in line.

Only when the train was gone and the last of the pods had lifted up from the ground and disappeared around the bend of a mountain to the south did she look up to see Fitz grinning at her.

"What?" she asked. She hadn't eaten yet; there was no way she'd gotten anything on her face.

"Nothing," he said, but he didn't stop grinning.

"I am not a hick," she told him firmly. "I live on a space station, thank you very much."

"Hey, flying trains are cool," he said. "It's the one thing attending this academy has going for it."

"I don't mind it here," Ritchie said. She looked around the platform and found Moreau standing just at the top of the steps that led down to the path, talking with Kristof Wyss. The rest of the cadets were headed up the mountainside to the campus, just out of sight behind stone outcroppings and wisps of cloud-like fog.

"That's because you've never been to any of the other academies," Fitz was saying, but she nudged him with her elbow then pointed at a fifth person who was also still standing on the platform with them. She was wearing a cadet uniform, but the material was stiff and new and she looked very uncomfortable moving around in it.

But there was something familiar about her. That hair...

"Tassa?" Fitz said, and the girl turned. It was indeed Tassa Sokolov, the train steward who had helped save Ritchie's life the year before. Her face was apprehensive at first, but then she recognized them and started grinning in giddy relief.

"Oh, I was hoping to run into you," she said, then hastily added, "both."

"I was looking for you on the train," Fitz said. "I thought I saw you in uniform, but I told myself I had to be going crazy. And yet here you are."

"Yes. Here I am," she said, lifting her arms as if to display her outfit.

"But... how?" Fitz asked.

"It's kind of a long story," she said. "The short version is I'm a cadet now. Cadet Sokolov."

"So no more calling her 'Tassa'," Ritchie reminded Fitz.

"Right," he said with a nod.

"It was Colonel Hansen's doing," she told them. "I had given up all hope of a career in the foreign service academy. Even now, the circumstances are not usual."

"How so?" Moreau asked. She and Wyss had drifted closer to find out what was keeping their buddies.

"Well, after what happened last year, the colonel thought it was a shame that I had never been accepted to any of the academies. And apparently you said something about it to him as well?" she said, pointing a finger at Fitz and giving him a teasing smile.

Fitz blinked in surprise. "Did I? Yeah, I think I did."

"So the colonel pulled some strings. Probably a lot of them. And I had to jump through more than a few hoops myself. I had to retake all the entrance exams to show my scores hadn't slipped. And I had to go through so many interviews that felt a lot more like interrogations. But in the end it was fine, because here I am!"

"You're a first-year, then?" Moreau asked.

"Sort of," Sokolov said. "I'm here part time as a cadet student and part time as an employee."

"An employee?" Ritchie said. She hadn't even known that was an option, or she might have applied for such a position back when she had been collecting rejection notices from all the academies. "What will you be doing?"

"I'll be working as Colonel Hansen's assistant," she said. "Actually, I'm supposed to be reporting to him now." Her cheeks were turning red in a way that had nothing to do with the chill wind blowing across the platform so close to the mountain's edge. Then she took a deep breath, as if screwing up her courage, and glanced Fitz's way. "Can you show me where his office is?"

Fitz blinked, then shifted his bag from one hand to the other. Ritchie had known him since they were little children. She knew what it looked like when he was tongue-tied, or just uncomfortable.

She had known Tassa Sokolov only briefly, but that entire time she had been clearly smitten with Fitz. Ritchie could see that hadn't changed. She suspected Fitz could see it too, as much as he had needed Ritchie to point it out to him in the first place. She didn't blame him for not knowing what to say to Sokolov, now that they were both cadets. Those sorts of relationships were not allowed in the foreign service academies, and were still strongly discouraged at the universities. Sokolov might not know this yet, but Fitz surely did.

Or he ought to. Rules and Fitz often seemed to have only a nodding acquaintance with each other.

"I can take you," Ritchie blurted out before Fitz could find his voice. Then she turned to thrust her bag into Moreau's arms. "I'll meet you in the barracks in a bit, okay?"

"Sure," Moreau said, struggling for a moment to sort out the two bulky bags.

"Great!" Ritchie said. "See you all at dinner!"

She had one last glimpse of Fitz's face in an almost comical expression of confusion. Then she took Sokolov's arm and guided her off the platform and up the long path to the school. Sokolov gently tugged her arm out of Ritchie's grasp but gave her a smile as she did it as if to say, "no hard feelings."

"Sorry," Ritchie said. "I didn't mean to drag you around."

"It's all right," Sokolov said. "I think I know what you're thinking about me, and I just want to say, I know I'm new here and there's a bunch of stuff I don't know yet, but I do know the rules. I read over the code of conduct several times."

"Oh," Ritchie said, and now she was the one blushing. "Of course you did. I'm sorry."

"You're just looking out for your friend," Sokolov said. "I get it. But you don't need to worry about me. I'm only looking to be friends with all of you too."

"Of course you are," Ritchie said.

Then Sokolov gave her a sly look out of the corner of her eye. "Not to say that in the future if our eventual careers should put us near each other but not in a direct reporting relationship, that I wouldn't be looking for more than that. With Fitz. Those eyes of his... you know?"

"Do I?" Ritchie said, genuinely flummoxed. She had known him for years, from the time they were toddlers until just after her twelfth birthday. Which definitely wasn't too young to notice if your best friend were attractive. But she never had. Even now, when she tried to call him to mind, she found herself thinking of the grubby kid she used to have adventures with, the one with the chaotic hair that resisted his mother's every attempt at neatening it up.

She knew his eyes were dark brown. But that was obviously not what Sokolov meant.

But Sokolov just kept talking as if she hadn't heard her puzzled response. "But that's years from now, if ever. And always assuming he's even interested, right? In the meantime, no worries. Are we good?"

"We're good," Ritchie said, grateful the conversation was taking a turn away from the uncomfortable.

"Great, because I'm going to need all the friends I can get," Sokolov said with a sigh.

They had reached the airlock doors that led into the main entrance through the library. Ritchie pulled one open to let Sokolov inside first, then crossed the space to open the inner door.

"Two sets of doors?" Sokolov said.

"It will make more sense on a windy, rainy day, trust me," Ritchie said. "You'll get used to the way your ears pop every time."

"Gotta love Oymyakon," Sokolov said, and followed Ritchie into the library.

The nooks and tables all around them were already filled with clumps of cadets. No one was studying, not yet, but there was a lot of laughing and talking to catch up on before classes started.

"What did you mean about needing friends?" Ritchie asked, as they left the unusually loud library behind and passed into the quiet of an empty corridor.

"It's weird," Sokolov said with another sigh. "I'm a year older than you, right? But I'll be starting as a cadet with kids who are three years younger than me. And I'll only be in half the classes. The rest of the time, I'll be working in the colonel's office. I'm not worried that the classes will be too hard for me. I mean, I know they'll be hard, but I'm sure I'll manage well enough. But I *am* worried that I'm never not going to be an outsider here."

"I felt a lot of that last year when I started," Ritchie said. "I get it. But you really don't have to worry. Moreau and I will look out for you in the barracks, and we'll introduce you to everyone we know. You'll totally have friends."

"Thanks," Sokolov said. "I feel a lot better."

"Good," Ritchie said, pointing out where the turn to the administration wing was. They turned down the corridor together. There was no sign of anyone about, but with the office doors all closed, it was hard to tell if that was actually true. "This would be the part that would make me nervous," she said. Sokolov raised an eyebrow at her, and she added, "working with Colonel Hansen all the time. I owe him my life, and he was a huge help in me getting caught up with the rest of my class when I started here. But he's intimidating, right?"

"Is he?" Sokolov said. "Maybe that's a cadet/colonel thing. I've been talking with him every couple of days since last year as he's helped me get into this academy, and he's not been intimidating at all. More like a doting uncle or something."

"A doting uncle? Really?" Ritchie said. "Maybe a doting uncle who can occasionally be really scary? You definitely don't want to get caught breaking any rules around that uncle."

"It's like we're talking about two different people," Sokolov said.

"Maybe we are," Ritchie said.

"I wouldn't be here without him," Sokolov said.

"Me neither. And to be honest, he's probably my favorite instructor here. And I haven't even taken a class from him yet," she added with a laugh. "I just hope now that you're a cadet and see the colonel side of him, you're not disappointed."

"I'm sure I'll be fine," Sokolov said.

"This is it," Ritchie said. She expected the door to be locked, but when Sokolov grabbed the knob, it turned easily. The lights flickered to life as she stepped inside.

"I don't think he's here yet," Sokolov said, moving around the assistant's desk to set her bag behind the chair. She moved like she was already familiar with the space. Like she belonged here.

"The train *was* early," Ritchie said. The door between the assistant's office and the colonel's personal office was standing open. Sliding her hands into her pockets, Ritchie stepped through the doorway to look around. The lights in that space too came on the moment her toe crossed the threshold.

"I feel like I should object to you doing this," Sokolov said as she followed Ritchie into the inner sanctum.

"I've been in here before," Ritchie said. "But only ink, um, stressful circumstances. I never got to really look around."

"You wanted a chance to admire his array of certifications?" Sokolov asked as she looked up at just that, hanging on the wall behind the colonel's chair.

"Not really," Ritchie said, moving to the bookcase that stood along the back wall. There were a variety of objects displayed there, but none of them had any kind of label to explain themselves. It was like being in a museum where someone had taken all the plaques away. She knew some of the artifacts were historical things from different planets of the Union of Free Worlds, but others were just plain alien.

"He's been everywhere," Sokolov said, moving to stand shoulder to shoulder with Ritchie. They both looked and resisted the urge to touch.

"That can't be his first service weapon," Ritchie said, pointing with her chin at a heavy-looking sidearm. "There's no way he's that old."

"I don't know, look at that picture," Sokolov said, also pointing with her chin. There was a photograph in a frame just behind where that gun rested, three cadets in uniform.

Three cadets in very old-fashioned uniforms.

But she recognized the earth tones of Oymyakon.

"No way," Ritchie breathed. "He attended this academy? How did I never know that?"

"That's definitely him there on the left," Sokolov said. She sounded very confident. At first Ritchie wanted to disagree. The kid in that photo was so gangly, his hair almost too long for regulation and definitely shouldn't be falling into his eyes like that. She wanted to argue that the face was all wrong.

But of course the face was all wrong. The intricate network of scars that criss-crossed the colonel's face wasn't anything he had been born with. They were still in the future of the boy in that picture.

And those were definitely his steely eyes.

Ritchie was just leaning in closer to try to read the nametags of the other boy and the girl that were standing with him in the photo—the girl in particular also looked strangely familiar—when she heard someone clearing his throat just behind them. She snapped to attention before she even knew for sure it was the colonel.

Better safe than sorry.

"Cadets," he said as he moved around the desk to set his steaming mug of tea near his chair. "Quick trip this time, I see?"

"Yes, sir," Ritchie said.

"Cadet Ritchie, thank you for assisting Cadet Sokolov in finding my office, but I'm sure the two of us can take it from here. You are dismissed."

"Yes, sir," Ritchie said, and saluted before hustling out of his office.

But not fast enough to avoid hearing him say, "Tassa! Just this once I will call you that, and you can call me Ieuan one last time. Henceforth I will be Colonel Hansen, no exceptions."

"And just one hug, Ieuan?" Tassa asked. Her voice was almost teasing, indeed very like a fond niece cajoling her favorite uncle.

But Ritchie didn't hear his answer. She was already out the door and halfway down the hall.

She made it all the way to the top of the sloping corridor that led to the barracks before she realized why the girl cadet in the photograph with young Hansen had been so familiar.

It had been Colonel Coralie Devereux, the officer in charge of the history and tactics classes.

Stranger still, in the entire time she had been at the Oymyakon Foreign Service Academy, she had never seen the two of them so much as speak to each other. But once they had been close friends. What was up with that?

Ritchie knew she was grinning like a fool as she jogged to her room, but she couldn't help it. Now she had a case to work on, clues to dig out, connections to investigate. Only this time, there was no dead body driving that investigation.

This time, it could be just for fun.

4

FITZ WONDERED if what existed between him and Kristof Wyss at that moment could be referred to as a companionable silence.

It didn't exactly feel like he was being shut out. They were technically eating together, like buddies were supposed to do. And it wasn't like there was a stack of books between them.

No, there was just a single tablet propped up on the table in front of Wyss' plate. His pale blue eyes never stopped scanning it, not even to look down at whatever he was stabbing with his fork and shoving into his mouth.

There had to be a dozen windows open on that tablet, and Wyss moved between them, scrolling through one, then paging through another, seemingly at random.

Fitz knew better than to give him a hard time about class not even having started yet. He wasn't sure why Wyss bothered to show up to classes at all. Not only were they largely beneath his skill level, his program of self-education was far more rigorous than anything the Oymyakon Foreign Service Academy had in store for him.

They had barely spoken together in the sleeper car back on the train past a cursory hello and confirmation that they were indeed now assigned buddies. Fitz had hoped that finally having a buddy was going to relieve the isolation he had felt all the year before, but he was having second thoughts about that now.

He wondered what Wyss felt about the two of them being paired up. He wasn't sure who had been Wyss' bunkmate the year before or what might have happened to him, just that he hadn't returned for his second year. The only other cadet he had ever seen Wyss hanging out with had been Keller.

And Keller had been crazy. Actually, legally insane. She was in a secure facility, only a step away from being in prison.

Fitz knew that Ritchie had been in some limited contact with her. He wondered if Wyss had as well.

If someone had told him that Wyss too had spent the year-end break in an isolation ward on a remote space station, he would've believed it. A lot of the returning cadets around them were sporting tans, if none so dark as Fitz's. But Wyss was as pasty and pale as ever.

Fitz decided none of those thoughts were good jumping off points for getting a conversation going, but when he tried to sneak a peak at what Wyss was reading on his tablet, he quickly realized that was no good either. Some of the text he couldn't even recognize as letters.

"If I asked what you were working on, would I understand your answer?" he asked.

"Depends on which thing," Wyss said. His voice sounded kind of vacant, like their conversation was slotted in his range of attention under every one of those open windows on his tablet. But then, eyes still glued to the tablet, he added, "here come Moreau and Ritchie."

Fitz looked up to see the two of them just leaving the end of the food line with trays in hand. He waved until they saw him and crossed over to the table where he sat with Wyss.

"Good to see you," Fitz said, as they set down their trays and slid into their seats. He hoped that didn't sound too emphatically relieved, but even if it had, Wyss was too absorbed to notice.

"It's been less than an hour," Moreau said, as deadpan as ever.

Fitz laughed an awkward laugh, then pushed his hair back out of his eyes. It was a nervous tic, and it immediately fell forward over his forehead again. He vaguely remembered his mother saying something about a haircut before he had left, but nothing had come of that.

As if their presence somehow gave him permission to finally eat, he turned his attention to the food on his plate and stabbed his fork into his potatoes.

Then Moreau said, "did you just *squeak*?"

Fitz looked up, but she wasn't talking to him. She was talking to Ritchie, who was blushing a deep shade of crimson.

"Sorry," Ritchie said, covering her flaming cheeks with her hands as if the sight of them might offend.

"What's going on?" Fitz asked, looking from her to Moreau and back again.

"Beats me," Moreau said, but there was the slightest curve to her mouth. As close as she ever got to looking amused.

"Please stop looking at me," Ritchie said miserably.

Moreau put a bit of chicken in her mouth and chewed, but she kept glancing over at Ritchie as if eager to see whatever she did next.

Somehow, this was even worse than eating in silence next to Wyss. He had no idea what was going on.

"I messaged with my mother," he said, desperate for a change of topic.

"That's interesting," Moreau said.

"About the Berwegers," he added. "Why they were here."

That got her attention. She sat up straighter. "And?"

"She didn't know," he was forced to admit. "But she's going to ask around. She has friends who are friends with their parents. Someone must know something."

"We'll probably know soon enough just from scuttlebutt around here," Moreau said. She looked around the cafeteria, and Fitz did the same, but there was no sign of the twins among the cadets currently eating dinner.

"I saw something intriguing in Colonel Hansen's office today," Ritchie said. Her cheeks were still pink, and he could tell that she was working to sound like her normal self. "Did you know that he used to attend this academy?"

"Yeah," Wyss said without looking up from his tablet. "He excelled at the alpine maneuvers training. That's why they moved him here to this academy. It has the most rigorous program."

"That's not what I heard," Moreau said. "I heard he was transferred from one of the more prestigious academies because of some sort of scandal."

"They could both be true," Fitz said.

"There might be another reason he ended up here," Ritchie said. She had that gleam in her eye, and Fitz knew she wasn't going to stop until she had revealed whatever it was that had her so keyed up.

"What's that?" he asked.

"He has a picture in his office of himself and two other cadets back in the day," she said. "One of them was a young Colonel Devereux."

She sat back in her chair as if she had just dropped a bomb of knowledge on them all. But Fitz just blinked at her. Moreau was focused on her food, although she was clearly waiting to hear more.

But to Fitz's surprise, Wyss tapped the side of his tablet to darken the screen and gave Ritchie his full attention. "They were friends?" he asked her.

"They looked like friends," she said. "Maybe what Moreau said is true, that there was a scandal at his last posting. Maybe she pulled strings to bring him here."

"Do I know who Colonel Devereux is?" Moreau asked between bites. Fitz was grateful she said it, so he didn't have to.

"She teaches history, strategy and tactics, and some of the diplomacy courses," Wyss said. "Mostly just to the last year students, with a few exceptions."

"Like you?" Fitz guessed.

"Keller and I had an independent study with her last year," Wyss said. Then he stared down at his plate, as if suddenly realizing that he had said her name out loud. Keller.

But Ritchie didn't seem bothered by the mention of her former stalker, almost murderer. She was too caught up in this new thing. "Have you ever seen the two of them together?" she asked.

"No. Not once," Wyss said.

"Oh, that's her," Moreau said. She had taken out her own tablet and was looking at a current image of Colonel Devereux as well as her public bio. "I've seen her in the hallways before. Never with Hansen, though."

"Isn't that weird?" Ritchie asked.

"Is it?" Moreau asked.

"If she really did help him out, why is he so cold to her now?" Ritchie asked.

"Who says he's cold to her?" Fitz asked. "None of us even noticed anything about the two of them before. Besides, they could be chatting together every evening and we'd have no idea. Why would they do it in front of cadets?"

"I'm not sure I understand what you think is going on," Wyss said. "They're colleagues now. They were in the past. But you make it sound kind of sinister."

"Maybe not *sinister*," Ritchie said, but trailed off without completing her thought.

"Bored already?" Fitz guessed. "Looking for a mystery to occupy our time?"

"This isn't the longest we've gone without a dead body entering our lives, you know," Moreau said to her.

Ritchie flushed again, but this time there was also a snap to her eyes. She wasn't embarrassed. She was worked up. "I'm not making trouble because I'm bored. I really think something is going on there."

"Like what?" Fitz asked.

"I don't know. But I'm going to look into it," she said. She stared down at the remains of her dinner, but Fitz could feel the irritation radiating off of her.

"If your instincts tell you something is going on, that's good enough for me. And you know we're always here to help you, whatever it is," he said. He reached out to touch her hand, but she pulled it away, tucking it out of sight under the table.

"I know," she said, and that pinkish glow was back.

What the heck was going on with her?

"We should go finish unpacking," Moreau said, and Fitz felt a stab of envy. He knew he and Moreau had the same impulse to get to the bottom of Ritchie's suddenly changeable moods. Only unlike Fitz, Moreau could drag her down to their barracks and demand some answers.

"Yeah," Ritchie agreed, and got up from the table at the same time Moreau did.

"We all have hand-to-hand training together first thing in the morning," Fitz said. "See you then."

"See you," Moreau said. There was a slight flutter to the corner of her eye as she brushed past him, but there was no way she had just winked at him. Not Moreau. Because that would be even more confusing than whatever was going on with Ritchie.

"Did you mean what you said?" Wyss asked Fitz the moment they were alone at the table.

"What?" Fitz asked.

"Did you mean it when you said that you trust Ritchie's instincts?" he asked.

"Sure," Fitz said absentmindedly. But then he added, "I mean, it certainly feels to me like she's trying to find a conspiracy that doesn't actually exist. But maybe it *is* something. Probably something mundane, like a long-past affair or whatever. But something."

"I don't think either of the colonels will thank her for digging into their personal lives," Wyss said.

"No, I'm with you there," Fitz said. "Let's just hope that once classes start, Ritchie will be too occupied to have time for extra-curricular investigations."

They bussed their trays, then walked together down the winding corridor to the barracks.

Maybe it *was* a companionable silence.

Once they were in their room, Wyss sat down at the desk and opened all the windows he had been looking at on his tablet. Fitz climbed up to flop down on his bunk and stare at the ceiling.

He supposed if he were going to be worried about Ritchie, he should be worried that she was about to get herself into a bunch of trouble for digging up info about the colonels. He knew firsthand the ire of a colonel who felt that a cadet had overstepped.

But all he could think about was the way she had looked, blushing that deep shade of rose, not once but twice.

It was definitely a new phenomenon. It hadn't been happening on the train. What had set her off? He would almost think it was from seeing the Berwegers, but they hadn't shown up in the cafeteria at all during dinner.

He started to fold his hands behind his head when he felt something brush against the back of his knuckles. He sat up on one elbow and reached under his pillow until he found it again.

A little message chip. It glowed in the visual overlay provided by his implant. So, a message for him.

He jumped down from his bunk to fetch his tablet, then slid the chip into the dock. The message then appeared before his eyes. An invitation written in an excessively flowing font. Some sort of special gathering of only a select few cadets from the upper two classes.

A secret gathering, down in the catacombs under the academy.

There were no names attached, but he knew in his bones where this had come from. The Berwegers. Clandestine meetings of only the most select invitees? That was totally their thing.

"Did you get an invitation?" he asked Wyss.

"Invitation to what?" Wyss asked, that faraway tone back in his voice. Fitz knew he was only being half listened to.

"Hey, mum's the word," Stucki hissed at him.

"What's that?" Fitz asked. Stucki grabbed him by the elbow and steered him out into the hall. Not that there was any privacy there.

"It's for the upper classes only. Didn't you read that?" Stucki asked him in a harsh whisper. He kept looking back over Fitz's shoulder to where Wyss still sat hunched over the desk screen, completely oblivious to anything happening around him.

"But you got one too," Fitz guessed.

"And Imhof," Stucki said, still whispering, if less furiously now.

"Are you planning to go?" Fitz asked.

"Well, yeah."

"This has the Berwegers written all over it," Fitz said skeptically.

"Well, yeah," Stucki said again, more emphatically. "You think I'm turning down an invitation from Feena Berweger?"

"But an invitation to *what*?" Fitz asked.

"Some sort of hazing ritual from the old days? Who knows?" Stucki asked.

"Did everyone get one? I mean, everyone in the top two classes."

"Probably not," Stucki said. "It said this was an exclusive event."

"Yeah, I really don't think this is my sort of thing," Fitz said.

"What do you mean? This is, like, how networking works," Stucki said. "This is how you forge the sorts of relationships that will really build your foreign service career."

"By excluding the unwanteds from the networking opportunity?" Fitz asked.

"Not everyone is officer material," Stucki said. "Especially not at the level the Berwegers are playing at."

"Their parents are admirals. They're still just cadets," Fitz pointed out.

"You know what I mean. Give them a couple of decades, and they'll be running the whole show."

"You know my dad outranks both of their parents," Fitz said. "By your argument, I'll be the one running the whole show."

"Not if you skip things like this," Stucki said. He gave him a significant look, then went back into their barracks.

Fitz didn't know whether to scowl his disapproval or just to shrug it off bemusedly, like he had always done. But if Ritchie longed to uncover a conspiracy, this was a much better place to start than with whatever had happened between the two colonels years ago.

But his gleeful eagerness to talk to her about it over breakfast was gone in an instant, as the thought occurred to him that if he mentioned it to her, she might have no idea what he was talking about.

What if she didn't get an invite?

If it went to kids of prominent parents, she ought to be a shoo-in. Her father had been one of the most highly regarded diplomats in the Union of Free Worlds.

Had been, until the day it had all gone so wrong.

Fitz knew it was an injustice, the way her father's name and reputation had been impugned. Even if he still lived, and no one knew if that were true, he was a prisoner of the yuffids, unable to defend himself or clear his name.

Moreau, he knew, was guaranteed to have gotten an invite, especially if the likes of Imhof and Stucki had. But Ritchie?

Would the Berwegers consider her potential based on who her father had been before that day, or after?

Fitz thrust his hands deep into his pockets and just started walking. He knew it would be hours before he could hope for sleep, if at all. Not with all the old guilt back on his mind, pressing down like a smothering weight.

He knew nothing he did could ever make things right again between him and Ritchie. Not in any way that mattered.

But if she hadn't gotten an invite to this secret meeting, he didn't even have to think about whether or not he wanted to attend.

Even if it meant his future career would be kneecapped by this decision. If Ritchie was excluded, so was he.

Not that he would ever tell her so. Because as much as he owed it to her, he could never tell her why. It would be just one more secret, another brick in the wall between the two of them. A wall she couldn't even see, but surely she must feel that it was there. Always there.

He sure did.

5

THE ACADEMIC YEAR had gotten off to an epically terrible start for Ritchie, and she hadn't even attended her first class yet.

Hoping that food would help her foul mood, she piled mound after mound of steaming scrambled eggs onto her plate. Moreau stood waiting for her, tray in her hands. She had a bowl of fresh fruit and a few squares of cheese and apparently craved for nothing more. She was shifting her weight from foot to foot and not saying a word as Ritchie added strips of bacon to her mountain of eggs.

"Do you mind if I...?" Moreau trailed off, sort of gesturing with her tray.

"Go ahead," Ritchie said, thinking she was anxious to get to the coffee at the end of the cafeteria line.

But when Moreau headed instead straight to the table where Fitz and Wyss were eating together, Ritchie couldn't exactly say she was surprised.

Something was going on. Since the night before, cadets were gathering in twos and sometimes threes, whispering together, eyes darting all around to be sure they weren't overheard. Whispers that stopped suddenly when she got too close. That would be tolerable, and far from the worst thing Ritchie had dealt with in a school.

But Moreau was clearly part of it. Whatever everyone was whispering about, Moreau knew. But when Ritchie asked her what was up, she had denied anything was going on.

The first time Moreau had shrugged it off, just before lights out the night before, Ritchie had rolled with it. Perhaps she *was* just being paranoid. Sure, she had seen Moreau whispering with Frei, but that could be about anything.

Then Ritchie had come back from the showers that morning to find Moreau, Grof and Frei all in a tight huddle. Their frantic whispers had cut off abruptly when Ritchie had come in the room. This time, when she asked Moreau what was going on, and she said she had no idea what Ritchie was talking about, she was sure that Moreau was lying.

And now Ritchie could see her leaning over her tray as Fitz did the same on the opposite side of the table. Whatever they were discussing was intensely serious, to judge by the look on Fitz's face as he spoke.

Wyss, for his part, didn't seem to even notice they were there beside him. Ritchie wished she could channel just a fraction of his rise-above-it attitude.

She finally got a turn at the coffee machine and brought her breakfast over to set it on the table next to Moreau's untouched tray. Or maybe "set" wasn't quite the right word. It clattered loudly, making the other two jump guiltily, which would've been more satisfying if she hadn't sloshed out a good third of her coffee in the process.

"All right, Ritchie?" Fitz asked.

"Fine," she said as she sat down. She didn't dare look up at him. Yesterday had been embarrassing enough.

Damn Sokolov for planting thoughts in her head. Now, when she looked at her oldest friend, she no longer saw the scrawny kid she remembered getting into so many adventures with. No, now, thanks to Sokolov, she saw a young man who really filled out his cadet uniform in all the right ways.

And she knew what Sokolov had meant about his eyes.

But worst of all, in Ritchie's book, that chaotic mass of hair she had remembered so fondly from when they were kids had transformed into something that was just barely held in check, thick and unruly. And when he was upset or nervous and he pushed it back in that unconscious way he had, it fell back forward over his forehead in a single thick lock that just did something to her.

Nope. She was not looking up at him. Maybe never again.

Damn Sokolov.

"You don't look all right," Fitz said. She could feel him leaning towards her and knew he wanted to make eye contact with her, but she looked at Moreau instead.

Then she remembered her anger.

"I know you two are hiding something from me," she said. "I really wish you would just tell me what's going on."

"It's nothing," Fitz said before Moreau could answer. "It's just this stupid thing... absolutely not worth your time troubling about."

"He's right. It doesn't matter," Moreau said. "It's not so much a secret as an aggravation that you don't need."

"So I'm supposed to thank you for looking out for me?" Ritchie asked, her tone much sharper than she had intended. "If you don't tell me, then it *is* 'so much a secret'. But have it your way." She shoved a forkful of eggs into her mouth and was almost annoyed to find they were still hot and buttery and exactly what she wanted. She resented the soothing qualities of breakfast.

"I'm not invited either," Wyss said to her in his soft voice.

"Invited to what?" Ritchie asked, then took another bite of her eggs.

"The big to-do for the chosen ones," he said with a shrug. "I gather being a second-year I'm too young, but I doubt I'd make the cut even if I were in your class. My parents don't have the right sorts of postings."

"Oh," Ritchie said, and set her fork down. "I'm not chosen either, then."

"It's stupid, like I told you," Moreau said.

"But you're invited," Ritchie said. "You don't have to tell me. Of course you are."

"I don't think being chosen by the Berwegers means anything to me," Moreau said. "They don't know me. They don't have the knowledge to properly judge me or rank me among others. To tell the truth, I'm more than a little annoyed by it all. I came here to make my own way, not piggy-back on who my parents are."

She was holding her fork as she spoke, and Ritchie could see she was gripping it so tightly her knuckles were going white. Her voice was steady, but there was a fire in her blue eyes, and Ritchie knew that "annoyed" was too small a word for what her friend was actually feeling.

"So you're not going to whatever it is you were invited to?" she asked.

"Definitely not," Moreau said, and stabbed at a piece of shining pineapple that dodged out from under the tines of her fork.

"But what is it exactly?" Ritchie asked.

"The invitation is vague on that matter," Wyss said.

"Um, not to be rude, but how would you know?" Fitz asked.

"The Berwegers didn't encrypt those invites. I saw a bunch of messages flood the system all at once. Was I supposed to *not* be curious?" he asked in the blandest of voices.

"Yeah," Moreau said leadingly. "They were private?"

"Not really. Every single one had the exact same text. Only the delivery addresses would be private," Wyss said. "I might've ignored a normal message, maybe, but they all contained some additional digital information that intrigued me."

"What kind of information?" Ritchie asked.

"Well, since the invite gives a time but not a specific place, I'm guessing at the appointed hour the invitees will be directed through their implants to the actual location of the event," Wyss said. "The invite just says it's in the catacombs under the academy, but I know you've been down there. The place is like a maze. No one will find it without help, especially if they are planning to meet somewhere deep. Which, given the number of people invited, they would have to be. That's where the larger caverns are."

"How deep have you been in the catacombs?" Ritchie asked with a frown. She had hated her own brief time down in those caves. That feeling of being inside a mountain, swallowed up by rock, about to be crushed, still came back to her in her nightmares.

"Personally, not far at all," Wyss said.

"You sent in drones?" Fitz guessed.

"I sent in drones," Wyss agreed.

"So, is this just like a party, then?" Ritchie asked.

"Maybe," Moreau said, but Fitz was shaking his head.

"No, it has to be more than that. This, whatever it turns out to be, has to be the reason the Berwegers are here at all," he said.

"That sounds ominous," Ritchie said.

"Or paranoid," Moreau said.

"No, they are gathering people for a specific reason. I just don't have a clue what it could be," Fitz said.

"I guess you'll find out tonight," Ritchie said.

"Are you kidding me? There's no way I'm going," he said.

"But you really want to know what this was all about. Isn't just going the best way to find out?" Ritchie asked.

"Maybe, but I don't care," he said. "I'm not going anywhere that doesn't have the sense not to exclude the likes of you. Not even as a spy."

Now she did look up at him, and his dark brown eyes were filled with a fierce loyalty. Their friendship meant everything to him. She had known that on an academic level before, but she felt it now in her gut. She wanted to tell him that she felt the same. That he was and would always be her first and truest friend. That nothing would ever get between them, least of all her inappropriate new feelings of attraction.

That last bit had her blushing and looking down at her plate again. No, she could never mention that. She knew how much his future career meant for him. She would never jeopardize that.

Assuming he even felt the same way. Which she really didn't think he did. Maybe he was where she had been up until her conversation with Sokolov. Maybe when he looked at her, all he saw was the little girl she had been back on Buennagel.

She felt them all looking at her, and could see the questions on Moreau's face through the corner of her eye. But before any of them could say a word, the cadet captains Blaser and Wyder announced the end of breakfast, shouting and clapping their hands to urge haste, particularly from the first-year cadets. Ritchie shoveled in as much egg as her mouth could hold, then followed Moreau to drop off their trays before heading off to their first class.

The day went by in one big, stressful blur. Hand-to-hand combat was all right, almost relaxing compared to all of her other classes, although she regretted having all those eggs in her belly. By the afternoon she was weighed down both physically and mentally by extensive syllabi, tablets of material too sensitive to be networked to her all-purpose tablet with staggering reading assignments to match, and even a couple of quizzes promised before the end of the week.

And the whispering had continued all day. She had never quite managed to tune any of that out.

She had just decided to skip eating in the cafeteria, preferring to study in the barracks with the last of the food she'd smuggled off the train, when she nearly collided with Fitz, who had been waiting for her at the top of the sloping corridor to the barracks.

"Sorry," she said as she stumbled back a step. "Look, I'm skipping dinner. Too much to do."

"Already?" he asked, incredulous. But then he shook his head as if to clear that line of questioning out of his mind. "Listen, I had a thought," he said.

"Okay," Ritchie said, hiking the strap of her heavy bag a little higher on her shoulder.

"I know that invite didn't have a plus one, but who's going to notice you don't belong if I just sneak you in?" he said.

"What are you talking about?" she asked.

"I'm talking about you and I crashing this party or whatever," he said. "My invite will direct us to the location, but we don't have to go inside. We can lurk and eavesdrop. You know, spy."

"You really want to know what they're up to," Ritchie guessed.

"Don't you?" he countered.

Ritchie sighed and rubbed tiredly at her forehead. Was this a good idea? She had been turning things over in her head all day, and she had decided that if the Berwegers were judging her by her parents, so be it. But if there was a chance that they really were choosing the future movers and shakers of the Union of Free Worlds society, maybe missing this first party or whatever wouldn't be such a big deal. They didn't know her yet. Lots of people misjudged her before they knew her. But so far, she had changed every single mind about her. Given enough time, surely she could bring them around to seeing her real value.

Of course, the fact that neither of them was in any of her classes was going to make that a little tough. But in Ritchie's life, nothing had ever come easy.

Still, sneaking around, stealing invitations, spying? That was never going to put her in anyone's good graces.

On the other hand, what if they never changed their assessment of her? What if she was always one of their unchosen? And what if that ended up mattering?

Fitz waited patiently as all of these thoughts raced through her mind. But in the end, he grinned as she gave him a reluctant nod. "Yeah. I think I do," she said.

"Then it's a date," he said. "I'll meet you here an hour after lights out." He started to head down the other corridor but turned back to add, "and hey, if this little conspiracy turns out to be nothing, we still have your mystery of the two colonels."

"The friends who never speak to each other," she agreed, but as she hauled her bag down to her room, all she could think was how little time she'd have for investigations this year. Not with this load of classwork.

And she had thought the last year was tough. This year just might be more than she could handle.

6

FITZ FOUND himself sitting alone in the cafeteria at dinner, and he wasn't sure why.

Ritchie had said she was skipping it to study, although it seemed very early in the year to start that sort of behavior. He guessed Wyss was doing the same, if more likely pursuing some academic pursuit of his own than an assignment for some class.

Moreau's absence was a mystery. Perhaps with Ritchie skipping the meal service, she decided to do the same.

But aside from being alone, he wasn't even sure why he was there. He wasn't particularly hungry, and the food on his tray wasn't calling to him in the slightest. Meat of some sort in a brown sauce with a side of mashed potatoes as dense as concrete. He wished he hadn't scarfed down all the kyaw fritters on the shuttle ride to catch the train. He could really go for some of those now.

Fitz jabbed his spoon into the mound of potatoes, but when it resisted coming out again, he took it as a sign and just left it there with a sigh.

Maybe he should be studying as well.

No, that was crazy talk.

"Shackleton Fitz IV," a male voice said. Fitz didn't even need to look up to know who had approached him. The rippling silence of the cadets around them had preceded Finn Berweger like the quieting of a crowd before a royal figure entering a room on state business.

"That's me," Fitz said, sitting back in his chair. He folded his arms as he leaned back to look up at his fellow cadet, but the youth in question opted to sit down across from him. Only first he spun the chair around and swung a leg over to straddle it backwards, resting his arms on the back as he leaned in to lock eyes with Fitz.

As usual, the effect of looking at that angelic visage made even Fitz blink twice, despite his best efforts to be unmoved. He just managed to keep his voice from squeaking and summon all the latent sarcasm he could muster to say, "Finn... Berweger, right?"

"Right," Finn said with a slow grin, unbothered by Fitz's attempt at humor.

"Right. We met at one of Guy Travert's parties," Fitz said, nodding. "More than one."

"Yeah? Your memory is better than mine," Fitz said. He tried to pick up his spoon to toy with it, but it still refused to pull free from the potatoes. That undermined his projection of cool more than a little bit.

"Your dad is stationed on Nisi now, right?" Finn said. He phrased it like a question, but Fitz suspected he already knew all the facts from the date of the Fitz family arrival to the precise current location of his father down to which room in the palatial villa on the coast he was standing in right that minute.

"Last I heard," Fitz said. "I doubt he'll take the governorship if they offer it to him, though."

"No, he didn't when they did," Finn agreed. "Not the kind of action your old man craves, is it?"

"I guess not," Fitz said. But his irritation with this roundabout conversation was getting hard to hide. "Is there something I can help you with?" he asked.

"Just making sure you'll be at our little gathering this evening," he said.

"Desperate to see me and catch up, are you?" Fitz asked.

"Well, I confess, I'm here now because my sister wanted to be sure you were there," he said with a grin. "She was very particular about that. Very... insistent."

Fitz almost smiled, imagining how this conversation would be going if Finn were having it with Stucki. But Fitz was less moved by Feena Berweger's charms. Aside from that initial jolt, of course, the one when he first saw either of the Berwegers and realized his memory of their attractiveness had faded, and the reality before him was so much more. It was a bigger jolt from Feena than it was from Finn, but for Fitz it was still only a momentary thing. He always just held his ground and let it pass.

"I wasn't planning to, no," Fitz said casually.

"Because we didn't invite your friend?" Finn asked, still grinning at him like they were sharing some sort of joke. "You know she's a definite no, right?"

"For you? I gather that's true," Fitz said.

"It's not personal," Finn said. "I'm sure she's great as a, um, 'friend.' But she's not going to be anyone who ever shapes the future for the Union of Free Worlds."

"Neither am I," Fitz said. "Better cross me off of your list too."

Finn looked around them, and several nearby cadets who had been not so subtly listening in on their conversation quickly turned back to each other and pretended to be carrying on with their own discussions. Finn edged his chair closer to the table and leaned over it to speak in a lower voice. Despite himself, Fitz found himself also leaning in to hear his words.

"I know who she is," Finn said. Then he winked.

Fitz let a beat pass before he tried to speak. "Everyone here does," he said. "No one cares about that now."

"I'm not talking about what happened with her father," he said. "I'm talking about what she did to you."

"What do you mean?" Fitz asked, genuinely puzzled.

"Your whole path in life took a dramatic turn when you were twelve, didn't it? At exactly the point when her life nose-dived." He raised both of his eyebrows as if he had made his point. Something about this extra level of smugness just rubbed Fitz the wrong way.

"So?" he all but snarled.

"Hey, no judgments from me!" Finn said, holding his hands up in mock surrender. "I'm just saying, the reason you've flunked out of every other academy and ended up here, where you're barely hanging on to the last hopes of a career by your fingertips, is her. Tell me I'm wrong."

Fitz said nothing. And for once, it wasn't because he had promised his father not to speak of what had happened with Ritchie and her father. No, he owed it to *Ritchie* not to engage in this conversation.

But Finn seemed to take this as a point for his side in the debate Fitz wasn't joining him in. He lifted his hands again, an annoyingly fake magnanimous gesture. "See? And was she worth it? Is she?"

Fitz still said nothing. But he had to bite down hard on his tongue to do it. Ritchie hadn't ruined his life. His father hadn't either, if Fitz was being honest with himself. No, he had done that himself. But he wasn't going to tell Finn so.

"All right. Have it your way," Finn said with an unbothered shrug. "Just think about it. She's been pulling you down for years, but that doesn't *still* have to be true. You have two years left before heading to university. Lots of time to get in with the right sort of people, people who can pull you up to where you're meant to be."

"Why do you care?" Fitz asked. "Do you think my father's gratitude will be worth something to you?"

"You and I both know it absolutely would," Finn said, finally turning serious. But it only lasted for a flash, and then he was grinning again. "But can't it just be because I've always liked you, and it hurts me to see you this way? Alone and friendless?"

Then he was gone, leaving Fitz's mind racing through all the things he wished he had said.

His rational mind knew it was better that he had said nothing. The last thing he needed was for Finn Berweger to get curious about what had happened five years ago. That would be doing Ritchie no favors at all.

But the urge to run after Finn and tell him just what he thought of him and his sister was strong.

He threw his tray of mostly uneaten food into the return station and stalked back to the barracks.

But by an hour after lights out, his mood had improved somewhat. He heard Stucki and Imhof getting out of their bunks to head up to the main hall, then the sounds of other cadets moving through the corridor after them. Fitz rolled out of his bunk, still dressed, and dropped soundlessly to the floor.

"Are you going?" Wyss asked out of the darkness of the bottom bunk. He sounded surprised.

"Kind of," Fitz said. "I'm waiting for the others to go, then Ritchie and I are going to sneak in after them."

"Interesting," Wyss said. He sat up into the light from the corridor and Fitz saw that he too was still dressed.

"Were you coming too?"

"No," Wyss said with a yawn. "But I have my drone array down there, still mapping locations. I was curious which chamber everyone is meeting in."

"Can I get a copy of what you've mapped so far? It might come in handy," Fitz said.

"Sure," Wyss said, and got up from the bunk to head to the desk. He pressed his thumb to open up his individual set of screens.

Then Fitz had another thought. "Do your drones pick up sound?"

"Not these. They're too little. But the images are so clear my software can read lips. In case you want a record later of what they're saying down there."

"Definitely," Fitz said.

"My only worry is that they have to fly close to people to get good data for the software to run. Close enough for them to be seen."

"And get slapped out of the sky," Fitz guessed. "And you don't want to lose them."

"Exactly," Wyss said. "I have dozens of them, but not hundreds. And there are a lot more caves yet to be mapped. So I'll be doing a little manual directing from here. Their decision-making programming is good, but not weighing benefit of the images recorded versus cost of destruction good."

"Sure," Fitz said. The corridor had been silent for a few minutes now. It was time to go. "If you're asleep when I get back, we can catch up over breakfast."

"Yeah," Wyss said, but his attention was already on the many screens he was opening on the desktop.

Fitz crept up the sloping corridor to find Ritchie just about to turn to go back down the other way. She spun back around, and her face was tight with anxiety. And not the usual kind he watched her struggle with constantly, that she wouldn't be good enough to stay at the academy. No matter how high her marks, that worry never left her. It was as much a part of her as any physical part of her body.

No, this was a new thing. She really didn't want to be doing this. He knew she was only here now because he had asked her to go with him. And he suddenly realized that was actually kind of weird.

He knew why he would do anything for her. But why did she feel the same way about him?

"Fitz?" she whispered, as if she wasn't sure it was really him standing there awkwardly, staring at her without speaking.

"I'm here," he whispered back. "Ready?"

"I guess," she said. "Say, did you see Moreau at dinner?"

"No. Wasn't she with you?"

"I haven't seen her since our last class together."

"I'm sure she's fine," Fitz said.

"I'm not worried that she's in *danger*," Ritchie said.

"You think she's avoiding you?" he asked.

"If she had changed her mind about going to this thing and didn't want to tell me, avoiding me would be the best way to do that."

She sounded glum, as if Moreau had betrayed their friendship. He took a step towards her, reaching out to touch her arm, but before he could speak, a map suddenly exploded over his visual field.

"What is it?" Ritchie asked.

"Time for the party," Fitz said. "I'm getting the route information now. The others will already be moving along the path. We should hurry."

"Right," Ritchie said, suddenly all business.

They headed down the main hallway until it ended at a narrower, perpendicular corridor. They turned left and then left again, this corridor now running steeply downhill past the closed door after closed door of disused storage rooms. Ritchie walked easily by his side, not needing him to navigate yet. Then they reached the end of the corridor and crawled past the loose grate and through the meter-long tunnel to where the hallway resumed.

The lights were dimmer here, but the floors, walls, and ceiling were the same as in the corridor behind them. The only difference was that this corridor lacked doors, and at some point in the passing centuries had acquired a little stream that had worn a groove into the stone floor as it trickled its way downhill, deeper under the mountain.

"All right?" Fitz asked.

Ritchie looked surprised at his question, but nodded. "Did you remember to bring glow sticks?" she asked.

He nodded and pulled one out of his pocket to hand to her. "For when we reach the end of the lights."

"Thanks," she said.

The corridor took another turn to the left and continued running ever steeper, but this time it was down into the dark. The walls, floor and ceiling transitioned from finished corridor to rough-hewn mining tunnel before finally becoming mostly natural cave.

"Okay, we'll be following the directions from the invitation from here," he said, calling it up to the corner of his vision. Then they both clicked on their lights and a sickly green glow lit up the space around them. It didn't provide a lot of detail, but the night vision their implants projected over their fields of view filled in the rest in starkly drawn outlines.

It only took a few minutes to reach the cavern where they had found Kung sitting alone drawing pictures of his unrequited, now dead love Jeger.

Fitz knew the others were far ahead of them. They had all met together where the hidden hallway lights ended, but that had been several minutes ago. Normally this wouldn't be a problem, and had in fact been what he had intended so that they could be sure to not be seen.

But the directions he was getting were only one step at a time, and the previous steps were deleting as each new one appeared in his visual field. His implant was refusing to hold on to any of the information. He could, of course, still remember it with his own brain. But he hadn't used his brain for rote memorization since... well, probably ever.

The caves lost all semblance of constructed hallways well before Kung's cavern, so the directions had to be more than a series of left or right turns. And the steps all had colorful names for landmarks to watch out for. It was hard to miss the sparkling stone waterfall or the rock formation like a king's throne. He knew they were on the right track at first, but the further along they walked, the further apart the landmarks became. And the more times he had cause to worry, they had missed a turn.

"Are you okay?" Ritchie asked him. He looked over at her. She looked unusually pale, even by glow stick standards, and he remembered too late how much she had hated being underground before.

"Fine," he lied. No way was he going to tell her that he was increasingly afraid they were going to get lost.

"It's just, you were mumbling to yourself," she said.

"Was I?" he said, but he knew full well he had been. He had been repeating the directions, each cycle adding the next step.

But now, in the time it had taken to answer her twice, he had lost track of where they were going. He ran through the list again, ignoring her increasingly worried look. He still had all the steps. His memory wasn't completely shot from disuse.

But he had gotten no new ones for several seconds now.

He blinked, but the map refused to return to his visual field. He checked his inbox, but even his copy of the invite was gone, as if it had never existed.

"Fitz?"

"We're nearly there," he said. He tried to give her a reassuring grin, but he was pretty sure it was a wobbly one. "I know you hate this."

"I won't lie. I don't love it," she admitted, hugging herself. "But I'm doing okay. Really."

Despite her words, she was looking paler than before. But then the yellowish-green light the glow sticks cast over everything wasn't remotely flattering to anyone.

He only hoped it would help him see some sign of the passage of all those other people. "This way," he said, and guided her through a narrow channel between two jagged rock faces then into a cavern filled with strange lumpish stones that looked like petrified mushrooms. The floor of the cavern sloped down and ended in a sort of chute of smoothed stone like a slide.

"If we go down, how do we get up again?" Ritchie asked.

"I'm sure there's a way," Fitz said, although he was far from sure of any such thing. But this part was still on the directions he had been receiving. The others must have come this way. "Do you want to go first?"

She looked down the chute, then up at him, and he could see that she was shaking.

"Do you want to go back up?" he asked. He knew he could find their way back to the entrance. That history hadn't been erased from his data.

"No," she said, but he could see that she was working hard to muster up her courage.

"There's room enough for both of us to go down at once if that's better," he said.

She gave him a grateful smile, and the two of them sat down on the stone floor. They had to scoot for several meters on their backsides before they reached a point where the stone was smooth enough and steep enough to carry them down.

But all too quickly it became smoother still and even steeper, and they were flying down a spiraling tunnel that was growing narrower around them by the second. He grabbed Ritchie and pulled her closer to him, wrapping his arms around her even as they both stretched out as long and as straight as they could. If that tunnel got any narrower, they were going to be wedged in.

And that was the best-case scenario.

He heard laughter in his head, a boy's and a girl's together. Completely superfluous. It was now abundantly clear that the others hadn't come this way. That the Berwegers had given a set of directions just for him. The only thing he didn't know was where they were sending him and Ritchie. On a wild goose chase? Or to their deaths?

He held Ritchie tight in his arms as they picked up speed through the darkness. He had gotten her into this. Whatever it took, he would get her out again or die trying.

But he was really hoping despite current circumstances it would be the former.

7

RITCHIE WAS the farthest thing from a daredevil. She found no thrills in going fast, in facing the possibility of death at every sharp turn, of not knowing when the ride was going to end.

She flew her glider almost daily and could execute whatever aerobatic maneuver she was instructed to perform, but left to her own devices, she would most enjoy a gentle gliding through the air, at most slowly banking around in lazy circles around the landing field. Of course, then, she was always in control.

This? This was the very opposite of control.

And she was enduring it all while knowing, knowing with every shrieking cell of her nervous system, that they were the entire time plunging ever deeper under that mountain.

She could feel her mind wanting to just break. If it snapped, she wouldn't have to be aware of anything at all.

It was so tempting. But she forced her mind to stay as it was. Lost in the dark, the glow sticks long gone ahead of them or behind, but either way completely out of sight now.

And they were moving far too quickly for her implant to lend her night vision any useful information at all. All she had to focus on was her hands gripping fistfuls of Fitz's tunic. That, and his arms wrapped around her. She could feel the jostling and knew he was taking the brunt of the impact from dozens of outcroppings in the rock. He was going to be black and blue by morning.

Then they started spinning in a tight spiral that had the gorge rising in her throat. But she quickly realized this was a good thing. Well, not the threat of vomiting all over Fitz. But the tight spiral was finally slowing their momentum.

She had just a split second to dread the thought of climbing back up through that chute. They must've been sliding for a kilometer or more.

Then they were out of the chute, firing out into open air. Ritchie yelped and held on to Fitz even more tightly, and he did the same to her.

And then they were falling again, this time straight down. But before she could even open her mouth to scream, the air around them was just gone. They were plunging through an icy cold mass that sucked the breath from her.

Now she really wanted to scream, but raw survival instinct kept her mouth clamped shut as they torpedoed straight down through the water.

It felt like they hung there for an eternity. Her whole world was shockingly cold and wet and she couldn't breathe and she had no idea which way was up, which way she should be kicking towards.

And the entire time that feeling of the mountain over her just waiting to crush down on her never, ever went away.

But Fitz still had a hold of her. She felt a lurch as he started kicking towards the surface she still couldn't sense. She kicked out too, following his lead. But even with both of them swimming together, it felt like there was no end to the water over them. The pressure was building against her ears, and she was really afraid that they were swimming down and not up. And how would she even know the difference?

It didn't matter. Fitz knew. And she trusted Fitz. Just that thought calmed her.

Her lungs were on fire when she suddenly felt the water flowing away from her face and could hear Fitz sucking in breath after breath. She did the same, over and over again. The air was nearly as cold as the water, but she didn't care.

"All right?" Fitz asked out of the darkness. They were both treading water, but he had kept a hand on her elbow so that they wouldn't lose each other.

Ritchie made an answering sound, sort of a sputter that she didn't even know the meaning of. She tried looking around them, but her implant refused to superimpose any outlines to mark out their surroundings on her field of view.

"I can't see," she said.

"Me neither," he said. Then she heard a click and saw him holding a glow stick over his head with the hand that was not on her elbow. It glowed its sickly green light with all of its might, but it illuminated nothing but the two of them struggling to stay afloat in the midst of an endless inky black sea.

"Where are we?" she asked.

"Exactly where the Berwegers wanted us to be, I'm afraid," he said. He gave up looking around for any hint of their surroundings and turned his attention back to her. From the sudden look on his face, she guessed she wasn't looking well. "I'm so sorry, Ritchie. This was all my idea. I practically had to drag you here with me, and now look at the mess we're in."

"You never had to drag me with you anywhere in all the years we've been friends," she said, hating the sound of miserable guilt in his voice. "This time is no exception to that. So forget about who's to blame. What do we do now?"

"Pick a direction and start swimming, I guess," he said, looking around them again. "Any direction is as good as any other."

"You can let me go, now," she told him. "I'm not planning to ditch you."

"Oh," he said, as if he hadn't realized he was still clutching on to her arm. He let her go with a sheepish grin, then inclined his head to his right. "This way?"

She nodded, and they swam together through the darkness. Even with the warming exercise, Ritchie could feel her teeth chattering from the cold. She knew it would only feel colder once they found the shore and got out of the water and into the air.

But the alternative was much worse.

"The Berwegers led us here, then?" she said as they swam. "You didn't get lost?"

"No, I was following their directions with no hint we weren't following all the others to the party until the very moment on the chute when we were sliding too fast to stop or go back."

"What did they say?" Ritchie asked.

"Nothing. They just laughed. Both of them," he said through gritted teeth.

"So they know where we are?" she asked half-heartedly.

"I don't think so," Fitz said. "I think they knew about the top of that chute, but I doubt they've ever come down here."

"Still, from the chute, someone could send down help," she said. "They wanted to keep us away from their gathering, but not to *kill* us. Right?"

He didn't answer. She hated that he didn't answer. But she didn't press. Something was bothering him, as if he had done something more than just try to crash their party, something that had led them to retaliate in this way. But he would tell her what it was when he was ready. She knew he would. There were no secrets between them. Not since they were kids.

They swam on in silence a little longer. The first time Ritchie heard gentle splashing from somewhere ahead of them, she was sure it was wishful thinking, just her imagination. They were both swimming in smooth, even strokes, but they weren't exactly silent. She was probably just projecting some of that sound they were making off into the darkness.

But then it grew louder, and she could see by the eager look on Fitz's face that he heard it too. They both found the energy to swim just a little faster, and a few minutes later they were rewarded with the feel of slick stone under their feet and hands.

Then they were crawling up a pebbly shore that ended almost at once in a sheer stone wall that reached up far past the light from their glow stick. But it didn't matter. They had enough space to flop down together and catch their breath.

Unfortunately, the cold seeped into her body far faster than the fatigue left her exhausted legs.

"I can't get through to anyone," Fitz said from where he lay sprawled beside her. "We're too deep for our implants to reach."

"I didn't think that was possible," Ritchie said, and now she was shivering for two reasons. She hated that word. *Deep*. Nothing good came from being deep. Deep under the ground, deep under the water. It was all bad. "We have to get out of here," she said. "We have to figure something out to get us out of here."

"I'm working on it," he said. "I'm broadcasting a distress call at the very limits of my implant's range. It's easier to focus on that if I'm not walking at the same time."

Or talking either, Ritchie guessed, but she couldn't sit quietly and wait. "Why would you try that? We already know we're too deep to call for help," she said.

"Too deep to reach the school systems," he agreed. "But I'm not trying to reach the school. I'm trying to reach Wyss."

"Or any of the kids at the party," Ritchie said, and instantly tried to reach Moreau. But there was no response.

"I think we're too deep for wherever that party is either," Fitz said.

"Then how will Wyss hear you?"

"He has a drone array down here, mapping the tunnels," he said. Then Ritchie felt him send something from his implant to hers. She opened it and saw an intricate map of caves and caverns floating hologram-like in her field of vision.

"Has he been here?" Ritchie asked, scanning the image.

"I don't think so, but there are a lot of places he hasn't poked into yet," Fitz said. "Then there's the fact that this map is already dated. Just from a few hours ago, but still. One of his drones might be close enough even now."

"If we can find ourselves on this map, we can get back to the school," Ritchie said.

"That's what I'm hoping." Then he sat up straighter to look her in the eyes. The glow stick he had left shining on the pebbly beach cast his face mainly in shadow, and she imagined she looked much the same to him. "Dry yet?" he asked.

"Yes," she said, touching the material of her pants and tunic. Even her boots were moisture-free. She wondered about that. They never felt dry enough when she was running outdoors in the Oymyakon weather, but they could handle swimming through a subterranean sea just fine?

"Good, me too," he said, getting to his feet and wiping the grit from the beach off the seat of his pants. Then she felt him send something else to her implant, and she blinked hard to open it. Her map now had an addendum, an area he had marked in a green blobby highlight. "Do you see what I'm looking at?" he asked.

"Yes," Ritchie said, as she stood up. "The tunnels Wyss' drones have mapped so far have a couple of chutes that head off in this direction. A shame none of the drones have followed them yet."

"It means there must be more than one way out. I wished we had a drone with us to scout a path out for us, but I guess we're on our own. We'll just follow the shore and see what we see."

They started walking along the pebbly shore. In some places it was wider, in others it was so narrow they had to splash through the water, but always the stone wall before them was sheer and extended further up than they could see with glow stick and night vision.

Ritchie didn't like how helpless this was all starting to feel. Not that she was the kind to give up in despair. But still. "Any way out is going to mean a climb up. If all the chutes drop out over the middle of that sea..." She couldn't finish her thought. It would mean there would be no way for them to get back out.

"I don't think that's the only way," Fitz said.

"I really don't need false hope right now," she said.

"It's not false hope. Haven't you noticed how very straight and smooth this stone wall is?"

Ritchie didn't understand him. Then she looked at the stone wall, not as an obstruction in her way but as a thing in and of itself. "It really is a wall, isn't it? Shaped by people."

"More likely machines, but yeah," Fitz said. "The school is built on top of an old fortress, remember? And no one has learned all of its secrets."

"But why a fortress wall down here?" she asked.

"To protect from invasion from below," he said, and gave her a wild grin.

She supposed she ought to find the prospect chilling. Battles down here in the deep? And what matter of creature would come *up* to here?

But to her surprise, she found herself returning that almost manic grin. Because it was good news. If there was a wall down here, there had been people down here. And that meant there had to be a way up.

The beach narrowed away to nothingness again, and they splashed around a jutting corner of that stone wall to find themselves facing a long, narrow canyon. The fortress wall was on their left, as ever, and the more cave-like rock to the right was just as impassably tall and steep.

But between the two ran a pebble-strewn path that just had to lead to somewhere.

"Shall we?" Fitz asked with an elaborate bow.

"Might as well," she said, but she was still grinning like a fool. She had never heard of anyone getting hypoxic underground, but then she knew very little about such environments. "Our implants would tell us if we were getting hypoxic, wouldn't they?" she asked Fitz.

"Why, do you feel sick?" he asked.

"Not quite myself," she said.

"Just how should yourself be feeling after everything that's just happened? Keeping in mind we're still in it," he added.

"I have no idea," she admitted.

"There you go," he said.

"So you feel normal? Sober? Whatever?" she asked.

He stopped and looked at her as if trying to tell if she was joking with him. But why would she be joking? She could see in his eyes that he mentally tested then discarded a series of possible responses before shrugging and turning to continue following the path.

"Fitz?" she asked.

"It's not weird for me," he said back over his shoulder, and she jogged to catch up with him before he could disappear around the next curve in the narrow canyon. "It just feels like we're together again, having another adventure sure to get us in tons of trouble. Or me, anyway."

"We remember our shared childhood very differently," Ritchie said. "Trouble? Really?"

"Me? Always. You? Not so much," he said. He was still walking so fast that she had to keep jogging not to get left behind.

"But your trouble was always because of your dad. It wasn't because of anything *we* did. Right?" she prompted when he didn't respond.

He stopped so suddenly she collided with him. But he didn't turn around. He just stared transfixed at the path ahead of them.

She had said too much, and in too joking of a tone. She remembered well how he had felt about his father when they were kids. From what he'd said in the last year, that relationship had only soured in the intervening years. She absolutely hadn't meant to make light of that. "Fitz? I'm sorry. We don't have to talk about your dad. I know how you feel about that."

"It's not that," he said. He turned to face her, but at the same time he took a step away so that she could see the path ahead of them. "It's just, I was more right than I knew about our adventures ending in trouble. I mean, look at that." He pointed at what he must've just avoided tripping over.

"That's a dead body," Ritchie said.

"That's a dead body," he agreed.

The body was wearing a cadet's uniform, but it was no one they knew. She was absolutely certain about that. These half mummified/half skeletal remains had clearly been down here for quite some time. Maybe even decades.

Suddenly she felt warm, really warm. Like her whole body was aglow with the fire of her curiosity. This was even better than the mystery of the two colonels or whatever conspiracy the Berwegers were recruiting for. This was a real thing she had to get to the bottom of.

Fitz seemed less enthused as he watched her face, but she just couldn't dampen down that glow. "You know, finding dead bodies is more of a thing of our youth than our childhood days together," she teased.

"Whatever," he said, throwing up his hands. "Let's go take a closer look. Maybe we can figure out who this poor kid used to be."

"The first step in finding him justice," Ritchie said.

8

FITZ HANDED Ritchie a fresh glow stick, his last one, then stepped back to let her examine the body on her own. Her interest was clearly a little ghoulish, but that fear that had been in her eyes since they'd left the last hallway of the academy behind was finally gone now. Focusing on the body was driving all claustrophobic thoughts from her mind. He knew it wouldn't last, and he still had no idea how they were even getting out of these caves, but for a moment anyway it felt good to see her a little closer to her usual self.

"This is a very old-fashioned uniform," she said, carefully not touching it as she leaned in close with the glow stick. "The piping isn't something any of the academies have used in more than twelve years, and the colors are just a little off."

"Okay," Fitz said to her, even as he tried sending out messages with his implant again. Still nothing in range to respond.

"Did he just fall asleep here? His hands are folded on his belly like he was relaxing, and I see no signs of injury," she said.

"If we're careful, we can try turning him over," Fitz said, moving to stand over her as she knelt beside the fallen cadet.

"Voet," she said, and he realized she was reading the name tag on his uniform. "Why does that sound familiar?"

"I don't know anyone of that name," Fitz said. "We can search the databases when we get back upstairs." He saw her stiffen and regretted his words. He hadn't intended to remind her of where exactly they were.

But then she saw something else, leaning forward to examine the ground beneath the body. "Is this dried blood?" she asked.

"It's hard to tell in that light," he said. "Let's roll him over on his side and see what's under him. I'll take his hips, you take his shoulders. If we keep his body in alignment, I think he'll hold together."

Ritchie's mouth was a tight line, but she nodded. He knelt down beside her and gently slid his fingers under the hip of the body. "Ready?"

Ritchie slipped her fingertips beneath the bony shoulder. "Ready."

They lifted as one. It was lighter even than he expected, but it didn't crumble. In an instant, they had the bony body resting on its side.

And could see the dozens of tiny slashes in the back of the uniform, each stained darkly, the fabric held in stiff waves.

"Definitely a murder, then," Fitz said.

"Do you remember any legends of a missing student?" Ritchie asked even as she moved her glow stick from stab wound to stab wound, searching for more clues.

"No, but I'm not really up on such things," he admitted.

"These are all different," she said.

"They all look the same to me," he said.

"No, the depth of penetration is different. The angle, the locations. I don't think he was stabbed a dozen times by one person. I think he was stabbed once each by a dozen people."

"That's a horrid thought," Fitz said.

"Like a ritual," she went on.

"You might have conspiracies on the brain," he said. "Considering why we were down here in the first place. Or actually before that. You were obsessing about that picture in Hansen's office even before the invitations went out."

But she didn't seem to have heard him. She just kept examining the body in front of her, centimeter by centimeter. But there was nothing else for them to see. She finally set her glow stick aside. "My gut says this cadet was killed by a dozen people who took turns stabbing him then left him here where no one would ever find him." She rolled back onto her heels and looked up at the sheer stone wall that still loomed over them. "I want to know more about this fortress."

"The fortress predates the academy by centuries, Ritchie," he pointed out.

"But it has a history, and that history travels through time with it," she said. "It means things to people. Potentially," she conceded before he could even argue.

"If the body was never found, then someone got away with murder. At least one someone," he said.

"Wait, what were you saying a minute ago?"

"About what?"

"Conspiracies? No, after that..." she said, but she tapped a fingertip to her chin as if hoping to summon more of a memory. Fitz had no idea what she was searching for, so he just waited. Then her face lit up, and he knew she had it. "The photo in Hansen's office," she said triumphantly.

"What does that mean?" he asked.

"This cadet. Voet. He was in the picture. That's why the name sounded familiar to me. I'm sure I'm right."

"Colonel Hansen has a photo in his office of himself as a cadet with both the future Colonel Devereux and this unfortunate soul before us?" Fitz asked skeptically.

"If you don't believe me, we can sneak in there and I'll prove it to you," she said.

"If you say you saw it, that's good enough for me," he said. "But what does it mean?"

"For one, it means we probably shouldn't say anything to anyone upstairs about what we've just found," she said, and all the manic energy drained out of her. "He was left here for a reason. To be forgotten. Dredging it back up again, we should know what that might lead to before we say anything. For all we know, Hansen and Devereux are responsible for two of these stabbings."

"Hansen? No way," Fitz said. "Frankly, I find it hard to believe Devereux did this either."

"But they might know who did," Ritchie said. "And if they do and have never said anything about it, maybe there's a reason they kept it secret."

"I don't know, Ritchie. That's a lot of hypotheticals," he said.

"So let's start working up better theories," she said. "I'm not saying we hide this forever. Just until we know what the consequences of revealing it are."

"It's the first day of school, and you're already stressed out about the classwork," Fitz reminded her. "Do you really want to throw another investigation on top of that?"

"Why not?" she said carelessly. "I think it helps me focus."

Fitz barked out a laugh. "Sadly, I think that's true."

"We can always find this place again in our implant histories," Ritchie said. "But for now I guess we should get back to finding a way out."

"Right," he said, and looked up at the sheer wall again. At some point there had to be a way inside of that thing. Even a defensive wall had a gate somewhere. But after so much time, it could be buried in fallen rock or deliberately destroyed before the fortress was abandoned or just not findable anymore.

"Do you hear that?" Ritchie asked suddenly, her voice a mere breath of a whisper.

He didn't dare speak, just lifted his eyebrows in unspoken question. She lifted a finger for him to wait, her eyes faraway as she focused all of her attention on her hearing.

Then he heard it too, the softest of whirring sounds.

He immediately sent a call out with his implant. He had never attempted to communicate with one of Wyss' drones before, and he had no idea what response to expect. The complete lack of one was disheartening.

But the whirring grew louder. Ritchie straightened up to stand beside him, and they both scanned the shadowy darkness above them in the narrow canyon.

Something dropped down to hover in front of his face, too close to his nose. He almost swatted it away, but stopped the impulse just in time. The little machine was the size of a largish insect, but surely no insect of such size could live in this place. What would it eat?

"Wyss?" he said out loud.

"Can he hear what they hear?" Ritchie asked him.

"No, but they read lips," he said. Then he couldn't help grinning at her. It sounded silly when he said it out loud like that.

"Okay," she said slowly. "What good does that do us?"

"He's manning the controls remotely," Fitz said. "Buddy, we need a way out of here. Can this little guy guide us back? Preferably by a route that wouldn't require us to fly."

The drone just hovered there in front of his nose for the longest time.

"Maybe he went to bed," Ritchie said. "Or he can't receive signals from this drone any better than he can from us. We're too deep." She shivered as she said that last word.

"The drones form their own network," Fitz said. "So long as they are within reach of each other, they form a chain between us and Wyss."

"I don't know. It sounds like a lot to hope for," she said. "Can it even work?"

Suddenly the drone dipped and rose, then dipped and rose again in rapid succession.

"Was that Wyss nodding?" she asked.

"I think so," Fitz said. "Quick, tag it with your implant so it shows up on your night vision display. We don't want to lose sight of it, tiny as it is."

At first they followed it at a run, further up the canyon. The path grew narrower but also steeper, leading them ever closer to the surface.

Then it took a turn, and the canyon was gone. They were standing at the edge of a large rocky slope like the side of a hill, steep enough where they needed hands and feet both to get up it. They sent showers of pebbles scurrying down behind them, as well as the occasional larger rock.

Then Ritchie cried out as the rock she was using as a foothold rolled out from under her and she slammed down hard on her belly, sliding a few meters back down the hill.

"Are you okay?" Fitz asked, stopping to look back down towards her. He could hear the drone flying back to hover closer to his head. Good old Wyss was paying attention. He wasn't going to leave them behind.

"I'm all right," Ritchie said, and climbed back up to where he was. She must have bitten her lip or caught it on the sharp edge of a rock, but it wasn't bleeding too badly. He reached out to wipe it away, but she flinched back. "It's fine," she said, and dragged the sleeve of her tunic across her mouth. Now she had blood smeared all the way up her cheek to her ear, but he decided he should probably just let it go.

Then she looked up, initially to find her next handhold, but then too far ahead, and she saw what he had been hoping she wouldn't notice for a while yet.

The roof of the cavern was curving down before them to join the top of the hill. But they didn't quite touch. What they were crawling toward was no human-sized cave they would be walking through. No, for as far as his night vision could see, there was nothing but this same hillside of loose rock under an ever-lowering stone ceiling. There would be barely enough room to crawl on their bellies, and no sign of when they'd reach the other end.

"We're sure this is a way out?" she said. She didn't sound anxious or scared. No, she sounded like she'd just shut off every single one of her emotions. Like something robotic was running her body now.

"Wyss wouldn't take us where we didn't absolutely have to go," Fitz said. He reached out to touch her again, this time to grasp the hand that was closest to him. She didn't pull away.

She was shaking, even worse than they'd both been shaking after their cold swim, before their uniforms had dried.

"You can do this," he told her.

"I know I can," she said, but still in that robotic voice.

"And I'll be with you the whole way," he said, squeezing her hand even more tightly. "And so will Wyss."

"Wyss," she said, but as if the sound had no meaning for her.

"Right, Wyss," he said. "Wyss who's still in the academy, who can call for help at any point." Then a sudden thought struck him, and he looked up until he had pinpointed the drone's location. Then he mouthed some words without making a sound.

Wyss had to know *not* to call anyone, not unless he and Ritchie were in very grave danger indeed. A rescue would surely lead to others knowing about the body.

There was something hesitant in the way the drone nodded this time. Then it made a short jabbing forward and back motion, as if pointing towards Ritchie.

"Ritchie is okay," Fitz said aloud, all too aware of how the hand in his was still shaking, if less than before. Then he mouthed another question.

Did Wyss see the body?

The drone waggled in place. Fitz couldn't help grinning to himself. He knew that meant no, but he also knew it meant that Wyss was even now on a separate screen, rolling back the footage to look.

"Wyss, it has to stay secret for now," he said out loud. "Do you read me?"

The drone made the nodding motion again, then turned to face the top of the hill and started slowly flying over the surface.

"Have I ever told you how much I hate space stations?" Fitz asked.

"No," Ritchie said. Then, as if she was only belatedly hearing him, she looked up at him. "Wait, seriously?"

"Seriously," he said, and released her hand. They started climbing again, hand and then foot, hand and then foot. Ritchie was taking an extra second to be sure of her holds before taking the next step, but she was moving.

But they were still in the openness of the cavern. He had to keep her attention focused on his voice. That and the next handhold, that's all he wanted her to be thinking about.

"You know the regulations that govern space stations are nowhere near as strict as they are for spacecraft," he said.

"There hasn't been a significant accident on a space station in our lifetimes," she said. "Not even a deliberate act by a terrorist or act of war. They are as safe as houses on a planet's surface."

"Sure, says you," he said. "It doesn't feel that way to me. Every time

I'm on one, I can never stop thinking about the thin layer of metallic hull that is all that stands between me and the vacuum."

"There's more than the hull protecting you, you know," she said. "There are redundancies on top of redundancies. And they work! Again, no accidents in our lifetime."

"Still. It's chilling. I don't know how you stand it," he said. He looked back down at where she was climbing just a bit below him, but her face was intent on the task of find holds and puzzling out what he was saying. She wasn't looking up. That was good.

But in a few more meters, the ceiling was going to be brushing their backs.

"It's not my favorite thing either," she admitted. "But you get used to it."

"Me? Never."

"But you fly all the time," she said. "You're not freaked out, not even in jump space."

"I never said it was a *rational* fear," he said, and she huffed a sound that might almost have been a laugh.

"How much time have you spent on space stations, anyway?"

"How much time? Too much. Let's see, the first time was when I was a kid. And you're going to say this is the real source of my trauma, but I'm going to say it isn't," he said.

Then he went on to spin her an involved tale that had a kernel of truth to it—he had indeed been freaked out from the first time he had been expected to sleep in a cabin on a space station at the age of three —but was largely embellished.

He doubted she was fooled. But she was engrossed. And that was all he needed.

He was just starting to flail for more details about the time he had seen pirates threatening to push his cousins out of an airlock for being too petulant over being robbed when his grasping hand found not a handhold but open air. He panicked, certain he was about to tumble all the long way back down again.

Then he realized the air he felt was the end of the climb. He grasped the edge with both hands and leveraged himself up. It was a tight squeeze between the top of the ledge and the rocky ceiling, but once he was through, he was lying on his back in blissfully open space.

He could've happily stayed there, flat on his back, just enjoying the sensation of not climbing, for hours and hours.

Instead, he rolled over to reach out for Ritchie and help her through. She didn't take his hands, but he caught the back of her uniform and pulled anyway. The faster she made it through that last tightness, the better. If her hips got caught halfway through...

He couldn't even complete the image in his head. The idea of her panic scared him too much.

But she didn't get caught, and the two of them both flopped onto their backs and just laid there, looking up at the hovering drone.

Then the drone sent him a message. Ritchie, lying beside him with her head on his arm, flinched ever so slightly and he knew she had gotten it too.

An updated map of the catacombs. The path they were meant to follow was outlined for them, all easily walkable caves. They would be inside the school within minutes.

From the time when they got up and started walking, that was. Neither of them stirred. It just felt too good not to move.

But of course Ritchie sat up first. Not to get moving, but to look down into his face. "Thank you," she said.

"For what?" he asked. He started to say that it had all been his fault, because it absolutely had, but she put a hand over his mouth to stop his words.

"You know for what," she said.

"You're welcome," he said, or tried to. Her hand was still over his mouth.

She laughed, but then she really was standing up, reaching down to pull him up after her. "Come on. It's late. And it's way too cold and damp to sleep here. And we have work to do."

He groaned out loud at that last bit. He had just been looking forward to hitting his bunk.

But she was right. The murder might have happened decades ago, but he felt the same urgency she did to get to the bottom of it.

He just hoped that that bottom didn't contain two colonels under whose command they both were. Awkward didn't even begin to describe what that would lead to.

9

IT WASN'T ENTIRELY a surprise to find Wyss waiting for them in the hall outside the library doors. Ritchie knew Fitz had been communicating with him.

When he hadn't been keeping her calm, that is.

Technically, they were all violating lights out, but being in the library was usually excusable for studying purposes. That excuse would be flimsier than ever on the first night after only a single day of classes, but if they were quiet, they wouldn't get caught, so it wouldn't matter.

Wyss seemed to take entirely too long to get the door open. Ritchie quickly pushed in after him, dragging Fitz behind her. His look of confusion deepened when she stopped just inside the library and turned to face Wyss.

"Have you seen Moreau?" Ritchie asked him the moment the doors had clicked shut behind them.

Wyss blinked, as much an expression of surprise as he ever registered. "No. Is she meeting us here?"

"She's not answering me. I don't know where she is," she said.

"Probably still down there with the others," Wyss said with a shrug. Then he lead the way to the corner of the library where their personal meeting room was situated. Not that it had their name on it or anything, but everyone in the school knew that was their special place. Either out of respect for the murder they'd solved last year, or out of revulsion for the one place that the murderess Keller had haunted every day she had been a fellow Oymyakon cadet, no one but the four of them ever studied there.

Or maybe it was because more than half of the space was taken up by the equipment that Wyss and Keller had assembled together. He used it all by himself now, and had rebuilt most of the systems since Keller had gone away. Wyss insisted he wasn't afraid that she had left anything nefarious behind, but Ritchie knew an abundance of caution when she saw it.

Keller had tried to kill Ritchie, just at the moment that Ritchie had realized that Keller had been the one who had used her to murder Jeger. And yet somehow Ritchie knew that the person Keller had hurt the most had been Wyss.

What must it feel like to be betrayed like that by your closest friend? Ritchie looked up at Fitz as he opened the door to let them all in the meeting room. The corner of his mouth twitched, not quite a smile, as she brushed past him.

It would be completely devastating.

"So they're all still down there?" Fitz asked, as the three of them each took a seat at the table. Wyss tapped on the tabletop display. There was an array of windows, each labeled with a drone's identifying number. Several were showing tracking shots through empty caves. Three were recording a crowd of people gathered in a brightly lit cavern, but only from a great distance.

But nearly a quarter of them were just blank.

"They swatted down that many?" Fitz asked, running a hand over his face.

"Not by hand," Wyss said, and his face twisted into a frown. "Someone down there is wicked accurate with throwing rocks. I lost all of those in a matter of seconds. I suspect they know about the other three, but they're letting me watch from a distance."

"A distance too great for lip reading," Fitz said.

Wyss nodded.

Clearly this was picking up a conversation they had had earlier, without her, but she thought she got the gist of it. Still, she wasn't sure it made sense.

"You think they knew that?" Ritchie asked. "I mean, that's a bit of a leap for them to intuit that the drones are running lip reading software, and that there's a range past which they don't work."

"And what that range is," Fitz said, nodding.

"Maybe they just want them too far out for the mics—which the drones don't have, but they don't know that—to pick anything up," Wyss said. "Whichever is true, they stopped shooting when only the three were still in the cavern with them. I guess it worked out for the best, since I sent the extra drones I pulled out of that cavern to search for the two of you."

"Thank you so much for that," Ritchie said, and he blushed. It was probably as understated a response as his blink of surprise, but with his pale skin even the softest of blushes flared brightly.

"So we don't know anything that was said at that meeting?" Fitz asked.

"Not a bit of it," Wyss said. "They shot the drones before they walked up on that little stage-like rock protrusion thing."

"The space looks like a cathedral, doesn't it?" Ritchie asked. She was squinting at one of the feeds when suddenly all the drone windows disappeared and a holographic projection of the cavern burst to life over the tabletop. It turned slowly and seemed to be a live image, as the outlines of people standing on the floor moved ever so slightly.

"I had mapped this space more extensively earlier," Wyss said. "It's a natural cavern, but it's been worked over. A lot of stalagmites and stalactites were removed to leave just the rows that stand like pillars. The stage part is also natural, but parts of it look artificially worn smooth and flat."

"By the Berwegers?" Ritchie asked.

"No, older. A lot older," Wyss said.

"Like twenty or thirty years ago?" Fitz asked, trading a glance with Ritchie.

But Wyss was engrossed with another of his computer screens. "Older," he tossed over his shoulder.

"Like fortress old?" Ritchie asked.

That got his attention. He spun back around in his chair and considered the question. "The parts of the academy that are built into the mountain *are* the fortress. The back corridor of the school that connects to the catacombs as well as the hangar decks and a few of the other outbuildings. But why do I sense that's not the fortress you're talking about?"

"There's another, deeper fortress by an underground sea," Fitz said.

"I thought that was just a legend," Wyss said. He turned back to his screens. "So this space they're meeting in as not as old, I don't think. But I'll find out for sure. I just need to get the drones down deeper to map around that area, and double-check with some of the histories that I thought were more legend than fact."

"It would be good to get a timeline between that chamber, the fortress at the bottom of the catacombs, and the academy itself," Fitz said.

"Yeah," Wyss said, back to his half-listening voice.

Ritchie watched the hologram turn in front of her. She wondered if one of the crude little figures at the bottom was a representation of Moreau. "If Moreau was there, she can tell us what was said."

"*If* she was there," Fitz said. "We don't know that for sure."

"I don't know where else she would be," Ritchie said. She didn't want to speak her real fear out loud. But just what had the Berwegers decided to share with that select group of cadets? And what if it was persuasive?

What if Moreau was about to change to a whole new circle of friends?

She had seen it happen before, back at her old school. She had lost a friend or two herself. Interests changed, and time was always in short supply for students. Mostly it wasn't anything particularly dramatic. It wasn't even something she had noticed right away, even when it was happening. Friends just took different classes and drifted apart.

But this time it felt different. Like Moreau was being lured away from her.

"Hey," Fitz said, and Ritchie realized she had settled into a glassy stare at nothing. "You okay?"

"You don't have to keep asking me that," she said.

"It's been a rough night," he said.

"But the hard part is over now," she said. "Now it's research time. Let's get started."

"Already done," Wyss said.

"What?" she asked, disappointed.

"Well, just the first search," he said. The hologram of the cavern winked out, and a window of information appeared in front of her. The text was lined up with her orientation, and Fitz moved his chair closer so he could read over her shoulder.

"His name was Stans Voet," Wyss said even as the two of them scanned the information for themselves. "He attended Oymyakon Foreign Service Academy, but disappeared two weeks before graduation. He already had a placement with the diplomatic corps waiting for him, even though he hadn't been to university yet. He was handpicked by the head of the school of gastronomic communication to be a member of their accelerated program."

"Gastronomic..." Fitz started to say, then gave up.

"Some species communicate extensively through food. The taste, the texture, what foods are paired with what other foods, it's all rife with meaning," Ritchie told him.

"Voet had a genetic variation that made him particularly suitable for that line of work," Wyss said. "His taste covered a wider spectrum than normal for humans, and with greater distinction."

"You think someone killed him for that?" Fitz asked.

Wyss shrugged.

"Probably not the taste thing specifically," Ritchie said. "Maybe because someone wanted his spot in the program? But that makes no sense, since I'm sure he was killed by several people working together. You know, I really don't like to start with motive. It feels too... forcing the facts to fit the theory."

"Agreed," Fitz said. "Any suspects at the time?"

"Are you kidding me? Until you found his body, this was never even considered a possible murder. He was declared missing. Search parties combed everything for kilometers around the academy, but no sign of him was ever found."

"And the catacombs?" Ritchie asked.

"It says they were 'thoroughly searched', but I'm doubtful they went everywhere," Wyss said. "*I* haven't even been everywhere yet. At some point the search was just abandoned."

"When?" Fitz asked.

"Two years later. By order of..." But Wyss broke off, his face flaring even more scarlet than before.

"By order of whom?" Fitz asked.

"By your grandfather," Wyss whispered. "Shackleton Fitz II."

"What does that mean?" Ritchie asked.

"It means my grandfather was the governor of this sector of the Union of Free Worlds," Fitz said as he scanned the text. "It would've been his responsibility. And after two years of searching, it hardly feels like a suspicious call to me to stop spending the resources on a fruitless endeavor."

"Weird, though," Wyss said, still whispering.

"Both of you are seeing conspiracies everywhere," Fitz said. "I'm not sure that's going to be helpful in our mission to find justice for Cadet Voet here."

But Ritchie had a sudden horrible idea. It was so repellant she found herself shaking again, although the room was quite warm, dry and comfortable. No, it was her very bones that were chilled by the thought.

"Did the Berwegers lead us there on purpose?" she asked, and realized now she too was whispering. "Did they want us to find this body?"

"No," Fitz said. He sounded absolutely, unequivocally certain.

"They knew this other cavern was here, the one they threw their party in, and they just arrived with us on the train yesterday," Ritchie said. "What else might they know?"

"Their parents were cadets here too," Wyss said. "At about the same time, now that you mention it."

"No, that's not why they sent us that way," Fitz said firmly.

"But how can you be sure?" Ritchie asked.

He looked at her, and she saw something like anguish in his eyes.

"Fitz?"

"They sent us that way because they're cruel," he said, looking away from her. "They know how you feel about close, underground spaces, and they know how I feel about..." He broke off, mumbling a curse to himself. Then he sat up straighter in his chair. "They sent us down the deepest path they could find in a hurry, and they gave us no more thought than that."

"They certainly don't seem to be thinking about you now," Wyss put in.

"No, they don't," Fitz said. Then he swiped away the window of information on Voet. "Anything else turn up on the first search?"

"A lot of variations of the same information," Wyss said. "He was a kid. There isn't much about him in the system. We might want to draw up a list of fellow cadets, although how we're going to question them from here I don't know."

"Even Hansen and Devereux will be tough to talk to," Ritchie said. Then she found herself yawning, a massive yawn that came out far too loud. "Sorry."

"No, you're right," Fitz said. "It's getting late. The next step is going to be talking to the other cadets at the party, but clearly they aren't going to be available until morning. We might as well get some sleep."

"Go on without me," Wyss said. "I'm going to set up a few search programs to run while we sleep."

"Don't be late," Fitz said. Then he and Ritchie went back out into the cavernous quiet of the library.

But it was a pleasant sort of cavern. Sure, the sky visible through the rooftop windows was dark and stormy even for the middle of the night, but it was still sky, not stone. And she was warm and dry.

And safe.

But something was bothering her.

"Fitz," she said, catching his arm before he could open the doors that led out to the main hallway. He turned back, but he was definitely avoiding her eyes.

"Something is going on that you're not telling me," she said.

It took him a minute to come up with a response, and when she heard it she didn't exactly like it. "What makes you think that?"

"Well, just to start, you seem to have a finger on why the Berwegers did what they did to the two of us. And it was about more than you trying to sneak me into their private party?"

"It's just a guess," he said with an offhand shrug. "An educated guess, but still."

"Okay," Ritchie allowed, ignoring how certain he had been when he had made this guess. Like what he said was carved on stone. "But say you're right. How would either of the Berwegers know how I feel about being underground? That's not exactly common knowledge."

Fitz sighed and ran his hands through his hair. As if he knew how distracting that was. Her heart leaped, but she ignored it. It was getting easier, ignoring those responses. Murder *was* a powerful focusing tool for her mind.

"You don't know the Berwegers, but that's exactly the sort of information they make it their business to know," he said. "And they want to know those sorts of things so that they can use that knowledge. I'm sorry they targeted you."

She waved the apology away. It didn't matter now. "But you would never tell anyone anything like that, would you?" she asked.

Now he was looking at her again, earnestly. "Never, Ritchie. Never."

"Not even by mistake?"

"I..." he stopped himself and stood quietly for a long moment, and she knew he was casting back in his memory. For what, though? "No. Never, I swear."

"I believe you," Ritchie said, partly because it was true, but partly because it seemed like the best way to get him to stop looking at her so intensely.

But he didn't. If anything, he kicked it up a few notches. "Ritchie, no one is ever going to hurt you through me. You have to believe that."

"Okay," she said, a little too loudly. "I believe you."

"Truly."

"I said I believe you," she said. He still kept his eyes locked on hers. But finally he seemed to accept that she was telling the truth and gave her a relieved smile. "But you know what that means," she said as he reached for the door handle.

"What does that mean?" he asked.

"It means the only person who could've told them was Moreau," she said.

Because no one else knew. Not her mother or her grandmother, nobody. She hadn't even known it herself until she came to this academy built into the side of a mountain. Only Moreau knew and could've told the Berwegers.

But how Ritchie wished it wasn't true.

10

AFTER FAR TOO LITTLE SLEEP, Fitz woke up to find his whole body stiff and sore. His muscles still ached from the exertion of the swim and the climb. He slowly eased himself out of his bunk and onto the floor, then caught a glimpse of his reflection in the mirror mounted to his open locker door.

He was a mess. His hands were scraped raw, and every inch of him was covered in bruises. He even had an abrasion over his eyebrow. He had no idea how he had gotten that. Probably falling down that chute.

Luckily Imhof and Stucki weren't there, so he didn't have to explain anything. Their bunks were still neatly made from the day before, never slept in. He wondered where they had crashed after the party. Or if the party was still somehow raging on into morning.

Wyss was sleeping at the desk, head resting on his folded arms. The many windows he had opened were running a variety of programs, even as he drooled on the screen. Fitz nudged him awake before heading to the showers.

This was going to be a long day.

But if he thought he felt bad, it was nothing compared to how Ritchie looked when he and Wyss joined her at the cafeteria table for breakfast. She didn't look like she'd slept at all, and he could see from her face that Moreau had never turned up. Like Imhof and Stucki. But while Fitz was merely curious where his roommates had gotten to, Ritchie was deeply worried.

"It's almost time for class," she said. "She wouldn't be late on the second day, would she?"

"It's not just her," Fitz said. "Look around. A lot of people are missing. You don't think they're all still down in the catacombs, do you?"

"I don't know what to think," Ritchie said, almost despairing.

Then a murmur of voices drew their attention to the doorway at the far side of the room. The twins were sweeping inside, oblivious to all the eyes on them as they made a few selections from the food on offer and sat together at a table in the center of the room. Then they just sat there, eating without speaking, as if it were a perfectly ordinary morning.

They didn't even look like they'd been up late the night before, let alone up all night. They were fully alert, in perfect uniform, without so much as a hair out of place. Somehow it made Fitz's body and all of its many bruises and abrasions ache all over again just looking at them.

"They must know," Ritchie said, pushing back her plate. "I'm going to ask."

"No," Fitz said, catching her arm to keep her from standing up. The idea of Ritchie talking to Finn Berweger made his blood run cold. He told himself that he was worried Finn might say something cutting and hurtful to her, and he wanted to protect her from that.

But a little voice in the back of his head was mumbling something about jealousy.

He wasn't sure if what he was feeling was jealousy per se, but he definitely didn't want to be there to see it when Finn Berweger put the charm on her. No one was immune to that, not even Ritchie.

Ritchie, who was currently looking at him with both eyebrows raised, waiting for him to explain himself, or at least to let her go.

"There she is," Wyss said suddenly, and they both turned to see Moreau slinking over to their table, a steaming cup of black coffee in her hand. She sat down next to Ritchie and took a long drink.

Other cadets were trickling in as well. Nearly all of them looked completely rested, like they were looking forward to an amazing day they fully intended to tackle with all gusto.

Fitz looked at Moreau again as she took another gulp of coffee that was surely too hot to be downed that fast. She didn't look as bad as Ritchie, but she didn't look nearly as fresh as the others.

"Nothing to say?" Fitz asked her when it became clear that Ritchie was having trouble finding the words.

"About?" Moreau asked.

"Where you've been?" he prompted.

"Oh. I thought that was obvious. I went to the thing," she said. "You said you wouldn't go, so I figured *one* of us should be there to see what's going on."

"And?" Fitz asked.

"So that's where I was," she said, and took another sip of coffee.

"That's all you have to say?" Ritchie asked her.

"That's all I can say," Moreau said.

"They swore you all to secrecy?" Fitz asked jokingly.

But Moreau's face was deadly serious. "They didn't have to make us swear."

"What does that mean?" Ritchie asked. She was starting to sound seriously annoyed.

"I really can't talk about it," she said.

"What, like, physically?" Fitz asked.

"Pretty much," Moreau said, draining the last of her coffee. She looked down at the bottom of the cup for a moment, then got up without a word to get some more.

"Why is she being like this?" Ritchie asked.

"Maybe she's just tired," Fitz said. "Which is probably a good thing. Look at the rest of the cadets who were there last night. They look insanely good. Well rested, I swear more attractive than usual. Am I crazy?"

"No," Moreau said as she resumed her seat at the table.

"Did everyone get a hit of go-juice when the party broke up or what?" he asked.

"Not everyone," she said, but she cringed as she spoke, then set her coffee down to rub at her temples.

"Interesting," Wyss said. "You really *can't* talk about it, can you?"

She shook her head, but then flinched again, as if that motion had triggered another sudden headache.

"Are you okay?" Ritchie asked. The rigidity had gone out of her body language and she touched Moreau gently on the arm.

"It'll pass if you all stop asking me questions," she said a bit too savagely. Then she took a deep breath. "Sorry. But seriously. No more questions about last night."

"What did they do to you?" The words were out of Fitz's mouth before he realized that was exactly the sort of question she clearly couldn't answer.

"There are a variety of techniques to wipe memories," Wyss said. "Some chemical, some physical. Brain implants are supposed to be absolutely unhackable, but I think that's a real possibility. I mean, it's everybody who was there last night, right? Not just you?"

"I should go," Moreau said, reaching for her coffee cup. Her eyes were half-closed as if the lights pained her and she was having trouble finding the cup.

"You don't have to answer," Wyss told her, even as he reached across the table to put the cup in her hands. "We can figure it out easily enough by asking everyone else the same thing."

"Don't do that," she said. She started to get up, but Ritchie clutched at her arm.

"Don't go," Ritchie said. "We'll stop asking about last night. You really look like you should just sit for a minute."

Moreau thought it over, then sat back down on the chair. "You're not wrong," she said.

Fitz realized that Wyss beside him was staring fixedly at the Berwegers, and jostled him hard until he stopped. "Don't invite trouble," he whispered to him.

"Sorry," Wyss said. "I just have so many questions. You know those two, don't you?"

"Barely," Fitz said. "It's best not to draw their attention if you can help it."

To his surprise, Moreau laughed. "That's rich coming from you," she said. "What did you do last night if not make absolutely sure their attention was on you?"

"You can talk about that?" he asked.

She shrugged. "You weren't in the room ever, so I guess so. We all know you got led on a wild goose chase."

"A wild goose chase to the deepest part of the catacombs," Fitz said, pointing his chin at Ritchie, who was looking down at her own plate with glassy eyes.

"Oh," Moreau said. Her joking tone was gone in a flash, and now it was she who put a gentle hand on Ritchie's arm. "Are you all right?"

"I'm fine," Ritchie said, yanking her arm away.

"You don't look like you slept much," Moreau said.

"I was worried about you," Ritchie snapped.

"I'm sorry," Moreau said. "Still, were you two lost for a long time? I mean, I know how you feel about... you know."

"Yes, I know you know," Ritchie said venomously. Moreau looked genuinely perplexed by her attitude and almost, if it were possible for Moreau to feel such a way, maybe a little hurt.

"Ritchie, I don't think Moreau told anyone about that," Fitz said. "They just knew. They have a thing, some mysterious talent, to just know stuff." He wished they weren't having this conversation with the people in question sitting just a couple of tables away.

"No, Ritchie, I would never," Moreau said earnestly.

Ritchie nodded without speaking, but she didn't look remotely convinced. Moreau toyed with her now-empty coffee cup. Wyss, as usual, was in his own world, zipping through files on his tablet as he munched the last of his toast.

"So, we found a body," Fitz said.

Ritchie glared at him furiously from across the table.

"What?" he asked. "She's part of the team. She has to know."

"Where did you find this body?" Moreau asked.

"Down in the deep," he said with a vague hand gesture. "Doesn't matter."

"Are you saying the authorities went down into the catacombs to retrieve a body and never broke up the party?" she asked.

"No, I'm not saying that at all. We didn't tell anyone," Fitz said.

"Why not?" Moreau asked.

"We absolutely are not having this conversation in the middle of the cafeteria," Ritchie said. They all got up and dumped their trash, then headed to the doorway to the main hall. Fitz briefly made eye contact with Finn as they passed his table. He was deep in conversation with his sister and a few other cadets, but gave Fitz the slightest quirk of his eyebrow, as if acknowledging that he had indeed not expected to see him at breakfast. Fitz made no gesture in reply, but by the time the four of them were out in the quiet stillness of the main hall, his blood was boiling.

He took a few deep breaths until the pulse in his ears quieted down enough for him to hear Ritchie say, "so that's why we can't say anything yet. It could be something either one or maybe both of the colonels might want to cover up."

"Colonel Hansen? Seriously?" Moreau said.

"We just want to be sure first," Ritchie said. But the deeply skeptical look on Moreau's face didn't budge.

"You can't blame us for thinking there might be a conspiracy," Fitz said. "Not when half the school, including yourself, were conspiring last night."

Moreau opened her mouth to say something, but then bent nearly double, pressing her fingertips to her temples.

"That's really messed up," Wyss said. "The minute we know who we can trust in the academy administration, I'm reporting what those two are up to."

"I'm okay," Moreau said, straightening back up. Her face was ashen and tight, but her eyes were alert. "What's the plan, then?"

"None of my searches are turning up anything useful," Wyss said, glancing at his tablet as if something might have appeared when he wasn't looking then shaking his head.

"We need to find out more about Hansen and Devereux's cadet days," Ritchie said. "Sokolov is close with Hansen. It's not inconceivable that he might have reminisced with her about it. She might know something."

"Or be in a better position than us to ask him about it without raising suspicion," Fitz said.

"You should talk to Frei too," Moreau said.

"Why Frei?" Ritchie asked.

"She works in Colonel Devereux's office doing the same thing as Sokolov does for Hansen," she said. "Well, she switches it off with two other cadets, but she's probably more likely to talk with you than the others."

"It's too late to grab her now before class," Ritchie said. "I'll have to catch her in the barracks later."

"I'm going to keep running the searches, and also mapping the catacombs," Wyss said. "Who knows? There might be more than one body down there."

"Or more clues," Fitz said, then sighed. "I don't see anything I can contribute at all."

"Don't worry about it," Ritchie said. "This is just the first stage of the investigation."

"Moreau, you don't feel under any compulsion to tell things to the Berwegers, do you?" Wyss asked.

"I don't think so," she said, looking up as if testing something in her own mind. "No. But maybe I wouldn't know I wanted to until I was doing it."

"Do you really think the Berwegers have mastered mind control?" Fitz asked Wyss. He only wished he were joking.

"No, not *control*," Wyss said. "But influence? Maybe. I'm running some other searches now. I have a free hour after hand-to-hand. I'll do a deep dive into it then, see what I can figure out. What worries me is that Moreau doesn't seem, well, worried."

"I'm not," Moreau said with a careless shrug.

"Someone's been messing with your brain. They punish you for trying to speak words. How is that not worrying?" Ritchie asked with deep concern. But Moreau just shrugged again.

"Did you consent to this?" Fitz asked.

Moreau didn't even open her mouth to speak this time before she was crumpled by another sudden headache.

"Boy, I hope the answer to that is no," Fitz said under his breath.

The other cadets were starting to come out of the cafeteria now, and they were no longer able to speak privately. They all had the same first class, so they walked together out towards the athletic field. Because for some reason hand-to-hand was nearly always done outside, no matter what the weather.

Fitz wished that administrative decisions were the worst of his problems. But now it was looking like even a decades-old murder wasn't topping that particular list.

11

DOZING off during hand-to-hand combat wasn't really a possibility, but for the three classes she had after that before the lunch break, it had been a constant risk. Her eyelids wanted to close, always promising it was just for a second, just to deal with some eyeball dryness, but she wasn't fooled. She kept them open, not quite having to use her fingers to achieve that.

Her ears couldn't close on her, but her brain kept opting not to process any of what she was hearing into words or thoughts. It was only the second day of class, and the lectures were largely restating the reading she had just managed to do the prior evening before meeting Fitz. But being called on to answer a question was an ever-present danger.

Ritchie got through it by a combination of obsessively taking notes of every single thing that was said just to make sure her brain heard it and by poking her stylus into her thigh under the desk every time she caught herself still drifting off.

She had barely eaten breakfast and her stomach was rumbling loudly by midmorning, but when her last class before lunch ended she decided that she could get by on the protein bar she had at the bottom of her bag. What she really needed was a quick nap, or she was never getting through the afternoon.

She dug the bar out of her bag and ate it in three bites as she jogged down to her room in the barracks. Each of those bites took several minutes to chew. The academy protein bars might be packed with all the essential foodstuffs a growing cadet needed, but they were notoriously difficult to break down and swallow without choking on the dryness.

She was trying to do just that when she finally reached her room and nearly choked anyway when she saw it wasn't empty as she had expected. Frei was in there, her back to Ritchie as she rustled through her locker.

"Oh, hi," Frei said, glancing back over her shoulder.

Ritchie nodded, still working on swallowing down the last bite of the protein bar. She felt like a snake already committed to gagging down too large of a rat. Finally she had it down and could say, "hi. This is a bit of luck. I wanted to talk to you about something."

"Oh, yeah?" Frei said distractedly. She smoothed her hands over her dark black hair, carefully arranged in braids that swept back into a neat little bun at the nape of her neck. Ritchie was pretty sure if she looked up regulation hairstyles in the cadet manual, the first picture would match Frei's hair exactly. Then Frei slammed the door shut and turned to look at Ritchie. "I don't really have time, I'm already late for my work shift, but if you want to walk with me?"

"Works for me," Ritchie said, and immediately about-faced to head back the way she'd come.

Frei really was in a hurry, to judge by her swift steps, but she looked over to be sure Ritchie was keeping up with her. "This must be pretty important, whatever you have to ask me, because I'm pretty sure you came downstairs to catch a nap. And no offense, but you really look like you could use one."

"You're right on both counts," Ritchie said.

Frei looked over at her again and frowned ever so slightly. "Didn't you get the pickup juice or magic powder or whatever it is everyone else got to fool the faculty into thinking everyone got a solid night's sleep?"

Ritchie was confused at first, but then said, "oh, from the party? No, I wasn't at the party. Weren't you?"

"I was in bed when you sneaked out," Frei said.

"You didn't get an invite either?" Ritchie guessed.

"No. I think Grof did, but she claims she didn't. So neither of us went. But you and Moreau both did, I thought?"

"I went out to look for Moreau," Ritchie said, which was at least partially true. "But I got lost in the catacombs. It was early this morning before I got back. Still sooner than anyone at the party, though."

"You got lost down there?" Frei asked, her eyes wide. "Ugh. That must've been horrid. It's a good thing you found your way back out again. You know there are tons of stories about cadets who went down there and never came back up again. Tons. Some of them simply must be true, right?"

"Right," Ritchie agreed. They had reached the main hallway, and she fell half a step back to let Frei lead the way. She wasn't entirely surprised when she headed towards the administration wing. "You work as Colonel Devereux's assistant, right?"

"I'm one of three of them," Frei said. "The other two are both last years. I totally didn't expect to get picked when I put in for the job last year. I hope to work in administration in the future, so this is a really good opportunity for me."

"I swear I won't make you late," Ritchie said. "I just was wondering what you thought about Colonel Devereux?"

"About the colonel?" Frei said, sounding surprised. "She's the longest serving member of the faculty. She's been teaching here since her fourth year in the foreign service. Most educators are far older than that when they start. I expect in another year or so she'll move on to one of the universities. I'm not sure why she's still here, actually."

"That sounds like her bio in the academy faculty book," Ritchie said. Frei was picking her words way too carefully, and even then she was barely whispering them, as if afraid to be overheard. But they were the only two people in the hallway this far into lunchtime.

"It's only been a couple of days," Frei said, again with a carefully diplomatic tone.

"What's she like?" Ritchie asked.

"You mean as a colonel?"

"Sure, as a colonel. Is she super strict?"

"Not *super* strict," Frei said. "I mean, of course she's strict with all the cadets. But you know she mainly works with a select group of cadets. The one on the career path I'm hoping for, actually."

"Administration?" Ritchie said.

"Administration of various installations or just command more generally," Frei said. Then she blushed as she added, "I want to run a space station someday. One of the remote ones on the frontier."

"Does she select the cadets for her special program herself?" Ritchie asked.

"Everyone can apply," Frei said, again too carefully. "There is a faculty committee that reviews all applications. They choose the finalists, and then Colonel Devereux selects from that final pool."

"How many don't make the cut?" Ritchie asked.

"I don't think anyone outside of the committee knows that number," Frei said. "The whole process is a behind closed doors kind of thing."

"But you have some thoughts?" Ritchie guessed.

Frei didn't answer. They had reached the door to Colonel Devereux's office. The door was closed and when Frei touched the doorpad, it shone red. She keyed in a sequence, then palmed the pad again. This time it flashed green. She pulled the door open, and the lights clicked on. Then she looked back at Ritchie.

If only the walk had lasted a few minutes more. Ritchie was sure Frei had been just about to tell her something, maybe something significant, but not now. They had reached the destination she had been jogging to get to in time.

But to her surprise, Frei leaned back out into the hall to look both ways before pulling Ritchie inside and closing the door.

"She's going to be here any minute," Frei said to her, whispering again. "I gather you've never had a conversation with Colonel Devereux?"

"The few times I've been called into an office, it's always been Colonel Hansen's," Ritchie said.

Frei's lips drew into a tight line. "I've only been working here for a few days, but I knew before I started here what she was like. I'm surprised you don't as well."

"What do you mean?" Ritchie asked.

"She's one of *those* types," Frei said, rolling her eyes. Ritchie just shook her head, not following this at all. "She comes from one of the old families. Do you get me?"

"But that doesn't matter anymore," Ritchie said slowly.

"It does if you're one of the old families," Frei said. "Every cadet in her program this year is from an old family. Every single one. And I know last-year cadets that I'm sure were more qualified. They must've been passed on as finalists by the committee. Their scores are exemplary, they're model cadets in every way."

"Maybe the committee is the bottleneck and not the colonel?" Ritchie said.

But Frei very firmly shook her head. "No, no way. If you'd ever heard her talk... but never mind. I think I was a surprise when she found me here. I don't think she thought I was the one who'd get this position. She quizzed me my first day, who was my family, where was I from. You should've seen the look on her face when I said I was from Space Station Gamma Gamma Pi."

"That's bad?" Ritchie asked, totally confused.

Frei looked like she wasn't sure if Ritchie were joking or not, and was prepared to be very angry indeed if she were.

"I seriously don't know what you mean," Ritchie said.

"I believe you," Frei said. She said it was a tone of wonder, as if she were surprised with herself. Like she'd just admitted to believing Ritchie when she said fairies were real and she knew because some lived in her hair.

"Space stations are bad?" Ritchie asked again.

"You're from a space station. You don't know how rare we are in the student body? Even in this, the lowest ranked of all the academies?"

"I didn't know."

"Wow," Frei said.

"Old families don't come from space stations, I guess."

"They come from planets, and big, important planets at that. Like your buddy Moreau. Or your bestie Fitz." Then she laughed. "You know, last year I thought you were such a little toady, just making friends with the people you could use the most to climb up in the world."

Ritchie didn't know how to respond to that. She had always thought that Frei was aloof. She had chalked it up to the quiet girl preferring to keep to herself. But she had no idea her roommate had thought so little of *her*.

"Relax, I figured it out pretty quickly that that wasn't you at all," she said. "It's pretty obvious that your friends have a genuine regard for you, and that it's mutual."

"Fitz and I have known each other since we were babies," Ritchie said.

"Maybe that insulated you, then," Frei said. "But trust me, all the other cadets know exactly where everyone else grew up and who their families are. This thing with only the select few of us getting invites is just bringing it more out in the open. Did you think you got all that hate because you started late or something?"

"No, I pretty much assumed that was it," Ritchie admitted. "That, and being a murder suspect didn't help."

"Look, I can talk with you more tonight after dinner if you like, but you should really disappear before she gets here," Frei said.

"Can I just look in there real quick?" Ritchie asked, pointing to the inner office.

"Why?" Frei asked.

"I'm not going to touch anything. I'm just trying to see if she has a certain photo in there."

"A photo?" Frei asked. She sounded like she was intrigued. She opened the door to the inner office, the light clicked on, and they both went inside. "What kind of photo?"

"Her as a cadet," Ritchie said. "She went here, back in the day."

"I've never seen one like that," Frei said, scanning an entire wall of framed photographs that were arranged behind the desk chair. "She likes to put up pictures of herself with important people, the more recent the better."

"Yeah, it was a long shot," Ritchie said, turning to look at the book-shelves that ran along the back wall. At one end was a locked glass-fronted cabinet filled with medals arranged in displays. She had to squat down to see the bottom shelf. At first she saw nothing but an old wooden box covered in what looked like decades' worth of dust.

Then she saw it, pressed against the back of the cabinet, almost completely obscured by the largish box. If she hadn't already seen the full picture in Hansen's office, she doubted it would mean anything to her now. But she recognized the library steps, Hansen's arm raised to make a gesture to the camera, the very top of Voet's head.

"Do you have a key to this cabinet?" she asked hopefully.

"No," Frei said. "That's what you were looking for?"

"Yeah, but it's enough to see it from here," she said.

"Then you should really go," Frei said. She was getting increasingly anxious.

"Sure. I don't want to get you into any trouble," she said, and followed Frei back out to the hallway outside the outer office door. Frei pushed the door all the way open and locked it in place. Then she looked up and down the hall again before leaning in to whisper to Ritchie.

"Do you know what's weird?" she asked.

"What?"

"The cadet who's been to see her the most since the train arrived yesterday isn't even one of her select program students," she said. "It's Feena Berweger."

"That *is* weird," Ritchie agreed. "Any idea what they talk about?"

"No. They always close the door, and half the time the colonel sends me on some pointless but time-consuming errand first, as if I might try listening through the door. What do you think that's all about?"

"I have no idea, but I'd love to know more," Ritchie said.

"If I learn anything I'll tell you," Frei said. "You're investigating again, aren't you?" Ritchie said nothing, but Frei grinned anyway. "Yeah, I thought so. You have that gleam in your eye. Let me know if I can help. We space station brats have to hang together."

"I'm sorry I didn't know that before," Ritchie said. "I feel like I was letting you down, and I didn't even know."

"Forget about it," Frei said, then waved for Ritchie to get a move on.

She headed back down towards the main hallway, hoping to at least catch a glimpse of Colonel Devereux in passing, but whatever was detaining the colonel wasn't finished yet.

She had kept the photo, sort of. What did it mean, to leave it out and yet in a place no casual observer would ever see it? Was it a sign of complicated feelings? If they had all been friends, she and Hansen both must've struggled with the lack of closure. Voet had never actually been declared dead. So far as they knew, he might still be alive out in the universe somewhere.

If they were innocent, that would be true. But if either or both of them had been involved?

She really wanted to talk to Colonel Hansen about it. Her heart told her he would answer her honestly, if he answered at all.

But sadly, lunchtime was nearly over. She would barely have time to go get her bag out of the barracks before her next class.

She was going to need another protein bar for sure. This day already felt like it was a week long, and it was only half over.

12

FOR THE SECOND time in as many days, Fitz found himself sitting alone in the cafeteria at meal time. Which was annoying.

He hoped Ritchie had opted to get some sleep. The few times he had seen her that day, she had been looking rougher and rougher.

He guessed that Wyss was probably in the library working on ten things at once. But if he had found anything useful, he would've let Fitz know. Best to just leave him to it.

He was a little worried about Moreau, though. He had tried asking other cadets if they had been at the party last night, but all he had gotten in return was enigmatic smiles. Maybe because the cadets in question weren't even entertaining the thought of answering his inquiries.

Or maybe the Berwegers had done a little something extra to Moreau, because she was friends with Ritchie and Fitz.

He hoped not. But he couldn't quite make himself doubt it.

His first class after lunch was a mechanics of flight systems class. He had been flying gliders since he was old enough to reach the pedals, and his interest in maintaining or repairing the mechanical system hadn't lagged far behind. His father's personal mechanic had shown him a few things when tinkering with the family's private shuttle. Fitz wasn't sure if he had an actual aptitude for fixing things, but he knew pursuing it irritated his father.

It was a small class, but already on the second day it was all hands-on. He found himself paired with a last-year cadet he knew, if only slightly.

Leodegrance Kung.

"Fitz, right?" Kung said as they set their bags on the far end of the worktable, away from the engine they were meant to disassemble piece by piece.

"Right. We met in the catacombs last year," Fitz said.

"I remember," Kung said and winced ever so slightly. "Not my best day."

"No," Fitz agreed. "You get back down there much these days?"

"To the catacombs?" Kung asked, a tad aggressively. "Is that a roundabout way of asking me why I wasn't at the meetup last night?"

"You weren't?" Fitz asked.

"So you weren't either," Kung said and visibly relaxed.

"You know how you can tell neither of us were there?" he asked. Kung shook his head. "We're talking about it now."

Kung barked out a laugh. "Yeah, people are being weird about it, that's for sure. It's not like it was a secret or anything. Everyone knew it was going down."

"A lot of people involved for a conspiracy," Fitz said.

"Conspiracy? You think so? I figure it was just a bunch of kids who wanted to feel superior to the rest of us. Like they can't get enough of that during their fancy vacations over the semester breaks."

"So you weren't invited?" Fitz asked.

Kung looked over the instructions on the tablet that rested on the table, then looked up at the engine. Fitz was about to ask again when Kung finally said, "yeah, but who cares? Not my scene."

"What's the old quote? Wouldn't want to go to a party that would invite the likes of me? Yeah, I was invited but gave it a skip as well," Fitz said.

Kung was already working at removing the casing, but glanced up to give Fitz a smile of agreement.

"So, *do* you go down to the catacombs a lot?" Fitz asked.

"Not since that last time," he said. "Not really all that much before, either. I just knew it was the easiest way to get lost for a while. Walking away from the academy would be decidedly less pleasant."

"What brought you down there in the first place?" Fitz asked, reaching in to help Kung work a tight piece loose.

"Everyone knows they're down there, right?" Kung said, gritting his teeth as he torqued on the jammed screw. It remained immoveable, and he re-gripped the tool and leaned in harder. It gave way with a shriek, then he could turn it easily with his fingertips.

"It seems that way," Fitz said. "But maybe you've explored them more than most?"

"Maybe," Kung allowed. "I stumbled on a history of this location in my family library before I came here. Some old forgotten text in a really antiquated format. I had to use a half dozen programs to reformat it into something I could actually read. But even then the language itself was old and clunky."

"But still interesting enough to make you curious to go down there?" Fitz guessed.

"I made some extensive trips down there on free days my first year," Kung said. "But I never found what I was looking for, and my classes just got more and more demanding, you know?"

"What were you looking for?" Fitz asked.

"You know this academy was built on this mountaintop because it was a military location in the last war before Oymyakon joined the Union of Free Worlds," Kung said. Fitz nodded. "That's true so far as it goes, but there's so much more. This particular mountain has always been occupied for as long as there have been people on this planet. And *that* goes back a lot further than the official records indicate."

"Says this book you found," Fitz said.

"Yeah, so grain of salt and all that," Kung agreed. "Still, I really wanted to find the remains of the original fortress. It was built entirely within the caves. And do you know why?"

"To fight an invasion from out of the subterranean sea?" Fitz said and instantly regretted it. Kung had clearly been about to say the exact same thing with great delight, and Fitz had just stolen his thunder. "I like legends too," he added.

"They aren't just legends if you can find proof," Kung said. "Not that I ever did. But I gave it a go for a while there. That old fortress deep under the ground, apparently it was some sort of a sacred site before it was even a fortress. Warriors were brought there to be sacrificed."

"Sacrificed?" Fitz said. "To what?"

"That, I have no idea," Kung said. "Maybe whatever kept coming up out of the water." Then he gave Fitz a chagrined look. "I never actually finished reading that book. Maybe it says somewhere towards the end. It was just such a tough read. But the illustrations were cool."

"I bet," Fitz said.

"I still have it," Kung said, and his eyes rolled up and to the left as he scanned his inventory. "Yeah, it's here. I'll bounce it over to you."

Would you? Cool," Fitz said, far more excited than he had ever been to receive a data file before. Then he leaned in over the engine, making more of an effort to assist Kung, who was far better at talking and working with his hands at the same time than Fitz was. "So, human sacrifices?"

"Maybe other species too, but human for sure," Kung said.

"Anybody ever find a body?" he asked, hoping he sounded more casual to Kung's ears than he sounded to his own.

"A body? In the catacombs?" Kung said with a frown. "I don't think so. But you think someone would at some point, right? I mean, so many cadets have disappeared down there. There must be bodies all over the places."

"And yet you never found one?"

"Not for lack of trying," Kung said. Then his manic grin dropped into a more serious frown, and he motioned for Fitz to lean in closer. "Look, maybe I shouldn't have sent you that file. You really shouldn't go down there."

"Too dangerous?" Fitz asked in a joking tone.

But Kung was deadly serious. "Caves are caves. But that's not what I'm talking about. I mean... you know who I mean. Our two newest fellow cadets."

Fitz nodded. They had an entire year's worth of new cadets as well as Sokolov and a few random transfers, but just the fact that he didn't want to say any names out loud made it abundantly clear who he was referring to.

The Berwegers.

"Did they say something to you?" Fitz asked.

"Finn did," Kung said. "I don't think last night's do was a onetime deal. At any rate, he made it very clear that he knew I liked to go down there and very strongly hinted it would be best if I didn't go down there again. The entire catacombs are now accessible by his invitation only. And I turned that down, so..." He shrugged.

"How did he know that? That you liked to go down there?"

"Beats me. I've never met him or his sister before. I guess if they asked around about the catacombs, my name would come up."

But Kung was shifting his weight from foot to foot as if intensely uncomfortable, and Fitz knew it wasn't from anything going on in that classroom.

"What is it?" he asked.

Kung shook his head and started to turn his attention back to the engine. But then he glanced up at Fitz, a questioning sort of gaze. "It felt like no one had told him. When he was talking to me, it felt like he just knew. And that he knew a lot. He mentioned Jeger and... some other stuff no one knows about."

"I think it's just an act," Fitz said. "He likes the feeling of power he gets from making you think he knows all of your secrets."

"But he *did* know stuff," Kung said. "Stuff he couldn't know. And I swear he knew more even than he was saying."

"I've known them both a bit over the years," Fitz said. "I promise it's just an act. They are very good at reading people, but that's it."

"If you say so," Kung said, clearly not convinced. "Me, I'm going to go out of my way to stay out of *their* way. I'm just saying, you should probably do the same."

Fitz gave him a pained smile. Clearly it was already too late for that. He was definitely on the Berwegers' radar.

The rest of the afternoon was less fruitful, and Fitz had passed the time during two dull lectures scanning the text file Kung had sent him. It was indeed very long, very dry, but intriguing. He wasn't sure if it would give them any clues as to what had happened to Voet.

Unless whoever had killed Voet had read the same book, or something similar with the same old tales of human sacrifice in it.

But why leave him lying in the canyon like that? Wouldn't the shore be the more likely spot, if they were echoing the old days, propitiating to whatever lived in the subterranean sea? Or some sort of altar, perhaps inside those fortress walls?

Unless they hadn't found a way inside, either.

By the time he was done with his last class, he was practically hopping with impatience to talk to Wyss. But it wasn't exactly surprising that when he pushed his way into the library meeting room, he saw Moreau and Ritchie already there, pouring over Wyss's screens.

"Wyss, you need to send more drones down to the catacombs," he said, perhaps a bit too loudly.

"Why?" Wyss asked.

Fitz then told them everything Kung had told him, and what little he had gleaned from the text file so far. At Wyss's urging, he sent him a copy of the file, and Wyss immediately slotted it into one of his search programs. The program would pull out keywords they could scan for clues faster than any of them were going to get through the actual text.

"Are we sure this is relevant?" Ritchie asked. "What you're talking about was so long ago."

"Legends live on, Ritchie," Fitz said. "If we know about them, the cadets in Voet's day knew about them. Who knows what they might've been thinking, but copycat killers are not unusual."

"Killers in foreign service academies are a little unusual," Moreau said. "Or at least they used to be, before last year."

"Well, I can confirm that Colonel Devereux also has a photograph of herself, Hansen, and Voet in her office, but it's buried in the back on the bottom shelf of a dusty and sadly locked cabinet," Ritchie said.

"And that means?" Moreau asked.

"I don't know what that means," Ritchie admitted, but she was visibly excited at the prospect of finding out.

"I don't think you should be the one who talks to Devereux," Moreau said.

"No, I agree," Ritchie said, to Fitz's surprise.

"Why?" Fitz asked.

"Apparently I'm branded by my home being on a space station," Ritchie said. She sounded like she was testing to see how they responded. Wyss just shrugged, and Moreau gave a slow nod, but Fitz could feel his face burning hot. "You already knew?" Ritchie asked him, sounding almost hurt.

"Not about Devereux," he said, even though he knew that wasn't what she was asking. "Look, any sane person can see that you've earned your place here. I don't know a single cadet who doesn't respect you and all you've done here. No one thinks you don't belong."

"I don't know," Ritchie said. "I can think of two who would probably disagree with you. And they are winning converts."

"Forget about them," Fitz said fiercely.

"But we can't though," Moreau said. "In fact, after I talk to Devereux, I should really talk to Feena. And you should talk to Finn," she said, pointing at Fitz. He bit his lip, not willing to say that he already had. He wasn't in a hurry to repeat that experience.

"Are you sure that's a good idea?" Ritchie asked. "Your headaches, I mean."

"They've gone away," Moreau said.

"Because we stopped asking you questions?"

Moreau didn't answer, but she really didn't need to. The way she wouldn't meet anyone's eyes said enough.

"If we're going to do this, we're going to do it together," Fitz said to her. "You and I together, talking to Finn and Feena together."

"Isn't it worse when they're together?" Wyss asked, as if inquiring about the results of a scientific experience.

'Isn't what worse?" Ritchie asked.

"They have an effect on people," Wyss said. "I've been observing. The effects vary by the person, but when the two of them are together, it is consistently more than doubled. Objectively speaking."

"You have numbers on this?" Moreau asked sardonically.

"I can get them," Wyss said.

"Never mind," Moreau said with a wave of her hand. "I'll go with Fitz. We'll take our chances."

"Let's talk to the Berwegers first and get it over with," Fitz said with a sigh. "You can catch Devereux later."

"I don't like this idea," Ritchie said.

"We're not sidelining you," Fitz said.

"No, that's not what I meant," Ritchie said. "And anyway, I was going to go talk to Colonel Hansen on my own. I bet if I ask him about that photo, he'll just tell me the whole story. I should've done that in the first place."

"I don't like *that* idea," Fitz said. "And I'm not just being contrary. If he is involved, of course he's going to lie."

"And if he does, I'll know," Ritchie said. "We'll have an answer either way."

"How?" Moreau asked. "If he is involved and you make him suspicious, who's to say he won't remove all the evidence. And then what will he do to us?"

"Nothing," Ritchie said. "It's Colonel Hansen. It's no exaggeration to say he saved my life. I trust him."

"Fine," Fitz said. "Moreau and I will talk to the twins and see what they know about everything down below. Maybe get a hint as to why they're here and what they're planning. More likely not, but you never know. They might be feeling extra open."

"And I'll sound out Colonel Hansen," Ritchie said. She spoke confidently and with a firm nod to her head, but then she shot Fitz a shy little look that was quite unlike her. "You trust my instincts, right? If it doesn't feel right, I'll bolt out of there on some excuse. I won't mention the body until I'm sure of him. I won't say anything to raise his suspicions. I'll ease into it and be sure he's on the up and up every step of the way."

"Of course I trust your instincts," Fitz said. "Just be careful."

"Says the guy heading into the real danger," Ritchie said. "I know I've only seen those two from afar, but even from across the cafeteria I can see how they put the whammy on people. Seriously, be careful."

"I'm the closest thing there is to being immune to Feena Berweger," Fitz assured her.

It would've sounded better if Moreau hadn't snorted back a laugh right after, but whatever.

13

RITCHIE'S STOMACH made a grumble of protest as she walked past the open cafeteria doors. The murmur of the cadets chatting together and the clatter of their cutlery as they ate had her mouth watering even before she walked into the scents of meatballs and brown gravy and freshly baked bread.

That protein bar had been in no way satisfying. But the odds of catching Colonel Hansen still in his office this long after the last class of the day was dismissed were growing slimmer by the minute. She had no time to waste, even to grab one of those crusty rolls to eat on the way.

His door was still open, the light within shining out into the hall, but when Ritchie stepped inside she saw the door to the inner office closed. Cadet Sokolov was still at her desk, but she looked like she was doing homework rather than any administrative duty. Not that Ritchie blamed her for taking advantage of having her own desk to study at. The barracks were often too loud for studying in, and the library was seldom much better. The other academies had wide green lawns that were perfect for sprawling out with a tablet, but even on the best days on Oymyakon it was less than comfortable to be outdoors.

"Am I interrupting?" Ritchie asked, and Sokolov jumped.

"No, just catching up on some things," Sokolov said, then gave her a wary smile. "Like the last two years."

"It gets easier," Ritchie assured her. "But don't let it overwhelm you to the point where you study through all your meals. You know there's always room for you at our table."

"Really?" Sokolov said. An image jumped to Ritchie's mind fully formed: Sokolov standing in the cafeteria doorway, not finding a single friendly face, and finding reasons not to go in.

"Well, usually," Ritchie said. "Tonight we're all working on things and none of us are in there, but usually at least one or two of us are at our regular table. You just have to walk up and sit down."

"I'll keep that in mind," Sokolov said. Then she glanced at the closed door to the side of Ritchie. "Were you here to see me or Colonel Hansen?"

"The colonel, if he has a minute. I don't have an appointment," she said.

Sokolov nodded, then tapped at a screen positioned out of Ritchie's view behind a privacy screen on the corner of the desk. Sokolov gave her a smile as they waited for a response.

"All right. You can go in," she said, waving a hand towards the door. Ritchie took a deep breath before turning the handle and letting herself into the inner office.

"Cadet Ritchie," the colonel said, as he closed window after window on his desktop screen. He folded his hands over the now-blank surface and gave her his full attention. "I think I know why you're here."

"You do?" Ritchie asked as she slid into the seat across from him. It seemed exceedingly unlikely that he did.

"I've just received an update from the Julius Henry Observational Center," he said. "I can understand why the news would make you nervous, but I don't think it's anything you need to be worried about. They are both young, far younger than the other residents of the center. That alone would draw them to each other. I don't think it's about you."

"Oh," Ritchie said. She could hear her usual cheery, I-don't-want-to-be-a-problem tone coming out of her mouth. It would be the easiest thing, to ignore this and press on with her actual business. But something in the way he wasn't quite looking up at her was off. He was telling her not to worry, and yet he clearly was.

And she had no idea why, because she didn't have a clue what he was talking about.

"I'm sorry," she forced herself to say. "You received an update about what?"

Colonel Hansen gave her a stern look. "What part wasn't clear?"

"Any of it?" she said and caught herself just before biting down on her lip. She thought she had kicked that nervous habit.

"They didn't contact you?"

"No, sir."

The colonel spun around in his chair to face the wall and ran a hand over his face. Then he turned back to her. "I thought you had heard something, and that was why you were here. I shouldn't have said anything. But since I have, I see no reason to leave you and your expansive imagination to try to fill in the blanks. The Julius Henry Observational Center is, of course, the institute where both Sidonie Keller and Cadmar Weld are currently being held. They've recently come into contact with each other. It seems like it was only a brief encounter, and they've both been moved to new quarters further apart on the station in the hopes that their paths won't cross again, or that they won't be able to seek each other out."

"And you think they were talking about me?" Ritchie asked.

"No, that's exactly what I *wasn't* telling you. It was a very brief encounter. As I said, it was probably more about the two of them both being young people that drew them together. I doubt they spoke long enough to realize they share a connection to you."

"Keller knew about Weld," Ritchie said. "I'm sure she even knew what he looked like. Probably where he was being held as well. She researched every single thing about me, and he was a big part of that."

"You may be right," the colonel said. "I have assurances it will not happen again. You've been in contact with Sidonie Keller, haven't you?"

"A little bit," Ritchie said. "She writes messages, and her chief therapist conveys them to me with her own notes about Keller's state of mind to provide more context. I have written very short responses, and I understand they also pass through her chief therapist too, so that I don't accidentally say something that might set Keller off or anything."

"You were worried she would keep asking about your father," he said.

"I was, but so far that's not been true," Ritchie said. "It's been like writing to a friend who's away on a school trip or something. I had pancakes for breakfast. I made a vase in art class. That kind of thing."

"Do you think she might write to you about meeting Weld?"

"I don't know," Ritchie said. "I guess we'll see."

"Now, cadet, if that isn't why you stopped in to see me, what was the reason?" he asked.

"Actually, sir," she stammered. Half of her brain was still worrying over what Keller might have said to Weld. She was certain that Keller had sought him out deliberately, and no matter what the staff at that observational center did, she would find a way to do it again. But why?

"Cadet?" the colonel prompted. His patience had limits, and she was making him late for dinner as it was.

"Sorry, sir. I was just wondering about that photograph," she said, pointing at where it sat on his shelf. "I saw it when I was in here the other day. That's Colonel Devereux, isn't it?"

She had tried to keep her tone conversational, cheery even, but the quizzical frown on his face had furrowed deeper into a dark glower.

"You knew each other as cadets? Is that how you came to transfer here?"

He didn't respond, but she would swear that the temperature in the room was plummeting. She had to change tacks and hope to find something he would answer to.

"The cadet with you, the boy called Voet? I've read a little about him. He was a cadet here at the same time as both of you, but he disappeared mysteriously one day and was never seen again. It's just, you don't have a lot of other pictures around. It's the only one. It feels important to you."

She paused to give him space to answer, but he still said nothing.

Now she really did bite her lip, hard enough to taste coppery blood on her tongue.

But still he just glowered at her.

This was not going well at all.

"Are you quite finished, cadet?" he asked icily.

"Yes, sir," she said, her voice barely more than a whisper.

"Are you certain? No other aspects of my personal life you've been researching? No other theories about my private affairs that you want to run past me?"

"No, sir," she said, even softer than before.

"I can see that my fondness of you has led you to believe that you're entitled to far more latitude than any cadet should aspire to," he said. "My past is no concern of yours. None. Neither is Colonel Devereux's, or any other member of the faculty here at this academy. For that matter, the private lives of your fellow cadets are none of your business. Am I being clear?"

"Yes, sir."

"No, I don't think I am. Clearly I'm not. How dare you approach me about this? Why?" his voice had been slowly rising as he spoke and that last question was fired out of him like shot from a cannon. Ritchie flinched and nearly threw her arms over her head in self protection.

"It's just, if Voet hadn't just disappeared, if he had been killed, wouldn't you—"

But he didn't let her finish. He was leaning over his desk now, the hands on the surface not flat but actual clenched fists as he loomed over her and roared, "enough! No more questions."

"The case was never closed," she said, unable to help herself. Was Fitz rubbing off on her? Why couldn't she just sit silently and wait for this storm to pass? Instead, she had to make it worse?

"No, the case is very much closed," he said.

"Other cadets have gone missing in the caves under the academy," she said.

"Everyone who's wandered off in those catacombs has eventually been found," he said. "Quite alive, I might add."

"So far."

"Cadet, you are really trying my patience," he said.

"I'm just afraid that history might be repeating," she said desperately.

"Who's missing now?" he asked.

She looked down at her feet miserably.

"Who, cadet? Tell me a name. If you think history is repeating, tell me who's missing now?"

"It could happen," she said. "Cadets go down there all the time. And most of those caves haven't even been mapped properly. It's insane."

"No, what's insane is me sitting here listening to you," he said darkly. "I will hear no more about this. None of this is any concern of yours. You're afraid of the catacombs? Then don't go down into them."

"But—"

"No!" he roared at her. "That's it. If you truly have nothing better to occupy your time than to try to dig up trouble, I will have to fill those hours for you. Your previous work schedule is being pulled. Expect an updated one from me shortly. I promise you, any job you hate to do, you're going to be spending hours and hours doing it every night from now until the end of the semester."

"Yes, sir," Ritchie said, fighting back tears. She barely had enough time to study now. If her work load was doubled or tripled? Just how many extra hours was the colonel planning to schedule her for?

"In the meantime, you may go," he said, waving his hand towards the door. Ritchie gratefully scrambled out of her chair, but before she'd even turned the handle on the door he said, "you may go out to the athletic fields and run laps."

As if the planet itself wanted to punctuate that sentence, there was a sudden clap of thunder, followed by a blast of wind strong enough to shake the building, and then a hammering of cold rain.

"Yes, sir," Ritchie said. "How many laps, sir?"

He glanced up at her, and his eyes were so cold they sucked her breath away.

"Just run. I'll tell you when to stop."

"Yes, sir."

"And one last thing, Cadet Ritchie," he said. She turned back again. His fingers were racing over the surface of his desk, tapping boxes and typing text, so he didn't even look up at her when he said, "if I so much as hear a hint of a rumor of you digging into the lives of any member of this faculty, but particularly either Colonel Devereux or I, I swear to you that you will be expelled that very minute. Am I clear, cadet?"

"Yes, sir," she said, and ran out of his office before he could say anything more. She just saw Sokolov out of the corner of her eye, her hands covering her gaping mouth and her eyes wide. How much had she heard?

But Ritchie turned her face away from Sokolov. She was blinking back tears already. A friendly show of sympathy would be too much for her to handle. She would absolutely lose it.

She ran down the hallway, through the library, and out into the storm towards the athletic fields that lay unseen through the heavy sheets of rain.

But the one thought that wouldn't leave her was that Colonel Hansen's response had been far too emotional. He was strict and believed in discipline, but that started with himself before others. He was always in control of his temper. His yelling was instructive, not angry.

But just now in his office, he had been very, very angry indeed.

The problem was, she had no idea what that meant. That he was guilty and thought she was closing in on him? Or that he was still grieving his friend after all these years?

Neither of those felt right. Something else was going on. But what?

She wished she had brought someone with her to the meeting, not to share the punishment with her, but to stay behind while she ran laps in the cold rain and see what Hansen did next.

14

FITZ AND MOREAU got to the cafeteria so late that Finn and Feena Berweger, who liked to wait for everyone else to get settled before making their grand entrance, were already at a table, eating and chatting with a bunch of other cadets. The cadet with the dark skin and platinum hair he already knew: it was Kung's buddy Vilem Blaser. The girl next to him with even darker skin but neatly arranged straight black hair also wore the insignia of a cadet captain, so she must be Milla Wyder.

There was another girl sitting next to Wyder, a squat but brawnily muscled blonde who must be her buddy. Her name tag read Joosten, and he remembered Stucki mentioning her on the train. But there was no sign of Kung. Given how he felt about the Berwegers, Fitz wasn't surprised. But it must be tough having a buddy you don't see eye to eye with. Especially if you had once been as close as Blaser and Kung had seemed the year before.

Fitz put himself directly into the line of sight of either of the Berwegers, who were sitting close together and eating off of each other's plates indiscriminately. Even so, it took a minute or two for Finn to finally notice him standing there with Moreau by his side.

"Can we help you?" Finn asked and flashed his most dazzling smile.

Moreau made a small meep sound, but Fitz blinked once, then said, "we were hoping to talk to you?"

"About?" Feena asked in a long drawl.

"A private matter," Fitz said.

"Well, you heard the gentleman," she said to the rest of the table. "We can catch up later."

The others gathered up their trays and moved away to other tables. Fitz sat down across from Feena, and Moreau sat down beside him.

He was worried about how she was doing. Was talking to the Berwegers directly going to set off her... whatever was giving her headaches?

Ritchie insisted that Moreau did have facial expressions that would give away her feelings, but to him her face was always a perfect blank. Her body language wasn't much clearer. She currently had her hands folded and was leaning in towards Finn ever so slightly. But was she feigning interest in what the Berwegers were about to say, or was she genuinely curious?

For all he knew, she was wildly curious and was dialing it back to the mild interest she seemed to be showing. Honestly, nothing about the arrangement of her features was giving him anything.

"Before you get started, I wanted to say something," Finn said, breaking the exhausting cycle of Fitz's thoughts.

"What's that?" he asked.

"Fee and I, we just wanted to apologize," he said, glancing over at his sister as if to confirm he spoke for both of them.

"We're really very sorry," she said with the smallest of pouts.

"It was meant as a joke, but we realize now we took it too far," Finn went on. "Or rather," he added with a little laugh, "you and your friend got taken too far." But his laughter was gone as quickly as it had come and he was all seriousness again when he said, "no hard feelings?"

"For throwing me and Ritchie down a bottomless shaft straight down to the planet's core? Why would there be hard feelings?"

"You got back out again," Finn said.

"I don't think there's any situation that Fitz can't finesse his way out of," Feena said. Fitz very carefully didn't look at her. He could sense her leaning in, and could only imagine what she was prepared to do with her eyes if he met her gaze.

Then Moreau beside him meeped again.

"That's what you should really be apologizing for," he said, pointing at Moreau but looking straight at Finn. "What the hell did you to do her?"

"Whatever do you mean?" he asked with an innocent blink.

"The headaches, just to start," Fitz said.

"It's nothing," Moreau said, but Fitz ignored her.

"Please, tell me what it is," Feena said with what really sounded like genuine concern. But before Fitz could answer, she got up and moved around the table to pull up a chair close to Moreau. Moreau turned to look at her, and Feena gazed intently into her eyes, as if she could see the source of the headaches through Moreau's retinas.

"You need to undo whatever you did," Fitz said. "Everyone else might be dealing with it okay, but you've really hurt her."

"That was never our intention," Finn said, and reached across the table to grasp Moreau's hand.

"Stop that," Fitz said, and pushed their hands apart. "Whatever you did, undo it now or I'm going to the administration."

"You're going to the administration to say what?" Finn asked.

"I know you did something to her, either chemically or somehow through her implant. Whatever it is, it's very wrong. But medical tests will get to the bottom of it, I'm sure," he said.

"It's really all right," Moreau said.

"It isn't," Fitz said.

"It's also not why we're here," she reminded him. For just a second she sounded more like herself, less addled.

"If you feel like you need to go to the administration, then you should do so," Finn said. "We won't stop you. It's nothing to do with us."

"Maybe I will," Fitz said. "But when I do, I'll be talking with Colonel Hansen. Not Colonel Devereux."

The blithe look on Finn's face was unchanged. But for just a split second, he had looked to his sister. Going to Hansen was clearly something they'd prefer he didn't do.

But Finn said nothing. He only shrugged, as unbothered as ever.

"If you feel unwell, you really should go to the infirmary," Feena said to Moreau. "My brother and I hold you in the highest possible regard. We are both very fond of you. We don't want to see anything happen to you."

"But what you really don't want is for her to tell anyone just what you were all up to last night," Fitz said.

"Last night was just a party. Beginning of school and all that," Finn said. "Not anything worth anyone getting hurt over. Well, maybe a few hurt feelings here and there."

"You split the entire student body in two, dividing everyone into invitees and non-invitees, specifically to hurt feelings?" Fitz asked.

"Do I look that petty to you?" Finn asked, and Fitz had to blink again. It was like Finn Berweger could summon a sparkling aura at will to really sell whatever he was saying. It was like a pressure on Fitz's brain, trying to force him to saying that everything was all right, nothing to worry about, just go with the flow.

"Then what was the point?" Fitz asked, pushing the words out past gritted teeth.

"You're asking the point of a party?" Feena asked him. She had Moreau tucked close beside her now, her head nestled on her shoulder. Feena was so tall she had no trouble looking at Fitz over the top of Moreau's head.

"He's asking the point of having a guest list," Finn said. "But he knows the point full well. His parents entertain on a regular basis, and those parties are not open to all comers."

"Those are more work functions than social events," Fitz said. He knew he was only feeling defensive because those parties were more his mother's purview, but the reason to have them at all was his father's career and his future aspirations.

"So was this," Finn said.

"Trouble is coming," Feena said, cutting off whatever her brother had been about to say. He closed his mouth, looking politely to his sister to continue. "Anyone who is paying any kind of attention knows this. Some say it will be war. Hopefully later and not sooner, but in the end, it will be war."

"War with whom?" Fitz asked.

"Does it matter?" Feena asked. "We will be called upon to defend the Union of the Free Worlds. We must be prepared to answer that call."

"Every last one of us must be prepared," Fitz said. "That's why we're all here, after all. Every single cadet."

"Yes, of course," she said with an indulgent smile. "But be serious, please. We will all have to make sacrifices, of course, but we won't all be the ones who make the decisions."

"There are many paths ahead of us in the Union," Finn said. "We need the right people in the right places to choose the right paths."

"It's as simple as that," Feena said. Then the two of them exchanged a smile that made Fitz's stomach roil uncomfortably. Luckily he hadn't eaten, or it would be threatening to come up again.

"I'm not following your argumentative leap from party to war," Fitz said.

"It's about choosing your future," Finn said.

"I thought that was what our time at university was for," Moreau said. "That's when we choose our paths."

"In normal circumstances, yes. But now, in these uncertain times? University is simply too late," Finn said.

"And we're not talking about a mere career choice," Feena added.

"So you two are here at the Oymyakon Foreign Service Academy to drum up recruits? For what, the resistance?" Fitz asked.

Feena laughed. "If anything, the resistance is what we're fighting."

"So there already is a resistance?" Fitz asked, getting more and more confused.

"A well-formed group with a name and a cause? Not yet," Finn said.

"But people of that ilk? Certainly. And they are working against us, against what's best for the Union of the Free Worlds."

"How?" Fitz asked.

"Too many planets are being allowed entry, and it's happening too fast. No one is assimilating properly. They are changing the very character of the Union of Free Worlds, and not for the better," Finn said.

"You know, if you just came to a meeting, we discuss this all at great length," Feena said, reaching around Moreau to put a hand on his thigh.

Fitz, with far more slowness than he intended, moved his chair until he was just out of her reach. Her hand slipped away from his thigh, but it was like she had left a burn behind. His skin still tingled where her warmth had been.

"Why Oymyakon, though?" Moreau asked. She sounded sleepy, but her eyes when she tilted her head to look up at Feena were downright besotted.

"Oh, we're sentimental," Feena said with a fond smile for her brother. "Our parents met here, you know."

"No, I didn't know," Moreau said. "Is it a passionate love story? Star-crossed lovers? Secrets and, well, hidden caves or something?"

"Romance is forbidden between cadets, you know. Has been since the dawn of the foreign service," Finn reminded her.

"What kind of story is that?" Moreau pouted.

"Oh, it's a good story," Feena assured her. "I can tell you all about it sometime."

"Why not now?" Moreau asked.

"It's quite long, and we've already lingered here too late," Feena said. "I'll just tell you that it involves a certain cadet, one who didn't abide by the rules against romances. He was thoroughly in love with my mother. You know it's true," she said to her brother as if cutting off an argument.

"True enough, but mother never encouraged him. She was a model cadet. As was our father. They knew each other then, and were fellow cadet captains and close friends, but never more than that until much, much later in their history."

"Once they were assigned to separate posts and the rules no longer held them apart," Feena said to Moreau in a loud whisper.

"But what happened with the other cadet?" Moreau asked. "He loved your mother, but then what?"

"He wasn't the right sort at all," Feena told her. "He never stood a chance, poor thing, but the wrong sort never seems to take a hint, do they?"

Fitz realized he was grinding his teeth and forced himself to stop. But it was maddening, watching Moreau look up so wide-eyed at Feena as she spun this pointless tale. He opened his mouth to speak, but shut it again in surprise when Moreau's foot kicked him hard in the shin.

"But how was he important in their story, then?" Moreau asked, her eyes never leaving Feena.

"Oh, well, just because they didn't have a romantic relationship in their academy days doesn't mean that their bond didn't start here," Feena said. "Sometimes a thing can happen, something small or maybe something bigger, but it changes the entire course of your life. And what happened with that cadet? It changed the arcs of both of our parents' lives. From that point on, it was only a matter of time until they got together and made us."

"I love a story with a happy ending," Finn said, but he sounded bored.

Then a sudden thought struck Fitz, and everything fell together at once. Not the least of it, the mystery of why Moreau was behaving so strangely. But as was usual with him he blurted out this thought before it had even quite congealed in his mind. "Oh, you guys are talking about Voet."

The mood at the table instantly shifted to something decidedly less friendly. Feena pushed Moreau up, then slid her chair away from her. For her part, Moreau was glaring at him furiously, and he kind of wanted to congratulate himself for reading her emotions much faster this time.

But Finn's icy stare was commanding Fitz's entire attention. "How do you know that name?" he asked. He was trying to sound casual. To most ears he probably did sound casual, like he wasn't really interested in the answer to his question, he was just making conversation.

But Fitz knew this answer mattered to him. Just the fact that Finn knew the name Voet was interesting. But this intensity? It spoke volumes.

"It doesn't matter, Finn," Feena said, resting a hand on her brother's shoulder. "It's time for us to go, I think."

"Wait, you forgot my invite to your next meeting," Fitz said.

Neither of them looked back at him as they sashayed out of the cafeteria. That strut was more than a little pointless; the only ones still sitting in the cafeteria were Fitz and Moreau.

"Sorry," Fitz said at once. "I missed what you were doing there."

"What I was doing?" Moreau asked, and her face was blank to him once more. Was she teasing him?

"You were just pretending all that, right?" he said uncertainly.

"Pretending," she repeated, as if tasting the word. "I'm not sure if that's quite right. More like I leaned in on what they were expecting me to feel. You probably didn't notice Finn kept touching my knee under the table."

"No," Fitz said. "Feena touched me once there..." Best not to dwell on that memory. He looked up at Moreau. "Are you all right?"

"Perfectly," Moreau said. "But we got our answer, didn't we?"

"Did we?" Fitz asked, still dazed by the thought of Moreau leaning up on Feena while Finn touched her knee. It was like completing a circuit or something. Shouldn't she have gone up in flames?

"The Berwegers know the name Voet, as you so cleverly ascertained," she said as they got up from the table and headed out into the shadowy main hall.

"Yeah, sorry about that," Fitz said with a grimace as they headed towards the library.

"Don't worry about it. I'm not sure how much longer I could've kept that up," she said. Then she caught his arm, keeping him just inside the library doors rather than heading towards the meeting room. "The point is, they know that name. Why would they?"

"Because they've heard it before," Fitz said.

"From their parents," Moreau said. "Who must've been here at the same time."

"The same time as Hansen and Devereux," Fitz said. "Just like Wyss said. But what does that mean?"

"I don't know, but it must mean something," Moreau said. Then she turned to look out the tall library windows, out into the darkening rainstorm. A rumble of thunder shook the glass and even set a few loose objects on the library tables to rattling.

"We should catch up with the others, see what they've found out," Fitz said, but Moreau once more caught his arm to keep him in place. Only this time she pointed out the windows, out into the storm.

"Hey, isn't that Ritchie out running in the rain?" she asked.

15

THE FIRST COUPLE of laps had been miserable. Her uniform was quickly soaked through, weighing her down, and the rain was so icy it hurt when it struck her face.

But after her body had warmed up a bit to the exercise, and she found her stride, it wasn't so bad. She kept up a steady rhythm, tuned out the weather as much as she could by focusing only on her feet slapping on the slick track. And she checked her implant for incoming messages. Not that her implant wouldn't alert her the minute she got a message, but something was clearly wrong somewhere.

Aside from not yet getting the command to stop running, it shouldn't be taking so long for Colonel Hansen to send her the new work schedule, should it?

The more she imagined him rubbing his hands together evilly as he thought up worse and worse assignments for her, the more nervous she became.

Then the run started to suck again. Her wet, cold clothes were chafing her entire body, and she was pretty sure there was ice forming in her hair.

But she never stopped running. Not until she looked up to see Fitz and Moreau blocking her path.

"Didn't you hear us calling you?" Fitz asked.

"Sorry," Ritchie said without slowing down. They stepped back to let her pass between them, then jogged to catch up with her.

"What are we doing, Ritchie?" Fitz asked.

"I'm running until the colonel tells me to stop," Ritchie said.

"But you went to talk to him before dinner," Moreau said. "That was like an hour ago."

"Feels like longer," Ritchie said. Her stomach promptly reminded her that she hadn't eaten anything since breakfast save that protein bar.

"He's making you run laps because you asked questions?" Fitz asked.

"This is just the start of it," Ritchie said. "He said..." But she couldn't force the words out. She stopped running, bending over with her hands on her knees as she tried to catch her breath. Or to keep the others from seeing her face as she blinked back tears. "He said I would be expelled."

"Expelled?" Fitz repeated. "For asking questions?"

"For asking personal questions, and digging into his private affairs. And Devereux's," she said.

"And the Berweger parents," Moreau added. "They were cadets at the same time."

"Seriously?" Ritchie asked, but immediately stamped down her own rising interest. "No, I can't be a part of this anymore. He was serious, and I can't risk expulsion. I just can't."

"But all we know is in the public record," Fitz said. "Even if you hadn't seen that photo and started wondering about it, we would know there was a missing kid from the same class year as Hansen and Devereux just from the school records. We haven't figured out a single thing that could possibly be described as private."

"We know where the body is," Ritchie said.

"You told him?" Fitz asked.

"No," she said. Then she straightened up to look down the track. Most of it was obscured by the storm and the darkness.

"Let's go back in," Fitz said. "Surely you're only still out here because he forgot about you. There's no way he actually intended to make you keep running in this weather."

"He was very clear," Ritchie said. But the idea of taking another step was too much. Her whole body was sore already.

"Let's go in and get dry," Fitz said. She gave in with a curt nod.

She wanted to run back to the library doors, but her legs couldn't manage more than a brisk walk. But then they were inside the airlock, and the second the door clicked shut behind them, the dryers built into the room around them turned on full blast and blew every last droplet of rain out of their clothes and hair.

Then the inner doors opened, and they passed through the dark, quiet library to the one room where a light was glowing: their usual meeting room. Wyss was sitting in the back corner among his array of computers. He looked up when they came in but just shook his head.

"Nothing new on my end," he said.

"We learned one crucial bit of information," Fitz said. "You were right. When Voet, Hansen and Devereux were cadets here, so were the Berwegers' parents. And they knew Voet for sure. Probably the colonels as well."

"Interesting," Wyss said, and started tapping at one of his tablets. "I'm going to run some information searches on them, see if they turn up any more connections. How did it go with Colonel Hansen?"

"Not well," Ritchie said.

"Can you give us more details?" Moreau asked. "It's not like him to punish you, let alone for something like this. I find that very curious."

"He was furious, absolutely furious. The minute I mentioned the photograph, it was like he just stopped listening to me at all. He shut me down. But I really think I should've told him about the body."

"He needs to know," Fitz agreed. "But maybe he shouldn't hear it from you."

"You he absolutely will expel," Ritchie said.

"No, I don't think so," Fitz said.

"I'm telling you, it was like he was swept up in this rage. It was scary," Ritchie said.

"And that really doesn't sound like him," Moreau said.

"It was like he was possessed," Ritchie said.

But Moreau shook her head. "No, I don't think so."

"Well, you weren't there."

"No, I wasn't," Moreau said. "But think about it. Does Hansen seem like the kind of guy whose best friend goes missing and he doesn't do everything he can to find him?"

"Colonel Hansen or Cadet Hansen?" Fitz asked.

"Both. When he was a cadet and his friend first disappeared, do you think he took that lying down? Or did he search the catacombs himself?"

"You think he already knows the body is down there?" Ritchie asked with a frown. "And he just left him? No, that doesn't sound like him at all."

"I don't know if he found the body or not. But what if he found out enough to know that he was better off not digging further?"

"You think he knows who killed Voet?" Ritchie asked.

"I don't know that either," Moreau said, then sighed in frustration. "Look, I just think that what you saw as him being angry with you was actually him putting real fear into you to stop investigating. And whether he knows something or just suspects something, he has left this matter unresolved for decades."

"You think he's afraid?" Ritchie asked, shaking her head. "No, that sounds even less like him than him being enraged."

"Not afraid for himself. Afraid for you. Maybe all of us," Moreau said. "He knew the Berwegers' parents. What do you think he thinks about them being here now? He probably has fears we can't even imagine. And he can't articulate them. So he's just trying to make you feel that fear, or just a taste of it."

Ritchie cast her mind back to those tense minutes in his office. He had cut off her words the minute he knew what she was driving at. His anger had been instantaneous. But he had also looked away from her. Had there been something on his face or in his eyes that he hadn't wanted her to see?

"He threatened to expel you," Moreau went on. "No one would take that more personally than you. He knows you well enough to know how you internalize everything. He knows with everything you said that you'll be stewing over what you did wrong and what you are going to do right in the future. There won't be room left in your head for finding out what he's trying to hide."

"That's a lot of conjecture," Fitz said.

"And I'm not sure if it helps us one way or another," Ritchie said. "I don't see that we have any choice but to drop the investigation."

"Or be way more sneaky about it," Fitz said.

"I have some information here," Wyss said, and spun in his chair, swiping whatever was displayed on his tablet over to the table in the middle of the room. There were dozens of windows, some text and some photos or videos. "The Berweger parents through the ages."

"They don't look much like their kids," Fitz said. "I mean, they're attractive enough but not preternaturally so." He grabbed one window and dragged it closer to him. It was a wedding photo. They were both in dress uniforms, he in the navy blue of a guardian and she in the ivory white of a diplomat. They were both captains at the time, and he had a couple of commendation ribbons already. "They look like kids in this. How old were they when they married? Or for that matter, made captain?"

"Thirty," Wyss said.

"They look younger," Ritchie said.

"A lot younger," Moreau said.

"This is a current photo," Wyss said, pushing another window at them. There was no wedding cake in this one, but they were still in uniform. Albeit they were both admirals now.

"Well, now they look thirty," Ritchie said. "How is that possible? They must be past fifty."

"There have been rumors for years that they engage in some health practices that are, shall we say, in legal gray areas," Wyss said.

"Like what?" Ritchie asked.

But it was Moreau that said, "harvesting organs or tissue from species that have not yet been declared sentient, although clearly are. Some even say that families like the Berwegers make sure that these sorts of species have a particularly arduous time being declared sentient."

"They slow down the bureaucracy on purpose to keep harvesting what they need," Wyss said. "I should stress those are just rumors."

"Very prevalent rumors," Moreau said.

"It's nothing compared to the speculation about their offspring," Wyss said.

"Sounds juicy," Moreau said, leaning in closer to hear what he said next.

"It's hard to tell which of the stories might be true, if any of them," Wyss said, scrolling through something on his tablet. "But the gist is that the twins were created in a lab to the Berweger parents' very exacting specifications. And alien tissue harvesting comes up a lot."

"That's why they don't look entirely human?" Ritchie guessed.

"Allegedly," Wyss said. "And I really want to take a closer look at one of them some time, because the rumors about those alien tissues are very interesting. It starts with the obvious extremely potent pheromones—I think we can all agree that *that* rumor certainly seems true from the way people respond to them—to the possibility that they have senses beyond the range of normal humans."

"What does that mean?" Ritchie asked.

"Again, these are just rumors, but it's possible that they can read people to an extremely accurate degree by reading their microexpressions. They might learn more about you than you thought you were revealing just by watching your face."

"Or they're crazy rich and can afford to hire the best, least ethical of investigators to research you," Fitz said. "I've heard that rumor as well."

"I'm really starting to hope that they continue to shun me," Ritchie said. "It sounds like I'm better off not drawing their attention."

"Agreed," Fitz said. Then he sat back and folded his arms as he regarded the others around the table. "So, what do we do now?"

Ritchie drew in a ragged breath. She knew what she thought, but she really didn't want to say it out loud.

"Ritchie?" he asked. She avoided meeting his eyes this time. The concern there for her was just too painful.

"I really think we should step away from all of this," she said. "It was decades ago. And it clearly involves a lot of very powerful people. We might find justice for Voet, but I think we're much more likely to just bring down a lot of trouble on ourselves."

"I'm sure Hansen would support that plan," Moreau said, but Ritchie just shrugged. Even if she told him, she was still going to be doing her extra work assignments, she was sure. Whenever they turned up in her inbox.

"We have to tell him we know where the body is," Fitz said. "He'll have to report it. It'll be brought up and there'll be an autopsy for sure. Then it won't matter that we've stopped investigating. The authorities will take care of it for us."

"Maybe we should contact the authorities ourselves?" Ritchie said.

"We will if he tries to stonewall us," Fitz said. "But I kind of want to talk to him myself. See if I think Moreau is right."

"You would be running the risk of expulsion," Ritchie said earnestly. "Do you hear me, Fitz? He could kick you out of here so easily."

There was so much more she wanted to say about how bereft she would be if he were sent away. Moreau was her buddy, but Fitz was her best friend. And she couldn't face the thought of losing him. Again.

But he looked up at her, and for the split second they held eye contact, she knew she didn't have to say any of that. He already knew.

"Ritchie, it'll be okay," he said.

"I'll go with him," Wyss said. "I have drone footage of the body that doesn't have the two of you in it. I can pretend that I found it on my own, if that helps. I mean, if his official story is that he got angry with you for speculating, he can't possibly get angry with me for starting with cold, hard facts and coming to him with them, speculation-free."

"I agree," Fitz said.

"Why don't we all go?" Ritchie asked.

"I certainly want to go. How come I'm the only one who doesn't get to face off with Hansen?" Moreau asked.

"No, you stay with Ritchie," Fitz said. "As soon as we know what's going on, we'll come back and fill you both in. In the meantime, I think it's better to keep Ritchie away from Hansen."

"I still haven't gotten the order to stop running," Ritchie admitted. "I guess you're right. But I don't like it."

"We'll go with you as far as the main hall," Moreau said. "We can wait there while you talk to him. But that way if the two of you get hauled off to the brig, at least we'll know what happened to you."

"Very funny," Fitz said.

16

WHEN FITZ and Wyss walked into Colonel Hansen's office, they saw Sokolov still sitting behind the desk, despite the late hour. Her homework was spread out before her, but she was staring at the closed door to the inner office with a glassy look to her eyes.

"All right, Sokolov?" Fitz asked, and she jumped.

"Oh, I didn't hear you come in," she said. She still sounded dazed.

"Is everything all right?" Fitz asked again.

Sokolov blinked and finally seemed to really see him. Then she smiled, genuinely happy to see him. "It's been a weird day. And a long one."

"I'm surprised you're still here. We thought we might have to track the colonel down in his quarters, but stopped here first just to check. What's he doing in there?" Fitz asked.

"I suppose you already know that he screamed at your friend Ritchie?" she said. He nodded. "Yeah, that was bad. She ran out of here so fast I couldn't even ask if she was okay."

"She's doing better now," he said.

"He's not usually like that," she said. "I mean, I guess I don't know him as well as I thought, but I never thought he could yell like that. It wasn't an officer dressing down a cadet. It was... personal."

"Yeah," Fitz said. "But what did he do after she left?"

"He shut his door without saying a word to me, and he's been in there ever since," she said. "I'm not sure if I'm supposed to go or stay here in case he needs me. I mean, it's almost lights out."

"Ritchie seemed to think he'd forgotten about her as well," Fitz said.

"She's not still running out on the track, is she?" Sokolov asked, a look of horror on her face.

"No, she's inside, warm and dry," Fitz said. "So he's just sitting alone in his office?"

"He's alone, but I've heard him talking, so I assume he's been sending out messages," she said. "I don't know to whom or what about. I can't hear him through the wall when he's not screaming. But there have been a lot of them."

Fitz glanced over at Wyss, who just shrugged.

"We wanted to talk to him about something that we hope won't set him off again," Fitz said to Sokolov.

"I'm not sure that's a good idea," she said. But before any of them could say any more, the door to the inner office opened and Hansen stepped out but immediately pulled up short.

"Oh. You're all here," he said with a frown, looking at Fitz then Wyss before finally seeing Sokolov still at her desk. "Cadet Sokolov, you're dismissed. I suppose you've missed dinner?"

"Yes, sir," she admitted as she hastily put her things into her bag.

"In the future, don't let me forget about you like that. You need to eat and study and get to bed on time," he said. His eyes darted down and to the left, the unmistakable sign of someone checking their chronometer. "And you have less than an hour to do it. Best get moving."

"Yes, sir," she said, hoisting her bag up onto her shoulder. But then she hesitated before stepping out from behind her desk. "Sir, these two wanted to speak to you."

"I'm not surprised," the colonel said. He sounded epically tired, but summoned up a smile for her. "You can go. Have a good night, cadet."

"Yes, sir. Thank you, sir," she said, and brushed past Fitz to run out the door.

"Cadets," the colonel said, and all the warmth that had radiated from his voice when he had spoken to Sokolov was gone.

"We have something to show you, sir," Fitz said.

Wyss gestured with his tablet, but didn't say a word. The colonel spared him only the briefest of glances before narrowing his eyes at Fitz.

"You're not here to tell me that everything is all your fault?" he asked.

Fitz summoned up a grin. "I think we can take that as said, sir."

But the colonel was not amused. "I don't think so, cadet. If this were minor league trouble, I would certainly assume that you put Ritchie up to it. But when it's something like this? No, *she* roped *you* into it. Not a doubt in my mind."

"It was mutual, sir. I swear it," Fitz said.

The colonel said nothing.

"Sir, we have something to show you," Wyss said, and then flinched when that drew the colonel's attention to him.

"Very well. Come inside my office," he said.

"Sir, did Cadet Ritchie tell you that I've been using an array of drones to map out the catacombs?" Wyss asked as he and Fitz sat down and watched the colonel first firmly shut the door behind them, then circle around to the far side of his desk.

"That might've come up," he said distractedly. He glanced at something on his desktop, then swiped it away. "I gather from what she was saying you've found some hazard down there. A danger to wayward cadets."

"We found a body," Fitz said. Wyss gave him a hard look. This hadn't been how they'd agreed to approach things. But he said nothing, just handed the colonel his tablet.

The colonel looked at it intently, then zoomed in on one of the images. "Voet," he said under his breath. Then he put a hand over his eyes.

Dead silence fell over the three of them, and Fitz could swear that his heart was beating too loudly. It felt like it was echoing throughout the little room. The colonel's breath came in jagged gasps, but he didn't move.

Fitz was absolutely certain that Colonel Hansen had not known what had happened to his friend until that very moment. He possibly had even been entertaining a hope that Voet still somehow lived. But that hope was gone now.

The silence stretched on, and Fitz could barely stand it. But the universe would end before he interrupted the colonel's grief.

Finally, the colonel lowered his hands from his eyes. They were red-tinged but dry. He looked at the image on the tablet again before handing it back to Wyss. "You found this with your drones? Just coincidentally?"

Wyss nodded, but Fitz couldn't stop himself from saying, "Ritchie and I found it first, sir."

"Why didn't she just say so?" the colonel asked, glaring at Fitz.

"To be honest, sir, we weren't sure if you didn't already know," he said. "I'm sure now, sir. If that helps."

"You cadets," the colonel said, shaking his head. "Why would you think your opinion of me could help me?"

"I was just trying to say—" Fitz began, but Wyss interrupted him.

"I'm not sure if you could tell from those images, but this was murder," Wyss said. "Cadet Voet was stabbed repeatedly. In the back. And then left there to die."

That brought a spark of anger to the colonel's eyes.

"And you didn't report this straight away because?" he prompted, holding his hand up at Wyss as if commanding him not to speak.

"Ritchie recognized his name," Fitz said.

"From my photo," the colonel said.

"Yes, sir."

"And so you thought...?"

Fitz swallowed hard. "We thought we should be sure first of you and Devereux."

"Cadets, these little investigations of yours are *not* why you're here."

"And yet, we keep stumbling into them," Fitz said, raising his hands as if giving up.

The colonel still wasn't amused. If anything, that spark of anger was reignited.

"Do you know who might have done this, sir?" Wyss asked. "It looked ritualistic. And we're worried because..." but words failed him. He looked to Fitz to pick up the thread, but Hansen spoke first.

"Because the Berwegers are here recruiting," he said. "Am I right?"

"Spot on, sir," Fitz said. "You're worried too?"

But the colonel just frowned as if at his own thoughts.

"Sir, if it was a ritual killing—" Wyss began.

"Put that thought out of your mind, cadet," Hansen said. "I know the legends, and I know it looks like some sort of ritual, but I promise you it's much more mundane than that. I know who likely did this and why, and they only made it look ritualistic in case he was ever found. No, this is a political conflict, not a cult thing."

"Ritchie is certain the evidence on the body points to about a dozen different killers," Fitz said.

Hansen considered this, then nodded. "Yes, that sounds about right. No one there would've been allowed to observe and not participate. That was why *I* wasn't there."

"So why was Voet in the catacombs at all?" Fitz asked. "And alone?"

"He wasn't supposed to be alone," Hansen said, his voice thick. "I wasn't there, but I was supposed to be with him. But when the time came, I backed out. I sensed things might go badly for the three of us. He went without me."

"Three of you? So the third was Devereux?" Fitz asked.

"Colonel Devereux," Hansen corrected him as if by impulse. "And I don't know. She always denied knowing what happened to him. I took that to mean she wasn't there. When Voet disappeared, my friendship with Devereux disappeared as well. I never spoke to her alone afterwards. I only ever saw her in crowds. I didn't want to believe… But I don't know. I just don't know."

"What was Voet trying to do?" Fitz asked.

Hansen passed a hand over his face again, and all signs of sorrow disappeared. "It was a different time. Before you were born."

"But we know the history of the Union, sir," Wyss said. Fitz had no idea what he was talking about, but tried not to let that show on his face. "There was a lot of political unrest during your cadet years. A lot of people thought the union was going to dissolve."

"It very nearly did," the colonel said. "How it held together, I don't know. There were so many working to bring it down."

"Like the Berwegers," Fitz guessed. "I mean the parents of the two here now."

"They were just cadets at the time, and not even a couple," the colonel said. "But her parents and especially Nico Berweger's parents, were openly advocating for a smaller union."

"They wanted to shed all but the core planets," Wyss said.

"Yes, nothing but humans in their union," the colonel said. "And not so very many of those. Only the ones on planets. No stations, ships with ongoing populations, or even moons. Only the wealthy who could afford to live at the bottom of strong gravity wells."

"And that didn't include you?" Fitz guessed.

The colonel gave him a hard look. "Hansen is my mother's family name. My father's family name I will not speak aloud, but you would know it if I did. I changed it before I even became a cadet. That's how long ago these winds started blowing, and how strongly I wanted to blow the other way."

"So you were invited but didn't go?" Fitz said. "I know how that feels."

"And Voet was not invited," Hansen said. "There was no place for my best friend in the glorious future they were trying to sell to me. I imagine you know how that feels as well."

"I do," Fitz said. A sudden wave of sadness washed over him, and now he was the one rubbing at his face. "Is this what history is? This constant cycling back to the same bad ideas?"

"They are trying again, sir," Wyss said. "Through their kids this time. They are splintering the cadets in this school into factions. How long before one of us ends up dead down in the caves?"

"That won't happen," the colonel said. "Don't you see? The last time cadets were meeting in the catacombs, that all stopped when Voet disappeared. I don't think his death was planned, and the killers were worried what would happen if he were found. Maybe they're still worried. They've been awfully quiet up until now. And I can't stop whatever those twins are up to. Believe me, I've tried. I can't expel them or move them or even shut them down. My hands are tied."

"Because Colonel Devereux has tied them for you?" Fitz guessed.

"Not just her," he said. "But yes. Short of the two of them committing another murder, which as I've said I doubt they'll do, there is nothing I can do. And even then, with their family's lawyers, it's unlikely they'll face real consequences."

"So far all they've done is talk to people," Fitz said. "Well, talk to people and then compel them to secrecy. Moreau gets headaches every time she tries to talk about it."

"I'll have to look into that," the colonel said. "If her implant shows signs of tampering, that would be actionable. But in the meantime, I suppose we should deal with Voet's remains."

"With this storm, no shuttle is going to be able to land for some time," Fitz said.

"No, and we won't touch anything until the authorities get here, but I would like you to show me where you found him."

"Of course, sir," Fitz said. "And I know you don't like when I say it, but I do understand what you're feeling, sir. You've lived with this uncertainty for decades, never knowing what happened to your friend. That lack of closure must have been brutal."

"Don't oversell it, cadet," the colonel said. "I knew he was almost certainly dead. He might've been in hiding or secretly become one of them and was living a double life somewhere, but those options never felt very likely to me. Today is just… confirmation."

"No, sir. It's just, I'm hoping you can remember that Ritchie is feeling much the same as you did, just a few years in to that uncertainty. On account of not knowing for sure if her father is dead or alive. She's living without closure too. And who knows if we'll ever solve that one."

"Point taken, cadet," the colonel said. "I'd send her the command to stop running, but somehow I think if she were still outside in the rain this whole conversation would've started very differently."

"I would've led with that, yes, sir," Fitz said.

"I tell you what, I'll divide up her extra work detail between the two of you," he said. Then he glanced over at Wyss. "Scratch that. The *four* of you. Moreau might not have been in this office, but somehow I just know she's tangled up in this as well."

"Yes, sir. She's part of the team," Fitz admitted. "Shall we?"

The colonel stopped to turn off the lights and lock his office, then the three of them headed down the main hallway to the back of the school and the entrance to the catacombs below.

17

RITCHIE AND MOREAU watched Fitz and Wyss disappear inside Colonel Hansen's office from where they were standing in the darkened main hallway. They could just make out the happy murmur of Sokolov's voice as she spoke to the two of them, but not well enough to make out the words.

"She's got a bit of a crush on our Fitz, doesn't she?" Moreau asked.

"Yeah, but she promised she'd keep it professional," Ritchie said.

"She promised *you*?" Moreau asked.

"Yeah, after we got off the train when I walked her to Hansen's office," Ritchie said. "Why do you sound so surprised?"

"That she'd keep it professional? I'm not surprised at all. But she told you specifically and not, oh, say, *Fitz*," Moreau said.

"What are you implying?" Ritchie asked, narrowing her eyes at her friend.

But then they heard Sokolov's footsteps heading their way. It wasn't after lights out yet, so they weren't breaking any rules. But just lingering in the main hallway this late at night was going to require an explanation that Ritchie didn't want to have to make up on the spot. So she grabbed Moreau by the arm and pulled her into the alcove behind a water fountain, where the shadows hid them from view.

Sokolov reached the point where the administration corridor met the main hallway and paused there, looking all around her. But then she nodded to herself and headed towards the barracks, away from Ritchie and Moreau.

"I would prefer she didn't bring it up with Fitz, actually, since he's totally oblivious to her attention, anyway. It would just be awkward all around," Ritchie went on as if they had never been interrupted.

"Sure." Moreau nodded as if in complete agreement. "I'm just relieved I'm not the only one who's seen it."

"Seen what?" Ritchie asked, with just the hint of panic in her voice.

"Murdina, I'm speaking to you as a friend here," Moreau said softly. "You and Fitz have known each other forever, and you're perfectly suited for each other in every possible way. If feelings grew out of that, it wouldn't be the weirdest thing in the world."

"Who has feelings?" Ritchie asked. "You know, when I first met you on the train I thought *you* were the one flirting with Fitz."

"I was," Moreau admitted, completely unbothered. "But flirting is flirting. That's not what I'm talking about now."

"It doesn't really matter, does it?" Ritchie said with a sigh. "We're both cadets here, and we'll be cadets together at university in another couple of years."

"I'm not accusing you of wanting to act on it. I'm just saying. You're awfully keen to chase everyone else away from Fitz."

"I am not!" Ritchie protested. "When have I ever?"

"Okay, okay," Moreau said in her most calming voice, hands raised in surrender.

"We work well together. I hope we continue to work together for years and years. That's all I'm focused on," Ritchie said. "And that didn't feel so impossible last year, but it's starting to feel more and more unlikely these days."

"Fitz has already turned down any opportunity that involved leaving you behind," Moreau said. "I don't see him changing that stance ever."

"So then I'll be holding him back. Or worse, pulling him down," Ritchie said glumly.

"You're letting this Berweger thing get into your head too much,"

Moreau said. Then she took a deep breath, as if bracing herself, and spoke through gritted teeth. "Most of the kids who were there last night were only curious. And they didn't find the speeches persuasive. It isn't a loyalty cult to the twins. At least, not yet." When she stopped speaking, she leaned back against the wall, pressing a hand to her forehead.

"It hurt you to tell me that?" Ritchie guessed.

"Not as much as it did before," Moreau said. "Whatever they did to me, it's fading away."

"That's good, anyway," Ritchie said. "I suppose I should be grateful I don't merit their attention. It seems like a poisonous thing."

"Not in the moment," Moreau said, and dropped her hand to look Ritchie in the eyes. "In the moment, when you have their full attention, it's the most glorious feeling in the world."

Ritchie felt a chill run up her spine, but before she could think of anything to say to that, they both stiffened and drew back into the shadows. They could hear the echoes of footsteps, but they weren't coming from the administration wing or from the barracks or library.

They were coming from the back of the school, from the entrance to the catacombs.

The steps grew louder as two figures approached. They were carrying a long, cumbersome object between them, the sort of duffle bag used to carry bo staffs for hand-to-hand combat drills out to the athletic field.

The figures drew closer, and Ritchie and Moreau both pressed as far back into the corners of the nook as they could. Ritchie held her breath and turned her face away, lest the shine of her skin give her away. Only when the figures were mostly past her did she dare sneak a peek.

It was the Berweger twins. But what were they doing at this hour? And what was in that bag? From the way they struggled to carry it between them, whatever was in there was quite a bit heavier than bamboo poles.

They walked past the nook and then turned down the administrative corridor. Ritchie and Moreau exchanged a glance and then sneaked out after them, keeping to the shadows on either side of the corridor and moving as soundlessly as they could. Luckily the

Berwegers were making no such efforts to be quiet, and the slap of their feet and the huffing of their breath covered whatever stray sound Ritchie or Moreau might be making.

They walked past the open door to Hansen's office, then let themselves in through the locked door just after it. Feena's palm and code opened the lock. It took a moment for the two of them to negotiate their awkward bundle inside, but once they were out of view, they didn't bother to close the door behind them.

"Closer?" Ritchie mouthed to Moreau. Moreau nodded. They paused outside of Hansen's office door, but the outer office was empty. The inner door was closed, and there was a murmur of voices from beyond it. Fitz and Wyss were still in there with Hansen, then. At least he didn't sound like he was raging at the two of them. Ritchie hoped that meant he was listening to what they had to say.

She and Moreau crept on. Moreau reached Devereux's door first and glanced inside before darting to the far side and pressing her back against the wall. Ritchie crept up to the doorjamb but didn't risk looking inside herself.

She could hear the twins talking. The answering voice must belong to Colonel Devereux. Ritchie had never heard her speak before that she could recall. It was a stern voice but calm, one that projected command with no need for added volume to drive her point home.

"Was this really necessary?" Finn was asking.

"You know it was," Devereux said.

"Yeah, but did it have to be us?" Feena said. "This wasn't exactly easy to retrieve."

"It had to be you," Devereux said. There was a tightness to her voice now, like she was masking a growing impatience. There was no question that she outranked the two cadets, but their parents outranked her. That wasn't supposed to matter, but if they were all so into the idea of the old families being better than everyone else, perhaps it did. If the Berweger line was better than the Devereux line. Ritchie had no idea. She suspected it wasn't even written down anywhere. The people that cared just knew who was better.

Suddenly Ritchie heard the sound of the door to Hansen's inner office opening behind her, followed immediately by the sounds of all three of them coming out to the corridor, chatting together. Ritchie looked over at Moreau in panic, but Moreau was shaking her head: it wasn't safe for Ritchie to try to dart across to the other side. But there was nowhere to hide where she was, trapped between the two office doors. All she could do was press back against the wall in the shadow around the light spilling from the open office door and hope for the best.

Moreau, on the other side of the door, did the same. There was a corridor she could slip around only a couple of meters behind her, but she wasn't going to leave her buddy behind. Ritchie appreciated that.

Hansen emerged from out of the hallway first, but he was looking at a tablet in his hands and didn't see either Ritchie or Moreau. Wyss was close at his heels, waiting to take that tablet back. He didn't see them either.

But Fitz, strolling out behind the other two with his hands deep in his pockets, saw Ritchie at once. He widened his eyes at her in unspoken question. She jerked her head back towards Devereux's office just as Finn made another complaint about the dampness of the caves.

He gave her the smallest of nods, then pulled his hands out of his pockets as he jogged to catch up with then pass Hansen and Wyss. He started jogging backwards, immediately launching into some sort of monologue designed to keep all attention on himself.

Ritchie and Moreau were safe.

Moreau gave her a knowing smile, but then they both turned their attention back to the conversation happening within the office.

"It had to be removed, and the fewer people who know about it the better," Devereux was saying.

"Yeah, but that still leaves you to go get it yourself," Finn said.

"I have my hands full already cleaning up after your parents," she grumbled.

"I'm sorry, what was that?" Feena asked in her sweetest voice. It was weird, the little shivers their voices sent up and down Ritchie's spine. When Wyss had mentioned all the rumors about their creation in a lab with alien parts and all, she had been willing to quietly dismiss it as just talk. But now she wasn't so sure. She could feel herself wanting to be manipulated by what they were saying, and they weren't even talking to her.

"I said you both know what's at stake here, correct? I don't have to explain it to you again, do I?" Devereux asked.

"No," Finn said, not remotely cowed by her domineering tone. "Tell me this, you've been working here for more than a decade now. So why wasn't this removed ages ago? Why is it still here now, when it absolutely must not be found? Why is that, colonel?"

"I don't answer to you," Devereux said.

"Why don't you treat my brother as an emissary from our parents and answer his questions, as they would be their questions if they were here to speak for themselves," Feena said.

"I didn't know it was even down there," Devereux said, annoyance creeping into her tone. "If I had, I assure you, it would've been taken care of, as you say, ages ago."

"We have the body but not the murder weapon," Finn said. "We looked around, but there was no sign of it. Any thoughts?"

"Did your parents leave it behind?" Devereux asked. "I always assumed they took it with them."

"Don't *you* know? Weren't you there?" Feena asked.

"Some of us were there," Devereux said evasively. "I already told you I won't name names. If your parents don't trust you with that information, then neither do I."

"Look, it's nearly lights out. What happens now?" Finn asked.

"It's not like the two of you need to worry about lights out. You have my blanket pardons for any infraction already," Devereux said.

"You want us to go back and look for the knife?" Feena asked, her voice almost a wail.

"No, I don't think so," Devereux said thoughtfully. "You said you looked already, right? If it wasn't there with the body, it could frankly be anywhere. A visual search is not the best use of your time."

"I don't disagree," Finn said. "But it must be found."

"Hmm, yes. That boy Wyss, he's already snooping in the catacombs with his drone array. Perhaps he should be assigned a specific task," she said.

"No," Feena said firmly. "No, we need to take the drones from him and run our own search."

"Telling him to look for anything at all would be suspicious enough. What if he actually found it?" Finn asked.

"Fine," Devereux snapped. "If you don't think I can bend a mere boy to my will, then fine. I'll figure out another way."

"Perhaps our parents should be informed," Feena said. "At least about what we've found already. They should be updated."

"Not just yet," Devereux said. "Hansen is in a tizzy about something. Until I know what, this is not the best time for sending encrypted messages that might raise eyebrows."

"Hansen is in a tizzy?" Finn repeated. "That sounds more than coincidental to me."

"To me as well," Feena said. "Colonel, are you on top of things here?"

"You know I am," she snapped. "I'll take care of Hansen and finding the knife. You two just take this bag and get rid of the contents."

"You sure like to make us do your dirty work, colonel," Finn said. "Afraid to touch things yourself?"

But Devereux didn't rise to his bait. "The incinerator is on the lower level of the school, on the opposite side from the catacombs. It's a very large room; I'm sure you'll have no trouble finding it. Run along, now."

"You better watch your tone," Feena warned her. "We're not following your orders here, you know. We're doing this for our parents."

"As am I."

Then Ritchie heard Feena and Finn both grunt softly and knew they had picked up that bag again. She immediately ran backwards to disappear inside the still open office of Colonel Hansen while Moreau on the far side of the door slid along the wall until she was gone around the corner of the cross corridor.

Ritchie just had time to manually shut off the office lights before the twins stepped out into the corridor with the bag between them. She stepped out of the doorway and deeper into the shadows, but this time she didn't turn her face away. She risked being seen to watch the two of them pass by.

Even in the dim light of the corridor, their faces in profile had that otherwordly terrible beauty. Like avenging angelic creatures, or at least very annoyed ones.

Ritchie didn't realize she had been standing there gaping until Moreau appeared in the doorway, waving for her to hurry and follow.

Yes, she was very grateful she had never been on the receiving end of their attentions. Just being in their presence was disoriented enough.

Ritchie spared a single thought wondering where Fitz, Wyss and Hansen had been heading off to. But then she forced herself to focus just on getting to the incinerator without being caught.

It seemed pretty clear that the twins had Voet's remains in that bag between them. And once those remains were consumed by the incinerator fires, there would be no way to ever know what had happened to him.

Or rather no way to prove that the admirals Berweger had stabbed him to death when they were just cadets, and one of them wasn't even yet a Berweger.

They had gotten away with it for decades now, but if Ritchie had anything to say about it, that ended today.

18

THEY DIDN'T GO BACK DOWN by way of the chute. For that, at least, Fitz was grateful. His whole body was still sore from the last time.

But Wyss's drones had not yet found a better route than the long, steep climb through the narrow chasm. Fitz felt a great reluctance to push his legs into that slash of darkness by the floor of the cave, almost hidden under overhanging rock formations. Then he had to crawl backwards, the rock catching at the back of his tunic as he moved.

Wyss had it easier, being barely tall or heavy enough to pass the cadet physical requirements.

Hansen with his wide shoulders and thick chest should've had a tougher time than Fitz, but he slipped through as if he did this daily. Which, for all Fitz knew, he might.

He was just glad that Ritchie wasn't there with them. He knew she would screw up her courage and force herself to do it, but he would be able to see in her eyes what it was costing her. The shrieking fear in her mind that never quieted. He almost thought that hurt him more than it hurt her. Maybe because he felt powerless to help her. Ritchie never felt powerless, not even in the face of her greatest phobia.

Wyss had sent both Hansen and Fitz the most up-to-date maps from his drone patrols. That augmented his implant's night vision, giving him better definition to the outlines of the rock around him to the point where he didn't feel like he needed a glow stick. The only light came from the drones themselves, a dozen of them all around the three of them as they picked their way down the rockfall.

Fitz wondered what Ritchie and Moreau had been up to. Spying on Devereux, apparently, but there must have been a reason. He had thought he had heard Finn's voice coming from inside. He didn't like the idea of the two of them getting caught. If it came down to it, getting caught by Devereux would be the better option. If she caught them spying on her, they'd just get tossed into the brig. Ritchie had been in the brig before. He wouldn't say it was no big deal, but it was certainly survivable.

But if the twins caught them? He couldn't quite imagine what the two of them would do. They had nearly killed Fitz and Ritchie for just trying to spy on them before. What would they do if they caught Ritchie succeeding at it?

What would they do to Moreau for betraying them?

Both thoughts made him shiver in dread, and he forced himself to focus on the task at hand.

But he was all too aware of the moment his implant lost contact with the academy systems above. He had never felt so cut off from everything he might need as he did in that moment.

Slowly the wall of rock behind him began to edge away from him, then opened up into the underground cavern. This time he could smell the briny smell of the water lost in the darkness below. He listened for the waves, but the sounds of rock sliding away beneath him and Hansen and Wyss covered up whatever soft lapping on the pebbly beach there might have been.

Finally, they reached the bottom of the rock face and could just stand on the sturdy ground. Fitz flexed and unflexed his hands over and over. His fingertips were raw and his knuckles were a bloody, scraped up mess. He was suddenly aware of just how many muscles were in the human hand as every one of them started to cramp up.

And they still had to climb back up again.

"Which way?" Hansen asked.

"It's not far," Fitz said, and led the way. The canyon was indeed far shorter than he remembered, but when he found himself looking down at the edge of the underground sea licking at the toes of his boots, he realized he had come too far.

"Cadet?"

"Wait a minute, something's wrong," Fitz said, walking more slowly back the way they had come.

This time he found it, or at least the blood-stained patch of gravelly path where it was meant to be.

"It's gone. The body's gone," Fitz said. He had a sinking feeling in his stomach that he knew why Finn had been in Colonel Devereux's office. His fear for Ritchie spiked.

"Are you sure?" Hansen asked.

"The location is marked on the map I sent you," Wyss said. "This is definitely the spot."

"The blood is still here," Fitz said. He found himself looking around as if he might've missed seeing the body somehow. But there was nowhere for it to be hiding. The canyon walls were sheer, with no nooks or overhangs, and there was nothing on the canyon floor larger than a pebble. "They took it."

"Let's not jump to accusations," Hansen said.

Wyss had his head tipped back as if trying to look straight up into the sky. Fitz was puzzled by this until Wyss put a hand up in the air and snatched one of the drones as it flew by.

"You have something there, cadet?" Hansen asked him.

"Maybe," Wyss said, connecting the drone to his tablet. "This one was down here when we got here. I think it might not have been high enough to back up to the system yet. It might've seen something that isn't on the latest map."

"Like what?" Fitz asked, moving to stand on Wyss' other side. All three of them watched as Wyss zipped through hours of video, the drone flying through endless loops of caves. He slowed down the playback as the drone followed the flat planes of the fortress walls, first flying high over the bank of the underground sea and then turning to run up the side of the canyon.

"There," Hansen said, jabbing a finger at the tablet even as Wyss paused the playback.

There was no question what they were looking at. Their backs might be to the drone, but no other cadets had such glowing blonde hair as the Berwegers.

The three of them watched as the twins gently, almost reverently, moved the body of Voet from the floor of the canyon into the interior of a duffle bag they must've taken from one of the gymnasium storage lockers. Feena even folded his hands back over his stomach, as they had been when Ritchie and Fitz had first found him.

Then she zipped the bag closed.

The two of them walked around the canyon for a few minutes as if searching for something, but in the end they didn't seem to find it. Instead, they just hoisted up the bag between them, again with great care, and started the long climb back up to the school.

"What were they looking for?" Fitz wondered.

"Murder weapon," Hansen said curtly. "Did *you* find it?"

"No," Fitz said, but then he felt like the planet dropped away from beneath him. He collapsed against Wyss's shoulder, staggering the smaller boy and almost sending them both down to the ground.

"What is it?" Hansen asked.

"They don't know that," Fitz said. "They don't know we didn't find anything. But they'll think we did. Ritchie..."

"Right," Hansen said. "Back up to the school, double time."

As much as he had loathed the idea of making that climb again, Fitz tackled it now with no hesitation. But he couldn't stop the circular racing of his thoughts.

Finn and Feena came all the way down here to remove the body. It didn't prove that their parents were the murderers, but Fitz knew in his bones that they were. And they had sent their children to remove the evidence.

They had the body, but not the murder weapon.

They hadn't removed the body before they started using the catacombs for their meetups. Why? Because they hadn't even known it was there. But they did now. Somehow, in that uncanny way they had, they knew that Fitz and Ritchie had found it. They could've waited until after lights out to retrieve it, but they hadn't. They hadn't wasted any time at all.

Fitz gritted his teeth. He hated that *somehow*. But he couldn't argue with it. Finn and Feena always knew things they shouldn't possibly be able to know.

So they knew who found the body.

But they would think that if the two of them had found the body, they had also found the murder weapon. And it would make sense that if Fitz and Ritchie had found it, they would have taken it back up with them. It was small and portable, unlike the entirety of Voet.

Now his worst-case scenario for if Ritchie got caught spying on them took a truly dark turn. Because they would believe that Ritchie knew where the murder weapon was. Nothing she could say would convince them otherwise.

And they would do anything to get the location of that weapon from her.

At last he reached the point where he could leverage himself up off the slope and take a moment to lie there flat on his back and get his breath back.

He didn't take that moment. He rolled back onto his feet and ran through the caves, back toward the school. He could hear Hansen calling for him, but he didn't slow his steps.

He emerged from the loose grate into the halls of the school proper and was about to run again when Hansen's hand closed around his ankle.

"Wait, cadet," he commanded.

"But Ritchie—" Fitz began.

"I understand your fear," Hansen said as he released Fitz to crawl through the grate himself and stand up beside him. "Where would she be now? The barracks?"

"Or the library," Wyss said as he joined them.

"No," Fitz said, shifting his weight from foot to foot. "No, I saw them just before we left. She and Moreau were outside of Colonel Devereux's office."

"Whatever for?" Hansen asked. Fitz shot him a desperate look. To his immense relief, the colonel understood him. "Right. We'll head there first."

Fitz jogged back to the administrative corridor, all the while sending message after message to Ritchie. She didn't respond.

The light was on in Colonel Devereux's office, but there was no sound coming from within. No sign of Moreau or Ritchie or the twins.

"Wait in my office, cadets," Hansen said, then went inside Devereux's office. Wyss took a step towards Hansen's doorway, but Fitz pressed his back against the precise spot on the wall where Ritchie had been some time before.

"Hansen," Devereux said. She was in her inner office, but her voice carried clear out to Fitz and to Wyss, now standing directly behind him. "I've been waiting for you to stop in."

"Have you? I must've missed your message," he said.

"Oh, I didn't send you any message. But you've been having a very busy evening, haven't you? I figured at some point you'd loop me in to whatever's going on."

"I doubt very much that you need to be looped in," Hansen said. "Where is it?"

"Where's what?" she asked.

"I know you sent those cadets down there with the express instructions to mess with a crime scene. I have proof they've done so. I don't imagine it will take long to prove you were behind it."

"How are you going to prove something that never happened?" she asked. "I never gave any such command."

"I won't have to prove it," Hansen growled. "The Berwegers have the finest lawyers in the Union of the Free Worlds. That, and no intention to ever see their precious children come to any harm. It doesn't bode well for you. But I know you weren't a part of this. I mean the original crime. You can still come out of this with some honor intact. But only if that body comes to no harm."

"You don't know anything," Devereux said.

"I know he was our friend. Your friend as much as mine, and I've had no friend since half as close as Voet was to both of us in our academy days. You helped with the coverup. I think you helped with the murder. In fact, I'm certain you did. But you never told me that you knew where he was and what had happened to him. You knew he was dead, and you never said a word."

"This was never about you, Hansen," Devereux said. Then she barked out a laugh. "It was never even about Voet."

"I don't care about your political schemings, Coralie. I've never wanted any part of them, and you know it. But I can't let you destroy what is left of Voet. That's not what he deserved. Now, where is he?"

Devereux said nothing. Fitz was pretty sure she could carry on saying nothing all night if need be.

It was time to try something else. But what?

But before he could even form a thought, he received two distress messages through his implant at once. One was from Ritchie, the other was from Moreau. From Wyss's sudden intake of air behind him, he guessed that they had called out to him as well.

He turned to look at Wyss.

"Incinerator room," they said as one.

Then Fitz leaned into the open doorway. He could see Hansen leaning over Devereux's desk, his fists thrust into the surface as he glowered down at her.

"Incinerator room!" Fitz shouted at him, slapping the wall as if to punctuate his point. But he didn't wait for Hansen to respond. He just ran, Wyss close behind him, as fast as he could, towards the back of the school.

19

RITCHIE HAD ASSUMED that Moreau had shared her sense of urgency. They had to stop whatever the Berwegers were about to do. So she was more than a little annoyed to find Moreau grabbing her arm and pulling her to a complete stop in the middle of the very end of the main hallway.

"They went this way," Ritchie said, and started to run again, making for the cross-corridor to the right.

"I know, but look," Moreau said, pointing to the left. That hallway was nothing but storage rooms, rooms that Ritchie had half-assumed were never used. But one of the doors stood open.

"They can't be in there. It's all dark," Ritchie said, but when Moreau headed over to it, she followed.

She wasn't keen on stepping into the darkened interior, but Moreau flicked on a light switch. They were looking into a closet, one stuffed with old sporting and combat equipment. The Berwegers weren't there, but it was a near certainty they had been.

The floor was littered with bo staffs.

"I thought they broke into the gymnasium, but perhaps these here would be less likely to be missed?" Ritchie said.

"They don't care. They left the door wide open," Moreau said. But then she bent and picked up two of the bo staffs, handing one to Ritchie. "Now we have weapons."

"Good call," Ritchie said. Then she stepped inside the closet to take two net bags off of one of the shelves. Each was filled with about a dozen of the sand-filled throw bags they used in training. Ritchie had never been particularly accurate when throwing them, but she knew when they hit with sufficient force they had a very distracting sting. They each tied a net bag to their belts.

Then they left the closet, continuing on down the corridor past the main hall, into a part of the school where Ritchie had never had cause to go before. "Where are we?"

"Maintenance rooms," Moreau said. "The laundry is through there, and the cleaning robots get charged and maintained through that door with the little flaps near the floor."

They kept walking, checking every door as they passed it. They all opened at their touch, but their dark interiors were empty of humans.

Ritchie gripped her bo staff tightly, grateful to have it in her hands. Even as she hoped not to have to use it. Not that she avoided violence when the situation called for it. She had had to fight to save her own life the year before, when she had been confronted by Keller with a gun. She was just worried that when faced with the prospect of marring the preternatural perfection of a Berweger face, she would hesitate to smash it.

"There," Moreau whispered, but Ritchie had already seen it too. The next two doors on the left side of the corridor both had a glow of light eking out from under them, lighting up the floor tiles with an orangish-red glow.

"The incinerator is already lit," Ritchie said. "Go to that other door. We'll go in at the same time. Maybe that will throw them off a little."

Moreau nodded, then jogged soundlessly to the far door. When she was in position, they both threw open their doors at once, charging inside with bo staffs at the ready.

But the twins were just standing there, waiting for them. Feena stood in front of Moreau's door, and Ritchie found herself face to face with Finn.

The strange otherworldliness was still there, but looking straight into his eyes changed everything about his face. They were an endlessly deep indigo. It felt like she was tumbling into them, like they were the sky itself. Not an Oymyakon sky, of course. More like the sky from her childhood home of Buennagel, the one she had long forgotten the shade of.

But it was that color exactly. She remembered now. Lying on her back, Fitz beside her, staring up into that cloudless sky. She wouldn't have described it as happiness, not as a kid when she had actually passed so many afternoons doing just that. But it had been. It had been the purest happiness she had ever known. Realizing it now almost made her feel sad.

But then Finn smiled at her, a warming smile, and the sadness left her. That sky had been bliss. And that bliss was in his eyes.

Then Ritchie bit her lip, hard. She was falling under his spell, wasn't she? This was precisely what she *didn't* want to have happen. With an almost physical sensation of anguish, she pulled her gaze away from his.

But the feeling of being under a spell was still there. It was muted, but still present.

It took far too long for her to realize he had a pistol trained on her. She had never seen that model of gun before, but she doubted it was anything less than lethal. Something of her alarm at seeing it must have shown on her face, because Finn was now smirking at her.

She forced herself to look past him, just for a split second. Behind him, the grate on the front of the incinerator was standing open, but the bag which held the remains of Voet was still on the floor, zipped up tight. She and Moreau were not too late.

But Ritchie feared that only meant she and Moreau would be there to watch as the evidence burned to ash. What could they with bo staffs and throw bags do against pistols?

"Cadet Ritchie," Finn said, drawing her attention back to him despite herself. He smiled at her again, not the smirk like when she had seen his gun, but the warm one that made her stomach all fluttery. He tucked his pistol away into the holster at the small of his back, then stepped towards her, his hand extended.

She gripped her bo staff more tightly and ignored his hand.

He dropped his hand but stepped up to her, well within the reach of her weapon. He didn't fear her, not even a little.

And she couldn't move. Why couldn't she move?

"Fitz has told me so much about you," Finn went on. "I feel like we're friends already. May I call you Murdina?"

"No," Ritchie said, but it came out only as a tremulous whisper.

She expected him to react to that, get angry or pretend to be offended or something, but he just accepted her word with a nod. "Very well. Ritchie. I know that name well, and not just in the last few years. Your father worked with our parents on more than one occasion."

"Finn, don't bring up her father," Feena said chidingly. "You know she's still hurting about what happened. And why shouldn't she be? It was a public tragedy for all the Union of Free Worlds, but so much more so for her family."

"I'm sorry," Finn said, putting a hand on her shoulder. "I should've begun by extending our condolences to you. It was such a loss."

"His disappearance, my brother means," Feena said. "There is no reason to assume your father has passed. In fact, our parents are certain that he still lives."

Ritchie swallowed hard. Her hands were so sweaty that the staff was threatening to slip right out of them. But she had to ask. She had to know.

She looked up at Finn and was at once caught in his eyes again. And he was so much closer to her now. His hand was still on her shoulder, but his arm was pressed against the length of hers. He had stepped around the upper half of her staff, right into her personal space. She could smell him, like woodchips and spice, an intoxicating combination of things she hadn't smelled once since she had gone to live on a space station. She could feel the warmth of him, he was so close.

Ritchie swallowed again. "Is there proof? Proof that he's still alive? Anything?" she asked.

"Only hope," Finn said, and the hand on her shoulder moved up to brush at her cheek as if to wipe away a tear. But she wasn't crying.

"It should never have come to pass, what happened to your father,"

Feena said. "The yuffids were light-years away from being worthy of joining the Union. The negotiation was, at the very least, terribly premature."

"Your father was put in an impossible position, fraught with danger, and then left to deal with the consequences all on his own. The Union let him down," Finn said. He had circled around her now, standing behind her with both his hands on her shoulders. His scent was enveloping her now, as if he had wings that he was folding around them both.

Ritchie clutched the staff in her hands like it was the only thing tethering her to reality. With Finn behind her, it was possible for her to close her eyes, and she did so. She squeezed them tightly and fought to get her thoughts back in order. What had she come here to do? It was hard to even remember.

Then another scent overpowered the woodchips and spice. The spice was still there, but it was counterpoint to an aroma that was intimately familiar to her. The roasted not-coffee and caramel and cream smell of an uber coffee bomb.

And she was feeling very warm indeed.

She opened her eyes to see Feena standing before her, both her hands on Ritchie's wrists. "We have connections, you know," she said to Ritchie. She could feel Finn's hands moving up her shoulders, his fingertips tickling against the back of her neck, sending shivers all over her body. It was hard to focus on his sister's words as she said, "we would love to help you find your father."

"Our father is so dear to us," Finn said, his mouth close to her ear. "We can only imagine how you feel being apart from yours."

"Would you like our help?" Feena asked. Ritchie still held the staff between them, but only with numb, nerveless fingers.

"Ritchie?" Finn said softly.

A loud metallic clang shattered the moment. Ritchie felt her mind clear. The scents of the twins were still all around her, but they were more like a standard perfume aroma than actually intoxicating. Finn stepped back away from Ritchie, and she sensed him drawing his pistol again. Feena in front of her spun around, also drawing her weapon.

"Crap," Moreau said, wincing as she stepped away from the now-shut incinerator. "I meant to do that a little more sneakily."

Feena looked back over her shoulder, past Ritchie to her brother. "She shut it down! Now we have to fire it up all over again."

"Relax. It'll go faster the second time," he said. Then his hand was on Ritchie's arm again, dragging her back against his chest. She felt the barrel of his pistol press up against her temple. "Drop the staff."

Ritchie let the staff fall from her hands to clatter at her feet. But the cold metal on her skin wasn't so much frightening as a wake-up call. It broke the last of his little spell. Her thoughts were finally clear, despite the timbre of his voice near her ear or the warmth of him pressed up behind her.

She sent out a call for help through her implant to Fitz and Wyss, and then belatedly to Hansen as well.

"Shut her down!" Feena yelled at her brother, her beautiful face terrifying when it was all apoplectic. "Her, too," she added, pointing her pistol at Moreau.

"You were supposed to be keeping an eye on her, dear sister," Finn said, but then made a move like he was cracking his neck.

Suddenly Ritchie felt like her head was stuffed with cotton. Her vision blurred. She felt off balance.

Her implant had gone silent. And not like it had when she had been deep in the catacombs with Fitz. That had just been a lack of connection to the school systems. Now her implant wasn't responding to any commands. She couldn't see the time, or summon up a guiding map, or anything.

Too late, she regretted not calling out to every implant connected to the school systems. Because she had no idea where Fitz, Wyss and Hansen had gone to, but she suspected it was those very catacombs.

And if they were in the catacombs, they had surely gone down to see the body. They would be too deep to hear her call, and too far away to come in time to help her and Moreau.

Moreau was shaking her head as if trying to get water out of her ear. Ritchie guessed whatever Finn had done to her implant, he had done it to Moreau as well.

But Moreau recovered quickly. The minute Feena took a step

towards her, still brandishing that pistol, Moreau straightened up, throwing a bag from each hand. Feena gasped as they struck her with a loud smack, one in the shoulder and the other full in the face.

Then Moreau was gone from sight.

"Feena?" Finn called, sounding equal parts concerned and annoyed in a way only a sibling could manage.

"I'm fine. Get her," Feena said. She had a hand pressed to her gushing nose and her eyes were winced half-shut, but the other hand still held her pistol. She waved it in the direction Moreau had been, but both Moreau and the bag that contained Voet had disappeared.

"I'll shoot your friend here," Finn said, pressing the barrel of his pistol harder into the side of Ritchie's head.

She was only going to get one chance at this, and it wasn't a particularly good chance. But she couldn't pass up the opportunity to take advantage of both his distraction looking around for Moreau and the force of him pressing that gun into her temple.

She moved as if she had practiced this particular maneuver a million times, simultaneously turning her head away to let the barrel slide past her, shifting her foot to plant it between his, and pulling on his arm until his whole body was moving in the direction of the gun, rolling over her now-outthrust hip.

She didn't throw him as she had hoped, but she did send him stumbling away from her. She bent to pick up her staff, but he recovered too quickly, slamming a foot down on it to pin it to the floor before she quite had a grip on it.

She didn't dare risk looking up at him. Instead she danced back, glancing around for anything to use as a weapon or cover from his weapon.

Then she heard him cry out in surprise and saw that Moreau, who was barely half his height, had tackled him out of nowhere. She didn't manage to throw him to the floor either, but she did knock the gun from his hand. It hit the floor, then slid off into the shadows in the corner of the room.

Ritchie slid headfirst after it. Her fingers fumbled, then caught it and she rolled onto her back to take aim at the others behind her.

But she was too late. She heard the zap of Feena's weapon just before she turned all the way over. For a moment, every one of them was frozen in place. Ritchie flat on her back with her gun trained on Feena, Moreau and Finn grappling together in the middle of the room, Feena with her gun in her hands but her eyes wide in horror.

Then Finn and Moreau both fell, first to their knees and then face-down on the floor.

And Feena started to scream.

20

FITZ HAD JUST REACHED the first door to the incinerator room and his hand was closing over the handle when a sudden chilling scream filled the air. It started as a shriek of surprise, lowered to a keening of sorrow, then ratcheted up to a bellow of rage, all before he even wrestled the door open.

Wyss crashed up against his back as Fitz flung the door out of the way, and the two of them charged into the room beyond, peering into a darkness barely lit by the dark red glow of a dying fire inside the incinerator. There were two figures sprawled out on the floor, but one was too tall and the other was too short to be Ritchie.

Then he saw Feena standing over them, some sort of pistol in her hands. He flinched, but she wasn't aiming at him. Her eyes were pure fury, but her arms held steady as she waited for her moment.

He followed the direction she was aiming and saw Ritchie with a gun in her hands, crouching behind a crate. But she was moving, straightening up to take a shot at Feena.

Feena, who was just waiting for Ritchie's head to appear over the top of the crate before she fired.

"Ritchie!" he shouted. Ritchie froze, and Feena shrieked again, this time all in fury, and pivoted on her heels to shift her aim from Ritchie, crouching behind cover to Fitz out in the open.

Fitz threw up his hands, as if blotting the weapon from his sight would save him. He felt Wyss ducking behind his back, using him for cover. Fitz was pretty sure Feena's shot would go through both of them as well as the wall of the corridor beyond the doorway behind him, but he couldn't blame Wyss for hoping for the best.

"Cadet Berweger, drop your weapon!"

To Fitz's surprise, the commanding voice from the doorway came not from Colonel Hansen but from Colonel Devereux. Which was a good thing; Fitz was in no way convinced that Feena would take orders from Hansen. Even now, she only lowered her gun. She didn't set it down or even holster it.

"What's happened here?" Hansen demanded. Then he saw the two cadets lying on the floor. "Someone get the lights on here. Wyss, gather up the weapons."

Wyss reluctantly left his cover behind Fitz to walk first to Ritchie. She handed over the pistol, then wiped her palms down her thighs as if touching it had sullied her. Then Wyss went to stand before Feena, holding out his hand.

"Cadet," Colonel Devereux said warningly. Feena sniffed loudly but handed over her weapon.

Wyss turned away from her to carry the weapons to Colonel Hansen. Only then did he start shaking in fear.

"We need medical help," Hansen said from where he was kneeling beside the two bodies. Then he gave Fitz a hard glare. "Didn't I ask for lights?"

"Right," Fitz said, and turned back to the door, feeling along the wall until he found the controls. The sudden flooding of light was so blinding it made his eyes water, but he heard Ritchie hiss in a breath as if it pained her. Squinting, he found her just where he had left her, crouching behind that dust-coated crate. He went to her side at once. "Are you all right?"

"I didn't think you'd hear me," she said, her eyes more closed than opened. "I was afraid you'd still be in the catacombs."

"Not after we knew the Berwegers had the body," he said. He looked her over. She seemed unharmed, but surely the twins knew ways to torture someone for information that left no mark. "Are you all right?" he asked again, gripping her arm to be sure he had her attention.

"I'm fine. Why do you keep asking me that?" she asked, annoyed with him. He let her go.

"I thought..." but he couldn't finish.

Ritchie gave him a puzzled look, but then Hansen spoke with great relief. "They are both only stunned. Wyss, I want to take a look at those weapons. Those *contraband* weapons."

"Yes, sir," Wyss said, and brought the pistols to Hansen.

"Interesting," Hansen said as he examined the weapons. "I've never seen one, but I've heard tell of them. Black market items. They fire an electrical charge. You're lucky these two both still have a pulse. They must've been in contact when you struck them. That diluted out the charge. Still, these guns are highly illegal. You and your brother are in very hot water indeed."

Cadet Feena Berweger said nothing.

"Stunned?" Ritchie whispered to Fitz. "The way she screamed, I thought they were both dead for sure. Or her brother anyway." She dropped her head back against the crate behind her as she slid to sit on the floor. "I can't remember the last time I was this tired."

"Yeah," Fitz said, looking down at his own scuffed up hands. Then he sat down, facing Ritchie. He still wasn't convinced she was all right. "I tried to respond to your message. I couldn't reach you."

"Finn did something to my implant," she said sleepily. Then she closed her eyes for a moment. "It's back now. I guess he knew I was about to call out to the whole school. Bring everyone here running." She opened her eyes and gave him a tired smile. "Should've trusted calling you would be enough."

"Did he hurt you?" Fitz asked.

"I wouldn't call it that," she said. "Is that what it feels like for everyone who talks to them?"

"I don't know," Fitz said. She had a wistful look on her face that was like a knife twisting in his gut. Like up until the gunfire started, she had been having a very lovely time chatting with Finn Berweger. In all his imagining of Ritchie being tortured for the location of the murder weapon, somehow he had never pictured this other, far worse scenario.

He reminded himself that she had, in fact, sent out a very urgent call for help.

"Ritchie," he said, taking her hand and squeezing until she focused on him again.

"Sorry. I think I'm still feeling some of the effects," she said. Then she rolled her head back against the crate, looking at him through half-closed eyes. "Do you always smell like that?"

"Me? Like what?" he asked, then immediately decided he did *not* want her to answer that question. "I mean, I did just climb all the way back down into the very damp and smelly catacombs and then climb back up with great urgency, before I sprinted here and am in fact still sweating. I certainly hope I don't always smell like this."

"Not that," she said, wrinkling her nose as if just now aware of what he was sure was a very powerful aroma. "I guess it's your smell, I mean. That woodsy thing. That smell means trust. It means home. How did Finn do that?"

Fitz shook his head as if to clear it, even though she was the one who was sounding rather addled. "I was really worried about you," he said, more accusingly than he had meant to.

"Why?" she asked.

"Because the Berwegers thought of something we hadn't," he said. "When they took the body out of the catacombs, they searched for the murder weapon."

"We didn't see one," Ritchie said with a frown.

"They didn't find one either," he said. "I was afraid they would think we had it. That you would know where it is."

"Oh," Ritchie said.

"That's all you have to say?" he asked.

"You thought they were going to hurt me to find out where we had hidden it?" she asked.

"Well, they certainly didn't know where to look for me," he said. "And even if they did, I was well out of their reach. I've been with Colonel Hansen the entire time. But the last time I had seen you, you were well within reach of Finn Berweger."

A team of medics came into the room with a pair of stretchers, but Fitz only caught a glimpse of them before Ritchie's arms were around him. He could feel her shaking, and knew that as usual she was only feeling fear when it was far too late for it to do any good in keeping her out of danger.

He just hugged her back as tightly as he could.

"I'm sorry I worried you," she said, her voice muffled against his shoulder. "I wonder why he never asked?"

There was a sudden metallic clang, too loud to be from the stretchers even if the medics had somehow dropped them in an uncharacteristic show of butterfingers. Ritchie stiffened, but Fitz was already on alert, letting her go and lunging to his feet to vault over the crate.

But he was too late. Feena was already turning away from the open grate of the incinerator. He could see a black duffle bag within, the one he had seen her and her brother put Voet's remains in.

He landed on the far side of the crate and ran towards her. She gave him one of her most dazzling smiles, and he just had time to marvel that the fact that someone had bloodied her nose was in no way diminishing her siren-like beauty before there was a flash, a bang, and a whiff of smoke.

She had used an explosive device to seal the grate shut. He knew it, but he still tried to fight it back open. Perhaps the metal hadn't warped closed yet...

But it was no good. He couldn't get it open. And then she had turned the flames back on and Fitz had to fall back, shaking his nearly singed hands.

"Hansen!" he yelled. But the colonel was already there, shoving him aside to struggle with the grate. He bellowed as he strained to lift it, and Fitz was sure he heard the metal groan as well. But it held.

Within a minute the last of the bag as well as its contents were reduced to ash, and all Hansen had to show for it were two badly burned hands.

"Oh, I'm sorry. Did you want that?" Feena asked. Her expression of innocence was so nearly convincing that Fitz had to remind himself he had seen everything she had just done, and she had absolutely done it deliberately.

"That is a pity," Colonel Devereux said with an exaggerated frown. Her acting was no match for the cadet's.

"You are going into protective custody," Hansen told her. "You and your protégées, all three of you."

"What could you possibly charge us with?" Devereux demanded.

"He said 'protective custody'," Wyss said.

"Just to be sure you're safe," Hansen said in a low growl. "Just until the murder weapon is found. There is a crime unit on their way here now, and I have the authority to detain anyone I feel may be a threat or may be in danger."

"But my brother is hurt," Feena said.

"He'll go to the infirmary as well as Cadet Moreau," Hansen said. "But I'm afraid you and Colonel Devereux will be bunking in the brig for the time being."

"And what about *your* protégées?" Devereux snarled.

Fitz looked at Ritchie. They both braced themselves for the inevitable. Hansen's cover story of protective custody to hold the others was going to necessitate it. But they had both been in the brig before and survived it. Provided they weren't expected to get through it with Berweger bunkmates, they'd be fine.

But to Fitz's surprise, Hansen only said, "they'll be safe with me."

He then sent Wyss, still holding the pistols, to accompany the medics as they brought Finn and Moreau to the infirmary. There was already a section of the infirmary that could act as a confinement cell in cases like this. It was a little chilling that anyone thought they'd need it at a school, but all things considered, Fitz just admired whoever had had the foresight to add that to the specs.

Then Hansen turned Devereux and Feena over to an armed security detail. He had already cuffed them both, but since the detail was made up of last-year cadets who had never yet used the weapons they were carrying outside of practice drills, it was understandable that they all looked like they were working hard not to puke from nervousness.

"I should accompany them to the brig," Hansen said to Fitz and Ritchie. "The crime unit won't be here until morning at the soonest. Are you two going to be all right on your own?"

He asked that in a soft voice, too low for Devereux and Feena behind him to overhear. Both Fitz and Ritchie just nodded.

Hansen nodded back, curtly. But then he leaned down closer to where they were sitting on the floor to ask, "any thoughts at all where that murder weapon might be?"

"I hadn't even thought of it until just now," Ritchie said. "It could be anywhere. It's been decades. If it wasn't near the body, where would we even start to look?"

"I wish I knew, cadet," he said.

"We'll have better luck in the morning when we're fed, rested, and alert," Fitz promised.

Hansen just nodded again, then spun on his heel to command the waiting security detail to march the prisoners out of the room.

"Hungry?" Fitz asked Ritchie.

"Like you wouldn't believe," she said.

"I'm dying for a shower myself," he said.

"I could use one of those. The library door driers are adequate for rain but are just terrible with sweat. I feel so sticky right now," she said. But she didn't move to get up. Fitz scooted over to sit beside her with his back against the crate.

It wasn't just dusty. It was greasy. Even through his uniform he knew it was layers upon layers of dust and grease. Layers that had accumulated over decades. They were probably older than Voet's bones, those layers.

Just what the heck was in that crate? Something no one thought to get rid of, and yet never seemed to need.

Just another mystery.

Ritchie rested her head on his shoulder with a little sigh, and all thoughts of the crate were gone from his head.

"Even that hard as hell bunk downstairs is going to feel good tonight," Fitz said.

"Yeah," Ritchie said, or made a sound that was in the vicinity of that word. But she made no move to get up.

Fitz tipped his head to rest it against hers. Then he let the exhaustion take him.

21

THE NEXT FEW days passed in a blur of too much schoolwork and not
enough updates on the ongoing investigation. Ritchie had to keep
reminding herself that no one, in fact, had to tell her or any other cadet
anything.

But it felt like she and Fitz had earned a little consideration.

Not to mention Moreau.

Ritchie went straight to the infirmary every day after classes and
spent as much time with her buddy as she was allowed to. She never
saw any sign of Finn, but she knew he was there as well, confined to
his own recovery room.

On the fourth day, when she went into Moreau's room, she found
Fitz and Wyss already there, standing around her bed. Moreau was
looking much improved even from the day before, and had her gown
down off her shoulder to show them the burn wound.

"So that's where you were in contact with Finn?" Fitz guessed, and
sort of mimed tackling Wyss to verify.

"Yep. And here's the exit burn," Moreau said, pulling her foot out
from under the bedsheet to show them the mottled purple spot on the
sole of her foot. "Good thing you came to see me in time. They're both

healing really fast and they say I won't even have a scar by next week. Which is totally unfair."

"So, wait," Wyss said. "That means Feena didn't shoot you. She shot her brother?"

Moreau just grinned maniacally. Whatever they were giving her for the pain was putting her in a very up mood.

Then she saw Ritchie lurking in the doorway and waved for her to come in. Fitz and Wyss turned to look at her.

"Hey," Ritchie said. "I didn't expect to see you two here."

"You've been keeping us up to date on her progress, but I figured she'd appreciate a personal visit," Fitz said.

"Thanks," Moreau said. "It's very dull in here."

"But I've been bringing you all the homework plus my notes," Ritchie said with a frown.

"That doesn't take me all day to go through," Moreau said. "And no one will tell me what's going on out there. So spill." She poked a finger at Fitz.

"What am I supposed to be saying?" he asked.

Ritchie sighed. "Moreau thinks I'm holding out on her. But the truth is, no one is telling us anything about what's going on. It's a criminal investigation and none of our business, apparently."

"Feena Berweger was back in her classes after lunch today," Wyss said, which got all their attention at once.

"Seriously?" Moreau asked.

Wyss nodded. "And Colonel Devereux was seen in her office too, apparently working. But she's not been teaching her classes. Yet."

"So that's the end of it?" Ritchie asked, confused. "They destroy the body and that's it? What about the blood on the stones down in the catacombs? What about the missing murder weapon?"

"What about what we saw and heard in the incinerator room?" Moreau added. "I'll testify to all of it. I know you will too. So what gives?"

"None of it is enough, apparently," Fitz said darkly. "Not when you're facing attorneys the likes of those who work for the Berweger family."

"The gun Feena shot me with is illegal," Moreau said. "My body is evidence of that."

"They don't have enough cause to continue holding them in custody," Wyss said. "That doesn't mean the investigation isn't still ongoing."

"Can you tell? From their communications over the academy systems, for instance?" Ritchie asked him.

Wyss shook his head. "They've upped the security. A lot. I can tell there's still chatter, so I think that means the case isn't closed yet, but beyond that I really can't guess."

"She could've killed me," Moreau said. "If I hadn't been touching Finn, if the entire electrical charge from the gun had hit just me, I would be dead now. And she'd still get away with it?"

"Maybe your family could sue for damages," Fitz said, his mood darkening by the minute.

"No. I don't see them doing that," Moreau mumbled. "We are not remotely in the same league as the Berwegers or the Fitzes."

"If it helps, since she shot her brother and not you, he's really the one who almost died," Wyss said.

But none of them were cheered by that thought. Feena had been aiming for Moreau, not her brother. If he had died, the attorneys would probably just find a way to blame his death on Moreau.

"I hate this," Fitz said, slumping into a chair and grabbing fistfuls of his hair.

"What's that?" Ritchie asked.

"This whole system. The whole way the world works. It's not the way it's supposed to work," he said. He glanced at her but then looked away, out the window rather than at her. Like it pained him to look at her. "But I really hate how the unfairness of it all is supposed to benefit me. I never asked for that. But not for a minute do I believe that my father isn't constantly pulling every string to shift things in my favor. I'm sure I only know a fraction of it. And no matter what I do, nothing makes him stop pulling those strings."

"I know how you feel," Moreau said. "There's nothing we can do to cut off those ties, is there? They'll always be there, our elders, waiting for us to take up our generational duty or whatever. Upholding the good family name. There's no escape."

"I hope you don't think it's any kind of party for the rest of us," Wyss said. He spoke lightly, like he was trying to brighten the mood, but he failed utterly.

"The Berweger twins might have gotten away with breaking the rules this time, but we'll get them next time," Ritchie said. "And there will be a next time. I'm sure of that."

"We might still get them this time," Wyss insisted. "They destroyed the body, and that was a lot of evidence, but Stans Voet is now officially dead, not just missing and presumed dead."

"He was stabbed by multiple people," Ritchie said. "Multiple people who got away with it and will still get away with it."

"Not if we find that murder weapon," Wyss said. "I'm building more drones by the day and sending them down there. If it's there, I'll find it."

"And if it was thrown into that underground sea?" Ritchie asked.

"I'll build submersible drones," he said. "I'm already working on a design."

"I'm not sure the murder is even the important thing," Moreau said. "I mean, it is huge, and I want justice for Voet too, but I'm more worried about what's happening now than what happened decades ago. Now that Feena is free in the school and Finn will be discharged the same day I am, will there be more meetings in the catacombs?"

"And is there anything we can do to prevent it?" Fitz said.

"Is there more you can tell us about that first meeting?" Ritchie asked.

Moreau touched her forehead almost unconsciously, as if in memory of headaches past. "Well, like I told you before, the twins gave a long-winded speech about the purity of the Union of the Free Worlds and the importance of preserving it. But the other cadets weren't really buying it. I could tell that the Berwegers wanted everyone to feel a lot more urgency, even fear, than they were."

"That seems odd. They've always been so good at swaying people. I've seen it over and over," Fitz said.

"I have too. I've even felt it. But that's always been in small groups, for small stakes," Moreau said. "Feena can absolutely get anybody at a party to fetch anything for her. She could probably even get them to fight with each other for her entertainment. But convincing a crowd of cadets to overthrow the world order? Maybe they aren't there yet."

"They'll hone their technique, you think?" Fitz asked.

"That's what I'm afraid of," Moreau said. Then she glanced at Wyss. "Any luck figuring out what the Berwegers even really are?"

"It's impossible to divide what might be based on fact from the outright fiction in the rumors about their creation," he said. "Having said that, I have a few theories as to some of the species they might have exploited."

"Do tell," Moreau said. Wyss grinned, then pulled out his tablet. She moved over so he could sit beside her on her bed and show her the images on his tablet.

But it would all just be speculation, Ritchie thought to herself with yet another sigh. And Fitz didn't seem inclined to listen either. He was still sitting in the room's only chair, his head between his hands. And those hands were gripping his hair so tightly it just had to be painful.

Ritchie put her hands on his, and he loosened his grip to look up at her. She tipped her head back, inviting him to follow her back out into the corridor.

"What's up?" he asked the minute they were outside the room, a concerned look on his face.

"Nothing with me," she assured him. "I just wanted to see how you were doing."

He gave her a confused look, as if she had accidentally spoken in some language he wasn't familiar with.

"You're very upset with your father. But so far as we know he isn't even implicated in any of this," she said.

"Oh," he said, dropping his eyes. "Well, he kind of is. He's implicated in anything that happens in the Union of Free Worlds, really."

"That doesn't seem to be what's upsetting you, though," Ritchie said. He didn't say anything. He had his hands deep in his pockets and was studying the toes of his boots. "If you don't want to talk about it, I understand."

"That's just it, I *do* want to talk about it," he said. His voice was emphatic, but he was still staring at his feet.

"Just not with me?" Ritchie guessed.

"You most of all," he said. Then he took a deep, ragged breath and looked up at her through his thoroughly mussed bangs. "I'm sorry. Finn had some things to say to me when this was all just getting started, and it's been eating at me."

"He seems like he's better at that than his sister," Ritchie said neutrally.

"Or more willing to use it," Fitz said. "Or she's just more inclined to trust in her other... charms."

"What did you want to tell me?" Ritchie asked.

Fitz looked up at her with anguish in his eyes. Ritchie wasn't sure if he was about to speak or to hedge again or what. And she didn't get to find out because Hansen turned around the corner and started coming towards them down the hall.

"Oh, good. You're both here," he said as he approached. "Cadet Wyss too?"

"He's inside with Moreau, sir," Ritchie said. She tried to catch Fitz's eyes again, but he was all business now, looking to Hansen.

"I have your work assignments for you," Hansen said. "Why don't we all go inside?"

Ritchie felt her stomach drop. She had forgotten about her punishment for meddling. Or at least she had hoped that Hansen had forgotten. But she said nothing, just followed him into Moreau's room and sat on the arm of the chair. Fitz did the same on the other arm. Hansen then closed the door firmly.

But when he turned back to face the four of them, his first words were, "how are you feeling, cadet?"

"Improved," Moreau said.

"Excellent," Hansen said. "Your new work assignments. Any previous rotations on your schedules are henceforth cancelled, by the way. You'll see that update on your implant calendars momentarily. That means no field maintenance, kitchen duty, guard duty, none of it."

"Yes, sir," Ritchie said, and her stomach dropped still further. She had no love for any of those things, but she had a feeling in the coming weeks she was going to miss the old, happy days of scrubbing cookware in the academy kitchens until the early hours of the morning.

"Moreau, your schedule won't begin until you've been discharged from the infirmary," Hansen said after glancing at the screen of his tablet.

"Yes, sir," Moreau said, clearly disappointed.

"Wyss, your work assignment will carry with it certain system access privileges," Hansen said. "Don't get too excited; mainly it's things you've been doing already. Only now, you'll have permission to be in those systems."

"Yes, sir," Wyss said. He had straightened up at this news, noticeably intrigued.

"Now, the warning," Hansen said severely. "You four all report directly to me and only to me. No chattering with other cadets about your work assignments. I cannot stress that strongly enough. What you are doing is not to be public knowledge. Consider it training for future classified field work. Furthermore, and I can't stress this too strongly, no researching anyone without my express permission. I am doing my own digging; I will take all the risk. Specifically, a certain twelve individuals who may or may not have committed murder some decades ago. No trying to figure out who they might have been. No following up on hunches. It's far too likely that will draw unwanted attention onto you, possibly even real danger. I take all the risks. Understood, cadets?"

"Yes, sir," they all said as one.

"Excellent," he said, consulting his tablet again. "Now, Ritchie and Fitz, your first assignment begins this very minute."

"How long will it take?" Ritchie asked. Hansen frowned at her sternly, and Fitz beside her was staring at her like she'd gone mad. "Sorry, it's just that, I have a lot of homework to get through, and—"

"This takes precedence," Hansen said. Then his tone softened. "I'll clear any tardy work with your instructors. But I expect you to do your level best to stay on top of your classes, no matter how involved these work assignments become."

Ritchie swallowed, but her throat was too dry to trust herself to speak. So she just nodded.

"Sir, what exactly will we be doing?" Fitz asked. But Hansen acted like he didn't even hear the question.

"Your credentials," he said, reaching into his pocket and pulling out two insignias. He handed one to Fitz and the other to Ritchie.

She turned it over in her hands and saw the widespread golden wings that representing the diplomatic corps. A golden scroll that fluttered beneath the wings read: ACTING DIPLOMAT.

She looked over at what was in Fitz's hands and saw the crossed spears of the guardian corps over a scroll reading ACTING GUARDIAN.

Then she looked up at his face and saw that it glowed with excitement. She looked back down at her own insignia and felt her throat close up still further.

She was the farthest thing from a diplomat, acting or otherwise. What was she going to be called on to do? And how was she ever going to keep from failing at it?

"There is a shuttle waiting for you already on the launch field," Hansen said. "There are uniforms on board for you to change into. Time is of the essence. This appointment was very difficult to arrange, and I don't expect I'll be able to make another if you miss this one."

"Yes, sir," Fitz said, closing his hand around his acting guardian insignia.

"Where are we going?" Ritchie asked.

"You can review your briefing materials on the way. I'm sending them to your implants now," Hansen said. Then he looked at her, and his face softened. "You're going to the Julius Henry Observational Center."

"To see cadet... I mean, Sidonie Keller?" Ritchie guessed.

Her stomach found a new, deeper place to settle into.

"Yes, but also Cadmar Weld," he said. "They've both had conversations with you that implied they were aware of and perhaps even part of some larger conspiracy. I need you to go there now and ask them both more about it."

"But why me?" Ritchie asked. She flinched at the shrillness of her own voice.

But Hansen just put a hand under her elbow to propel her up from the chair and towards the now-open door. "Read your briefing materials. Prepare your questions in advance. But do it on the shuttle en route."

The minute he let go of her elbow, she stopped moving. But then Fitz was there, taking her arm to pull her along with him.

"I know you're overwhelmed, but once we're on the shuttle and you have a chance to start working on this, you'll be fine," he whispered to her.

She could see how excited he was by this assignment. And on some level, she knew this was a huge thing. To work as a diplomat or a guardian on an acting basis, even just to conduct a couple of interviews, was more than resumé padding. It was paving a path to a very bright future.

And yet, she didn't want to be a diplomat. Her father had been a diplomat, and she had let him down in the worst possible way. The path to making restitution for that didn't lie in following in his footsteps. It just couldn't. Not for Ritchie.

She wanted to be the one protecting the diplomat. Not the other way around.

"Cadet Fitz!" Hansen called down the hall just as they were about to turn the corner out of the infirmary.

"Sir?" Fitz called back.

"I expect that you will take this responsibility very seriously," Hansen said. "Do you understand me? I will not so much as entertain the thought of any other possibilities."

"Yes, sir," Fitz said. Then he was propelling Ritchie forward again, so fast she was nearly tripping over her own feet. "You know I've got this, right?" he asked.

She looked over at him, still all aglow with excitement. "Yes, I know that," she agreed.

If he heard any of the glumness in her voice that she was feeling, he didn't say a word. Perhaps he was chalking it up to nervousness about the assignment.

But she really wished they could change places.

22

IT TOOK MORE than a day to reach the Julius Henry Observational Center from Oymyakon, even under optimal conditions. Which their takeoff hadn't exactly been.

It had looked like there'd be one of those rare perfect breaks in the always stormy skies that would let the shuttle launch straight to orbit. Then the storm had closed around them, and for a few long minutes Fitz hadn't been sure if they were going to live or die a fiery death on the side of a mountain.

But Ritchie in that turbulent moment hadn't looked half as stressed out as she did now, going over Colonel Hansen's briefing materials and her own notes for the umpteenth time. He could see her lips moving as she practiced what she wanted to say or ask. The first few times he had offered to help, she had brushed him off, but after catching a few hours of sleep that she had clearly opted to skip, he had to try again.

His half of the assignment had been reviewing the center's security protocols, which, given that it was where the criminally insane were taken for psychiatric care, was already top notch. He of course had nothing to recommend to the staff, no demands to make in the name of protecting his diplomat. He memorized the maps and could visualize the entire route from shuttle landing bay to the predetermined interview room and back again as well as every possible escape route should something happen on the way. He knew where the weapons lockers were, and the infirmary, and the communications rooms. There was nothing else for him to do except help Ritchie prepare.

"Can we go over what we're planning to do when we reach the center?" he asked as he brought her coffee and eggs. Personally, as far as study food went, he was all carbs all the time. But after more than a year at school together, he knew that Ritchie always preferred great big fluffy yellow mounds of scrambled eggs cooked in butter with just a hint of sharp Cheddar cheese. She didn't quite look up at him when he held out the bowl for her, but she did set aside what she was doing to take the bowl and breathe in the aroma before digging in. "Which of the two were we going to interview first?" he asked as he sat down across from her with his own food.

"Weld," Ritchie said around a mouthful of egg. Which was more than she had been willing to say to him the day before.

"Why?" he asked, pulling apart the sweet cheese pastry he had replicated for himself.

"Not my call. The center has them on set schedules. We will have a half hour with him and then a half hour with Keller, and that's it," she said. Her eggs half gone, she turned her attention to the coffee.

"We have a little time yet before we get there. Did you want to grab a nap?" he asked before she took a sip of what he knew was the strongest black coffee the replicator could serve up.

"I'll sleep on the way back," she said and took a long swallow.

"To be honest, I'm not exactly sure why we're even talking to Weld," Fitz said. "I mean, I read the briefing materials. I get that some of what he said to you on the train implies he was getting information from some unnamed source. But why would that necessarily connect to the Berwegers?"

Ritchie took another drink of coffee, but he could see she was thinking about how to answer him. Finally, she said, "on the train, Weld shut down my implant. Finn did the same thing to me in the incinerator room. It felt the same."

"You were cut off from everything both times. It makes sense they would feel the same."

"The diagnostic that was run after Finn blocked me matches the diagnostic that was done by the crew of the train and later at the academy infirmary after Weld blocked me. No one knows exactly how it was done, but the evidence patterns are very similar." Then she grimaced, scrunching up her nose and closing her eyes. "I don't exactly understand it? Wyss could explain it better than I."

"No, I get it. So do you think Finn learned it from Weld, or the other way around?"

"As far as anyone knows, they never met," Ritchie said. She glanced at her tablet and scrolled through a bit of the text but then set it aside again. "They come from very different worlds. But if I had to guess, I think they both learned it from a common source."

"Someone who is trying to manipulate cadets into doing... what?" Fitz asked.

"I don't know," Ritchie said with a sigh. "I can see Weld being an easy target for manipulation. He had a lot of anger after what happened to his family, and a clear drive for revenge. Although I'm not sure what was accomplished by what he did."

"I don't think he was following the plan," Fitz said. "Whoever was manipulating him clearly wanted him to get to the academy first and then make some sort of trouble. What happened on the train was unforeseen."

"And then there's the fact that Finn and Feena don't seem manipulatable at all," Ritchie added.

They fell silent for a moment. Ritchie finished her eggs, and Fitz pulled apart the rest of his pastry. He only ate a few bits, though. Suddenly the rich sweetness was the last thing he wanted.

"There's another thing that doesn't feel right," Ritchie said.

"What's that?" Fitz asked as he got up and gathered their plates to return them to the replicator for recycling.

"From what Moreau has said, the twins are advocating for a Union of Free Worlds that has no new alien worlds in it. The aliens are the part they are fixated on. They're too different to blend in with the human populations. But that doesn't feel like anything Weld would've been driven by."

"He killed the Felzkinder," Fitz said. "Okay, technically a constructed species and not an alien one, but still not human."

"He killed the Felzkinder to get at a human woman," Ritchie said. "A human woman from a human family who's human world had destroyed his."

Fitz sat back down across from her. "Maybe we don't understand this conspiracy yet. All we know is what Moreau heard on one night. The first night the Berwegers spoke. They were probably just getting warmed up. The real meat of their message might be coming yet. If it's just about being angry and redressing grievances, Weld might have signed on for that goal and then just got impatient when he saw Lady Fabron on that train. He wanted to deal with his own personal grievances first."

"Maybe," Ritchie said, but she didn't sound remotely convinced. "At any rate, whatever he did to my implant is what I intend to focus on. If we only have half an hour, I'm only going to get so many answers out of him. That's the one I want the most."

She then turned back to her notes, but she seemed calmer than before. Talking things through out loud had been something of a help, then.

Fitz went back to his cabin and picked up his own tablet. He had a message from Wyss. The search of the catacombs was ongoing, if still fruitless. But Colonel Hansen had sealed off the entrance and set a round-the-clock guard. No one was going down there save the drones. Fitz could imagine that was angering the Berwegers. Where would they meet now? Out under the open skies? They might find the attendance to their events taking a bit of a hit if that were the case.

Soon they were approaching the space station known as the Julius Henry Observational Center, and Fitz got into his guardian uniform. It wasn't all that different from his academy uniform. All the hidden pockets were in the same places, and he could move as easily in it if a fight were to break out. But the deep navy blue was quite striking, especially with the silver trim and buttons. He pinned his acting guardian insignia to his breast and took a quick photo to send to his mother. Then he headed out to the main cabin space.

Ritchie was exactly where he had left her, hunched over the table referring to two tablets at once. But she too had changed into her borrowed uniform. Hers was ivory with whitish-gold trim, which made her usual space station paleness look more peaches and cream. Nothing like the sun-kissed golden hue she had always had when they were kids and spent all their time under open skies, but warmer than he had seen her since. The browns of their academy uniforms really didn't flatter her at all.

She looked up at him and caught him staring at her. He quickly looked away, but there was absolutely nothing to direct his attention to. So he had to look back at her again. He thrust his hands into his pockets and searched for something to say. "Um, Wyss tells me that the colonel has sealed off the catacombs."

"That's good, anyway," Ritchie said. "Although I guess that means they haven't found anything down there yet."

"No, but give it time," Fitz said.

The voice of the pilot crackled over the PA system. His mic must've been further from his mouth than he thought, as nothing he said was remotely clear. But Fitz sat down across from Ritchie and buckled in as she gathered up her tablets and stowed them before doing the same.

"You look good in your uniform," he said to her, and she flushed a shade of red that spoke more of anger than embarrassment at a compliment. "I mean, I think we both look like the real deal. Very professional. No reason anyone should hassle us when we get there. Right?"

"We have the credentials, and all the clearances have been filed," Ritchie said. She kept brushing at the sleeves of her tunic as if trying to rid herself of something.

She wasn't wrong. Two members of the staff were waiting when they landed in the shuttle docking bay and escorted them directly to a room with a table that ran the length of the room, dividing it neatly in two. There was a single chair on either side, and after the staff members had left, Ritchie settled herself down into it and pulled out her tablet to go over her notes yet again.

Fitz stepped back to stand behind her, his back to the wall. The rules of the observational center didn't allow him to bring any weapons inside, which limited what he could do as a bodyguard. And it's not like Ritchie would need any help on that score. She took their hand-to-hand combat classes far more seriously than he did.

She glanced back at him nervously, and he gave her a smile and a nod of encouragement, then quickly made his face neutral again as a door on the far side of the room opened and Cadmar Weld came in.

He was a little thinner, and maybe even a little paler, although given how pale he had been when they had met, it was hard to be sure on that score. But he was as tall and wide across the shoulders as ever. His close-cut red hair had grown out to curl behind his ears. There were golden highlights in those locks that hadn't been noticeable before.

Then he looked up and locked eyes with Fitz first and sneered. Yep. Same old Weld.

"Cadmar Weld," Ritchie said, getting to her feet to extend her hand to him. "I hope you remember me?"

"How could I forget you?" Weld asked, ignoring her hand. She pulled it back, and they both sat down in their respective chairs.

"Have you been told why I wish to speak with you?" Ritchie asked.

"Sort of," Weld said, looking from Ritchie to Fitz and then back to Ritchie again. "Wasn't expecting the uniforms and all. Aren't you all fancy?"

"It's temporary," Ritchie told him. "Not just anyone is given visiting privileges here. It is a maximum security facility."

"I guess that explains my lack of visitors up to this point," Weld said.

"How have you been doing?" Ritchie asked.

"Like you care," he scoffed. But she just waited until he said, "as well as can be expected. I meditate. I read. I wait."

"What are you waiting for?" Ritchie asked.

"For them to decide to let me go," Weld said. "Don't worry. I know that's years away. But there's little else to do but wait, now is there? There's nothing in my future but that elusive goal of being declared not a danger to others and released back into society."

"What happens then, do you imagine?" Ritchie asked. "Rejoin your family? Get a job and live on your own? If all you're doing is waiting for that moment, you must've made some plans."

"Not really. I'm sure it will all work out in the end," he said. "When I say waiting, I just mean waiting. You know, watching the time pass. The numbers tick by, and I watch them. I don't spend my time daydreaming about impossible things."

"That sounds rather bleak," Ritchie said.

Weld just shrugged and studied his cuticles.

"I know you felt you had to kill me because I knew too much about what happened on the train," Ritchie said, changing tacks. "But before that, it seemed like you and I had a lot in common."

"Yeah, I don't think that's true anymore," he said.

"Why not? What changed?" she asked.

"Nothing changed. I just didn't know then what I know now," he said with another shrug.

"What do you know now?" she asked.

He looked up at her through narrowed eyes, and Fitz was certain he wasn't going to answer. But then he said, "you and I are nothing alike. I was a nobody who scrapped together enough skills to get a little bit of attention. Then I squandered what little potential I had managed to acquire. Hey, it happens. But you? You're playing on a whole different field, aren't you?"

"What do you mean?" Ritchie asked. Fitz could see her spine straightening as she sat up taller. He knew that meant she was bracing for Weld to say something mean or dismissive. He couldn't see her hands, but he knew her knuckles would be white as she clutched her tablet.

"Lots of eyes are on you," Weld said. "Lots of people want to see if you dare to try to take your father's place. Me, if I were you, I'd run as hard and fast as I could in the other direction. But I guess you have other ideas." He reached across the table to tweak at the end of the sleeve of her diplomat's tunic.

Ritchie pulled her hands back out of his reach. "Like I said, this is just temporary. It was necessary for me to speak to you."

"And to Keller," Weld said.

"So you know her," Ritchie said.

But Weld just shrugged again.

"Tell me, what do you think of her?" Ritchie asked. Fitz was surprised by this question. What could she possibly be driving at? But he said nothing.

"She's smarter than me," he said. Then he gave Ritchie a hard stare. "She's smarter than you."

"That's debatable," Ritchie said.

"If you *were* smart, you'd let her have what she wants," Weld said. "Let her take your father's place. You know she wants it more than anything. And she should have it."

"You talk like my father held some particular sort of office," Ritchie said. "He was a diplomat. A talented one, but just one of many. He had no place to be passed down to me or Keller or anyone else."

"He was the vanguard for the Union," Weld said. "He went in when no one else could to speak to the alien species who were the least like us."

"And you think Sidonie Keller should do that and not me?" Ritchie asked. She was keeping her tone carefully neutral, but Fitz could hear the undercurrent of hurt. She didn't like to be devalued in anyone's eyes, not even Weld's.

But Weld just laughed. "I think you should let Keller do it, yes," he said.

"Because I'm not good enough?"

"No, you're good enough," Weld said, his demeanor all seriousness again. "That's precisely why you should say no."

"I don't follow you," Ritchie said.

"Find a different line of work," Weld told her. "One that doesn't have quite so many people eager to see you fail. Or willing to do what it takes to make sure you do."

"Weld," Ritchie said, and her voice was suddenly all icy. "Do you know something about my father?"

"No, Ritchie. If I did I'd tell you, just for old time's sake," he said. "As to the politics of it all, you must have access to better information out there than I do in here. Look around and listen and wise up. That's all I'm saying. That, and find a different line of work. I think I'd like you better in navy blue."

"Like I said, this is just temporary," Ritchie said. Then she picked up her tablet and scrolled through her notes. Weld waited patiently for her next question, but Fitz knew what she was going to ask next. They were nearly out of time, and she had yet to ask what she wanted to know the most.

"Weld," Ritchie said, setting her tablet back down, then folding her hands together over it. "You were the first person to disable my implant. You know that's not even supposed to be possible? And yet it's happened to me twice now."

"I'm not surprised," Weld said. "Lots of eyes on you, like I said. Must be uncomfortable."

"I wanted to ask you how you did it," she said. "Did you work it out on your own, or did someone show you?"

Weld glared at her, but there was more than anger in his eyes. Fitz was sure he saw the glisten of a tear not quite shed. Then Weld lunged across the table, seizing Ritchie's wrists and pulling her towards him.

"Let her go!" Fitz said, at once at her side. He seized Weld's arm to keep him from dragging her across the table.

But that wasn't what he was doing. Instead, Weld pushed his own sleeve back, pressing Ritchie's hand to his scarred forearm.

Wait, those circular scars were new. Had he been burned? They were all in a line, all the same size, all burned to the same depth.

"Do you feel it?" Weld hissed at Ritchie. She nodded. He let go of her wrists, but she stayed half-sitting on the table, running the fingertips of both her hands over his forearms.

"What is it?" she asked, looking up into his eyes.

"The scars are from the chemical interrogations," he told her. "One scar for each interrogation. You only see the burn on the surface. When they do it, it courses through your whole body."

Fitz could see Ritchie swallow hard, but she kept her emotions in check. "I feel something else. Something under the surface," she said.

"Those are the worms," Weld said. "That's probably not their technical name, but it's not like they tell me what they're subjecting me to. But they move through my body, all the time, probing and prodding."

"Does it hurt?" she asked.

"Every damn second," Weld said, then stepped back, pushing his sleeves back down to his wrists.

"Why?" she asked.

"You think you're the only one who desperately wants to know how I shut down your implant? I get asked over and over again. If you want to call it asking. I'm sure that's how it's phrased in my official reports. They're going to ask me again, the minute I step out of this office. They'll ask me for a few hours before I get put back in my room. But I'll never tell. Not even you, Murdina Ritchie."

Ritchie nodded, pushing back from the table to stand beside her chair. "The... worms. How is that supposed to make you talk?"

"Research it," Weld snapped. "They wear me down in so many ways. I don't know up from down, day from night, being awake from being asleep. But they can't make me speak."

"Eventually you'll break," Fitz said. Weld looked up at him, but not with anger in his eyes. It was more like he was assessing Fitz, comparing who he was now from who he had been on the train, perhaps? Or comparing what he saw to things he'd heard? But he looked away again, not revealing a bit of his thoughts to Fitz's eyes.

"I won't," Weld said. He sounded absolutely exhausted, but Fitz believed him. He would never tell anyone anything.

Fitz was suddenly very curious about Weld's meditation practice.

Then Weld gave him half a smirk, as if reading his mind. "You know how it's done, don't you, Fitz? The secret to keeping a secret. Tell me."

"You never let yourself think it even just in your own head," Fitz said, and Weld nodded. Then an alarm sounded briefly, and Weld gave them both a mocking salute before exiting through the far door.

Ritchie stood motionless, as she had since asking Weld about the interrogation worms. Fitz really hoped that she was still thinking about Weld and her implant, and not the last thing Fitz had said. She had seemed like she had been tuning them both out at the end of the interview.

But Fitz couldn't leave it alone. If she was upset with him, he had to know.

"Ritchie?" Fitz asked.

"I need a minute," she said. Her hands were clenched at her sides and her head was down, the sides of her hair blocking her face from his view.

"You're not upset about what's happened to him? The interrogations?" Fitz asked. "That's not on you. That's all on him."

"I know," Ritchie said.

Fitz moved to sit against the edge of the table, closer to her, hoping she'd look up at him. "He doesn't know anything about your father or what happened to him. You can't let what he said into your head."

"I know that too," she said, still not looking up. He reached out to grasp her arm, but she flinched out of the way. "Please, Fitz. I just need a minute."

Fitz nodded, but he didn't step away. He stayed there, near her but not trying to comfort her. She truly didn't seem to have heard him pretty much confess to keeping secrets. That was a good thing.

But the rest of it was almost killing him. Because if Weld had upset her this much, how much worse was it going to be after talking to Keller? Keller, who knew Ritchie so much better than Weld?

Keller, who relished hurting Ritchie with a sadistic level of joy?

Then the alarm sounded again. Ritchie slid back into her chair, and Fitz moved to take his position against the wall behind her. They both took a deep breath at the same time, then looked up as the door started to open.

## 23

RITCHIE TOOK A DEEP BREATH, clearing her mind from everything that had just happened with Weld. She had to deal with Keller now, and if she wasn't at the top of her game, Keller was going to run all over her.

When she heard the door swish open, Ritchie raised her head to look at Sidonie Keller. She looked the same. Either she wasn't being subjected to chemical interrogations like Weld, or she just tolerated them better. Her thick reddish-brown curls were as chaotic as ever, her freckled skin no paler than usual.

If Ritchie had to bet, she would say Keller wasn't being interrogated. She had manipulated Ritchie into murdering Jeger by arming what was meant to be a dummy gun on her glider, but she hadn't done any specific thing anyone else couldn't replicate. And if she had known how to shut down Ritchie's implant, she surely would have. But she had only locked her in a room and held her at gunpoint.

"Hey, Ritchie and Fitz," Keller said with a grin as she sat down across from Ritchie. As if they were about to have lunch together in the academy cafeteria, just like old times. "I like your uniforms. I always knew you two would end up as a working team. Diplomat Ritchie and her loyal Guardian Fitz. Yep, exactly how I pictured it."

"This is just temporary," Ritchie said, but Keller interrupted her.

"I know. No one gets to see me without meeting certain guidelines and jumping a ton of hoops. I would think Colonel Devereux sent you, since she's a master at those sorts of hoops, but something tells me it was Colonel Hansen. Am I right? Am I?"

Ritchie ignored that question. She glanced at her tablet, totally unnecessarily. She had memorized all of her notes during the flight, but it was nice to have an excuse to break eye contact with the always over-eager Keller. "You worked with Colonel Devereux as part of your independent study. Is that correct?"

"Yeah, and I bet she's madder than anyone that I ended up here," Keller said, sitting back in her chair with her arms crossed. "I really trashed my potential in her eyes, I'm sure. I was supposed to achieve great heights. But you know, I don't think I really threw that away or whatever. I just traded it. I got you what you needed to move ahead. I'm sure you'll make it more than worth what I gave up. In the end."

Great. More talk about Ritchie's bright future. It was more than a little creepy, thinking of these two patients in an observational center who were meant to be working on their mental health issues, choosing instead to spend their time focusing on her.

Keller seemed to sense that she hadn't answered the question the way Ritchie wanted, and she sat forward and folded her hands on the table, mirroring Ritchie's posture. "Yes, I knew Colonel Devereux well. I worked with her daily for the entire semester and change that I was at the Oymyakon Foreign Service Academy. I found her to be a fine officer, stern but fair. She had high standards, but she provided me with everything I needed to achieve those standards. There, how's that?"

"Did she ever talk to you about political matters?" Ritchie asked.

"Did you finally figure out that she doesn't like you?" Keller asked, eyes widening with pretend shock. "Don't take it personally. I'm from a space station, too. With diligent effort both to schoolwork and to always saying the right sort of things, you can change her opinion of you. She just has to see you as a tool she can use, an asset in her plans for the future of the Union of Free Worlds. If you're useful, she can overlook little defects like a lowly birth."

"So she talked to you about her plans?" Ritchie asked. She squeezed her hands together more tightly, hoping she didn't let any of her sudden eagerness show in her voice.

"Isn't it common knowledge?" Keller asked. "Not that I think she's right about any of it, of course. But no one knows better than you where my interests lie."

"In alien cultures," Ritchie said.

"The more alien the better," Keller said, rubbing her hands together. "They don't give me much to work with here yet, but they will. It's just like with Devereux, really. If you say what they want to hear and excel at every task they set before you, if you really know how to jump through all their hoops and show yourself to be a useful asset, why, things usually start to roll your way. I'll have looser restrictions and more privileges in no time."

"If you are playing the game the way the counselors and staff here at the center want it to be played, why did you contrive to meet up with Cadmar Weld?" Ritchie asked.

Keller all but hooted in delight. "You heard about that? What am I talking about? Of course you did! And you thought it was about you? Come, now, Cadet Ritchie. You were never this full of yourself before."

"I don't know. I hear a lot of people have eyes on my future," Ritchie said.

"Ha, sounds like Weld," Keller said. "Not that we talked about you. I've just been reading his counselor's notes from their sessions together. He's very interesting, former Cadet Weld. And no offense, Fitz, but he's a total bad ass. He takes everything they throw at him and just keeps coming back for more. All right, I admit it, I was crushing on him a little bit. Just a little bit! But I *had* to meet him. You know how it is," Keller said.

Ritchie bit her lip to keep from frowning. Keller seemed a lot more manic than she had before, if that was possible. Were they giving her something that made her this way?

And why would Fitz possibly take offense to what she had to say about Weld? Ritchie just managed to resist the urge to glance back at him. They could talk about it later on the shuttle.

"Weld seems to think quite highly of you as well," Ritchie said. "In fact, he thought you'd be better at this job I'm doing now than I am."

"That's not what he said," Keller said, firmly shaking his head.

"Were you listening in?" Ritchie asked.

"No," Keller said, then gave her a wicked grin. "Not *yet*. But I know Weld, and that's not what he would say."

"What would he say?" Ritchie asked.

"Nothing to do with what's going on here today. But he would totally say that I should be the one taking up your father's mantle," Keller said, still grinning. "Please, don't feel bad. But it makes sense. You've turned your back on your father's work for years now. I mean, I get why, I promise you I get why, Ritchie. But you did turn away from it, and I didn't. I'm ahead of you now when it comes to understanding these aliens. Maybe not the yuffids specifically, but the most alien of species, definitely."

"I'm glad you understand where I'm coming from," Ritchie said, trying to project all the warmth she had never really felt for Keller. "But I confess I never understood you. Why would you be so interested in learning these things?"

"It's the hardest course of study, isn't it? There's nothing harder, nothing where the stakes of getting it wrong are higher. And I've always wanted to be the best of the best."

"That's it, then? Just for the accolades? No actual goal about what you wanted to achieve with these various alien species?" Ritchie asked.

"With? No, not with," Keller said. Some of the exuberance had leaked out of her and she was almost introspective now. "Colonel Devereux isn't wrong about what's best for the Union of Free Worlds. Not everyone can be a part of it. But that doesn't mean we don't have something to gain from exploiting other species."

"Exploiting?" Ritchie repeated. That was the last word she had expected to come out of Keller's mouth.

"Well, sure," Keller said. "And you're a fool if you think your father wasn't after the exact same thing."

Ritchie sensed Fitz behind her, tensing up like he was going to charge the table again. Ritchie held up a hand, hoping he took the hint without her having to turn and actually stare him down. Then she said to Keller, "my father was *not* looking to exploit alien species. I know that for a fact."

"You may have been his daughter, but I'm his disciple," Keller said with a shrug. "I think I know him just a little better than you do."

"Isn't this off topic?" Fitz asked from behind her.

"Aren't you supposed to observe and not speak?" Keller shot back at him.

"No," Fitz said with a scoff.

"Yes, you are. You're just here to back Cadet Ritchie up. Sorry, Acting Diplomat Ritchie," Keller said, then gave Ritchie what seemed to be a sincerely apologetic look. Like Ritchie actually cared about her temporary title.

"We're a team," Fitz said. "We're here to talk to you about some of the things you hinted at while you were still at school with us. We're not here to talk about Ritchie's father."

"Of course you'd say that," Keller said with an exaggerated eye roll. Then she leaned forward, catching both of Ritchie's hands in hers and whispering to her across the table, as if there were any possibility that Fitz wouldn't hear. "It *is* about your father. And about you. There are things you don't know. And just between friends, Fitz is part of the world that doesn't want you to know them. I know you trust him with all your heart, and it's going to destroy you when he really does betray you. Speaking friend to friend, I just had to try to warn you, even though I know you're not ready to hear it."

"Hear what, Sidonie?" Ritchie asked, holding her hand up again to signal Fitz not to interrupt.

But Keller had suddenly gone quiet. Ritchie even looked back over her shoulder to see if Fitz was putting a death glare on her, but he was standing with his arms crossed, staring glassily at a random spot on the floor. Like he couldn't bear to listen any further.

"Sidonie?" Ritchie asked again. Keller was blinking back tears now.

"I'm so sad for you," she said. "And now our time is up. I have to go."

"Tell me what you wanted to say," Ritchie said, and now she was the one clutching at Keller's hands.

But Keller slipped away, shaking her head regretfully, as she backed towards the door. "I'm so sorry, Murdina. I know how it hurt you, what I did to you. I didn't mean to hurt you, but I guess I did. But it's nothing compared to what you're going to feel when Fitz betrays you. And he will. In fact, he already has."

"Keller," Ritchie said, but she was already gone out the far door.

Never in a million years would Ritchie entertain the thought that Fitz had, or ever would, betray her. Not when the person telling her so was Keller.

But Weld had said something too, about keeping secrets. And Fitz hadn't exactly denied it.

Ritchie turned to confront Fitz. He tried to take a step back, as if her look was hitting him like a blow, but promptly ran up against the wall behind him.

"Not here, Ritchie," he said.

Trust him to find the one thing to say that would keep her quiet. She just nodded, gathered up her tablet, and marched out of the room. The two waiting members of the observational center staff ran to keep up with her as she swept back down the hall to the shuttle bay.

As much as she wanted to talk to Fitz, it was nothing compared to her desire to get out of that white uniform. She went directly to her cabin and yanked the insignia off of the breast of her tunic. By the time the shuttle had left the space station's gravity-simulating spin behind, she was back in her familiar shades of brown school colors.

Only then did she emerge from her cabin.

Fitz was waiting for her, also in his school uniform. He had two bulbs of coffee in his hands and sent one sailing across the common room to her.

"What was she talking about?" Ritchie demanded, catching the bulb by impulse. She didn't want it. Fitz just toyed with his own bulb, not looking at her. "Fitz?" she said.

"I've already told you I'll never betray you," he said, not looking up.

"I meant the part where she said you already did. It felt like she was referring to something specific. Any thoughts?" Her stomach was like a hot, dense rock as she waited for him to answer.

"I'm not entirely sure," he said slowly. "I can only think of one thing she might mean."

"And that is?"

"Last year, the day Jeger died, I told you I heard her and Bale arguing on the flight deck," he said. Ritchie nodded, rolling the warm coffee bulb between her hands as if it were some sort of stress toy. "What I didn't tell you is what they were arguing about."

"No, you did. You said it was about her training technique," Ritchie said. "That she was too hard on the cadets."

"True," Fitz said, "but that wasn't all of it. Jeger was talking about a coming war, and how we had to be prepared for it."

"We always have to be prepared," Ritchie said.

"Yes, but she was feeling a lot more urgency than that," Fitz said. "It wasn't some hypothetical to her, like maybe we'd have a border skirmish somewhere or have to put down another aspiring colonizer like Loindetu. She really thought that something was coming, and she was there at Oymyakon to prepare us all to meet this... whatever. Bale wasn't convinced she was right. But he didn't say she was wrong either."

"But Keller said it was something about my father," Ritchie said.

"That's why I didn't mention it before," Fitz said. He still wasn't looking up at her, and she wasn't sure what that meant.

"Tell me," she said.

"Jeger thought this coming war somehow was set in motion by what happened with the yuffids," he said.

"She thought we were going to go to war with the yuffids?" Ritchie asked.

"It wasn't clear, and I never got a chance to ask her," he said. He swallowed hard and gave her the shortest of glances through the tangles of his hair. "I never asked Bale about it, either. I probably should have. I think he knew what she meant. He might even have known why she thought what she thought. Like, what proof she had, if any."

"He's at university now," Ritchie said. "He's a bit more reachable than Jeger."

"You want me to ask him about it?" Fitz asked. He sounded eager for her to give him some sort of task, and Ritchie felt her anger slip away.

It was a little thing, a detail that wasn't relevant to what they had been investigating at the time. But that was precisely the sort of little thing that Keller would pounce on and blow all out of proportion. But was it just Keller not wanting Ritchie to have other friends? Or was she specifically trying to drive a wedge between her and Fitz?

Ritchie sighed and rubbed at her head. Lack of sleep wasn't helping her think clearly, and her feelings were in terrible disarray. She needed to shift the attention off herself, even if just for a minute. "This was hard for you, wasn't it? Just standing there, nothing to do but listen?" she said.

He shrugged, but he also mustered a grin. "Maybe Colonel Hansen just gave us each the task that matched our skills."

"Yeah," Ritchie said, but she couldn't return his grin. She really felt like whatever the colonel had wanted her to achieve, she had failed to achieve it. She hadn't learned anything, but she had so much whirling around in her head now she doubted she'd get a restful night's sleep for the rest of the semester. If ever.

"Ritchie, I'm sorry," Fitz said.

"For what?" Ritchie asked.

"For being maybe too excited about this assignment. You told me once that you didn't necessarily plan on becoming a diplomat, and I flat out forgot. You would've preferred for our roles to be reversed?"

"No," Ritchie admitted. "I mean, you're not wrong. I don't think I have what it takes to be a diplomat. And please don't argue with me about that. I really can't have another discussion today about my mythic potential."

"Okay," Fitz agreed. "Personally, I think you have what it takes to achieve any position you strive for. Because the qualities that define you aren't confined to just one job."

"Yeah," Ritchie said, not quite able to let that compliment sink in. She just couldn't process any more assessments of herself. Not even from him.

"I just always assumed we'd be working together. That's why this all felt so right to me," he said.

Ritchie didn't know what to say to that. There were so many reasons why that might not be their future, so many things that could drive them apart. Up until just that morning, she would've said her growing feelings that refused to be tamped back down were the largest obstacle.

But there was something else. She felt it now, but looking back, she sensed it had been there for some time. There was something going on with Fitz, something that was like a wall between them. Or more like a force field. She couldn't see it or even really feel it, but she knew it was there.

And there was nothing she could do about it.

Not for a minute did she believe Keller when she said that Fitz would betray her. Never. But she also knew that whatever was standing between her and Fitz, only he could tear down.

But she didn't know if he even wanted to.

"We're not kids anymore," she said after far too much silence had stretched out between them.

"No," he agreed.

Then she went into her cabin, and she didn't see him again until they reached Oymyakon.

24

IT TOOK the shuttle a day to get back to Oymyakon, and then two days to get back down through the atmosphere. Two long days where Fitz hid in his room, terrified that Ritchie would demand more answers that he couldn't give her.

But she never did. And that didn't make him feel better at all.

He still didn't know if she had been listening to his last words to Weld. That was maddening all on its own. It's not like he could ask. If she truly hadn't heard, that would be the very worst thing he could do.

He wished he could go back in time and force himself to keep his mouth shut.

He also wished he could go back and get just five minutes alone with Keller. Not to throttle her, although that was a temptation, but to figure out just what she was accusing him of. Because there was no way she knew what had really happened. But she must know something. She was stirring up trouble, that was par for the course with her, but getting this close to the truth? Not even the Berwegers with their preternatural skills could do that. And if she was making canny guesses, she seemed to be sharing her theories with Weld. Or else why would Weld have said what he did?

But no one alive knew what she seemed to be hinting at, except for

Fitz and his father. And Fitz would sooner believe he had told her himself and somehow forgotten than that his father had revealed anything to anyone.

For the first time in his life, he longed to see his father. Not to talk to him, just to observe him for a bit, to see if he was still himself or if he was unraveling somehow. But that was impossible until the next semester break.

The shuttle landing was all too reminiscent of the departure days before. A momentary break in the clouds disappeared before they were quite through it, and the winds were horrific, throwing the shuttle around like a toy on high seas. He and Ritchie hadn't spoken as they buckled into their flight chairs, but after the fourth time they had plummeted stomach-churningly through an air pocket, he had found her hand in his. Had he reached out for her, or the other way around?

He didn't know, and he didn't care. He just held tight to as much of her as he could touch for as long as she allowed him to.

At last they were within the cavernous shelter of the underground flight deck, and the whine of the engines died away. Fitz unbuckled his harness and turned to head back to his cabin to retrieve his things, but before he could take a step, Ritchie was in his arms, hugging him tight.

"Hey, we're down safe," he said, patting her back. "It's okay, Ritchie."

"I hate everything," she said against his shoulder. "I hate everyone who's trying to control our lives from afar. I hate your dad and I hate the Berwegers and I hate Devereux and all her faceless, unnamed cronies throughout the Union. But I really, really need to not hate you too."

"Ritchie, I'm never going to give you reason to. Okay?" he said.

"I wish..." she started to say, but didn't finish.

She didn't have to. It was in the anguish of her voice, what she had been about to say.

He doubted she had slept at all the entire flight back. She had been stewing over everything that had been said, turning it over and over in her mind without asking him about any of it.

He tried to look at her face to face, but she just stepped away from him, wiping tears from her eyes, and went to get her bag out of her cabin.

By the time he had his, she was already at the bottom of the ramp. Moreau was there, hugging her with one arm as she brandished a cane with the other. Wyss was hovering awkwardly beside them, but saw Fitz at the top of the ramp and gave him a nervous grin.

"Guess what?" he said as Moreau and Ritchie stepped apart.

"We have the murder weapon," Moreau said.

"Hey!" Wyss objected.

"You found it?" Fitz asked. "Please tell me it's going to seal someone's fate. Please, we need a win here." Oh, how he needed a win.

"Go ahead. Tell him," Moreau said to Wyss.

"Well, it's a ceremonial dagger—" Wyss started.

"—belonging to the Berweger family," Moreau interjected.

"Which we know because of the family seal on the hilt," Wyss said.

"But it's also been well documented as a family artifact for centuries," Moreau said.

"They're just going to say it was stolen," Ritchie said.

"Yeah, that's what they're saying," Moreau said, but there was still a happy gleam to hers and Wyss's eyes.

"Go on," Fitz said.

"The box which this stolen dagger belonged in was in Colonel Devereux's office," Wyss said, and Ritchie sucked in a breath.

"I saw that box!" she said, her hands over her mouth in shock.

"We figured you did since it was right there by the photo," Moreau said, nudging Ritchie joshingly with her shoulder.

"Is that enough to tie Devereux to it, though?" Fitz asked.

"Maybe not, but her DNA is all over the knife," Wyss said. "I mean, the parts that aren't covered in Voet's DNA."

"Just hers?" Ritchie asked. "Voet was killed by a number of people. I'm absolutely sure of that."

"She might bring up a few other names if she's looking to make a deal," Wyss said.

"I wouldn't bet on it," Fitz said. "In fact, I rather doubt she'll live to see trial."

"That's grim," Moreau scowled at him. "This is a win here."

"Devereux gone from the academy is a good thing," Ritchie agreed. "But the Berwegers are still here, right?"

"With no catacombs to meet in, and no colonel ready to cover up any of their misdeeds," Moreau said. "They've been keeping a very low profile while you two were away."

"That's something, I suppose," Fitz said. "But their parents? I'm guessing they aren't even being accused of anything."

"No, but Colonel Hansen says they've been keeping a low profile as well," Wyss said. "Whatever they were planning, they've put it on a back burner for now."

"Yeah, but for how long?" Fitz asked.

"Hopefully long enough for us to get to the bottom of it," Moreau said. "What do you think our extra work assignments are for?"

"What are they for?" Fitz asked.

"Colonel Hansen trusts us," Wyss said. "The same can't be said for nearly anyone else in the Union. Like, anywhere."

"He's going to fight a fifth column all on his lonesome with nothing but the help of four cadets?" Fitz asked.

"Five," Moreau said. "Sokolov is part of the team."

"Well, that's good news," Ritchie said, with a lot more optimism than Fitz felt. "I really need a proper shower. You know, the kind that only happens in the presence of gravity."

"We can meet up in the library later," Wyss said. "Sokolov is off duty after dinner, and we have some more material from Hansen to comb over."

"Sounds like a plan," Ritchie said. Then she turned and walked away, Moreau limping along beside her with the help of her cane.

"We agreed not to pepper you with questions straight off the shuttle, but that's probably going to happen the minute we're all in the library," Wyss warned him.

"Good to know," Fitz said. "In the meantime, I think I'm going to get one of those shower in the presence of gravity things myself."

Wyss walked with him back to the main school building, but his attention was focused on the tablet in his hands, as usual. Fitz didn't mind. It had been two days since their interview with Keller, but a friendly silence was still such a balm to his soul.

He and Wyss parted ways in the library, Wyss heading back to their meeting room and Fitz heading down to his room in the barracks. He had just tossed his bag on his bunk and was digging through his locker for a clean towel when he sensed someone standing in the doorway behind him.

He really wished he didn't have to turn around. He could smell the musky aroma of a Berweger even across the space of the room. He wasn't ready for this conversation.

But there was no avoiding it.

"Finn," he said, still looking for that towel. Was it possible he had no clean towels?

"Looking for this?" Finn asked, reaching over Fitz's shoulder to pull a neatly folded towel down from the top shelf.

"Indeed, I am," Fitz said, and kicked his locker door shut. "So, here to gloat?"

"To gloat?" Finn asked, as if in surprise. "Didn't you and your little girlfriend win the day?"

"You're free. Your parents are free. Most of the conspirators are free and have been for decades. The only person who isn't free is Devereux, and frankly she feels more like a ritual sacrifice than poor Voet," Fitz said.

"Yes, poor Voet," Finn said. "Don't feel bad about his remains. There was nothing more to be learned from them, and he's at rest now."

"If you say so," Fitz said.

"I heard about your little trip," Finn said, leaning against the locker door in a studied casual pose. "Ritchie and you, diplomat and guardian."

"Acting diplomat and acting guardian," Fitz corrected him. Finn just shrugged.

"You two are close," he said.

"Oh, are you upset I didn't respond to your 'girlfriend' crack before? We're professionals. Fellow cadets. I don't feel any need to be super defensive about that. Because we have nothing to hide."

"'We'?" Finn repeated, raising one perfectly sculpted eyebrow.

"We," Fitz repeated. But he felt the sudden strong need not to look Finn in the eyes. As Finn so clearly wanted him to. He was even touching Fitz's shoulder now, as if they were buddies. As if he were lending Fitz some comfort.

"I see what you see in her," Finn said.

"I don't think you do," Fitz said, then silently cursed himself. He should not be encouraging this conversation at all.

But Finn just laughed. "Yes, I see it. And I know I shouldn't tease you. But not because you think you're both 'professionals'." He made little air quotes and laughed again. But then he leaned in to whisper close to Fitz's ear. "No, I know what's really keeping you apart is secrets. Or rather, one big secret."

There was just no avoiding this anymore, was there? Fitz felt anger bubbling up inside him, but immediately swallowed it back down. That was just the sort of reckless response that Finn could use to his advantage.

Fitz pulled away from Finn, but only made it half a step back before colliding with the edge of his bunk. Finn had him, quite literally, cornered.

He kept his eyes on the floor, not looking at Finn, and tried to silently will him to leave.

But if Finn really could read minds, he ignored that directive. "That's why I laughed at your little 'we' there. Because I know Ritchie, and her heart and mind are as open as the prairies of your homeworld of Buennagel. That planet she so longs to see again, and yet is terrified to go back to. Has she ever told you how homesick she is? Probably not."

Fitz felt his hands clenching into tight fists. But even if he could land a blow, it would achieve nothing.

And, damn him, he really wanted to know what else Finn had to say. If only he would stop dancing around it.

"You want me to just tell you, don't you?" Finn asked, and Fitz finally felt his control slip. He looked up into Finn's eyes, letting all of this anger show. "You do. I can tell," Finn said. "You want to know what I know. Ask me. Go ahead, ask me. Ask me to tell you what I know."

"Tell me," Fitz said, just barely able to grind the words out.

Finn's eyes were laughing at him. Then he leaned in to whisper close to Fitz's ear again. "I know what happened that day. And I know what *didn't* happen that day." Then he stood back again to look Fitz in the eyes. "You know what I mean. I'm talking about what you failed to do, and the blame that Ritchie has carried in her heart ever since. How could you do that to her, Fitz? She doesn't deserve that."

Fitz blinked hard and wrenched his eyes away. But it was too late. There was nothing more for Finn to learn from him. He had it all.

"Don't worry, buddy. I'm not going to say a word," Finn said, clasping him on his shoulders like they were old comrades at arms. "I would never."

He gave Fitz's arms one last squeeze, then turned to leave. But he stopped in the doorway to pause for effect. Then he turned his head just enough for the light from the corridor to outline his perfect profile. Only then did he say, "Unless I thought she needed to hear it. Does she need to hear it? Fitz? Maybe it would be easier for her, hearing it from me."

But he didn't wait for an answer. He disappeared from the doorway, his big dramatic exit.

Fitz dropped the towel and ran after him. Finn was only a few steps down the hall and turned back with genuine surprise on his face that only deepened when Fitz grabbed his shoulder, spun him around, and pinned him with one forearm across his neck to the tiled wall.

"Shackleton Fitz IV, I had no idea you had it in you," Finn said. His eyes were laughing, but his voice was a bit hoarse. Fitz leaned in on his arm a little harder.

"You will not say a word," Fitz hissed at him.

"Of course not," Finn said, holding up his hands in surrender. "But thanks for the confirmation. It was just a hunch. Feena said I was crazy. But I could see it all so clearly every time the two of you were together."

"You still don't understand, do you, Berweger," Fitz said, and leaned in on his arm again. Finn made a choking sound, half in jest, but half in real discomfort. "You're going to keep that secret. You're not going to let even a hint of it pass your lips to anyone. Not even your sister."

"I'm not afraid of you," Finn said, his voice raspy.

"No? Well, how about my father?" Fitz said.

"Do you really think he'll have your back?" Finn asked with a hoarse attempt at a laugh.

"No, never," Fitz said, and backed away from Finn. Finn rubbed at his throat, once again trying to play off his response as a joke, but Fitz knew that Finn knew how close Fitz had just come to really choking the life out of him. He waited for Finn to finish his little show before saying, "you've got it all backwards, you see. I'm not saying my father is protecting my secret. Like he ever would. I'm saying I'm covering his."

Finn's eyes narrowed skeptically, but Fitz didn't give him a chance to respond.

"Ritchie didn't ruin my life. My father did that, by making me keep just one little secret. For the good of the Union, of course. I never even think about what I know, because what if someone saw it there in my eyes? I don't get close to anyone, not even Ritchie. Especially not Ritchie. But there was no hiding it from you, was there? Well, now you get to join me in this hell of never letting it slip. Because if you breathe a word of it to anyone, I promise you he will know. And I don't think even your parents can protect you from the wraith of my father."

Finn's face was still impassive, so Fitz leaned in on his arm just a little harder. "Tell me, do you think I'm bragging?"

"No," Finn said. "I won't say a word."

"I don't need your promise," Fitz said, and turned away, but Finn laughed at him as he walked back to his room.

"Don't you see it doesn't even matter what I say?" he said to Fitz's back. "It's a miracle you've kept a secret from her this long. What happens if she decides to start digging? How long before she knows? And what happens to your friendship then? You will have torpedoed your whole life for nothing. She may trust you now, but that can change just like that." He snapped his fingers, but still Fitz didn't look back.

He crossed his room to pick up his discarded towel, but then waited a minute before heading to the showers. He wanted to be sure Finn was gone.

It wasn't even like he needed Finn taunting him to know that his friendship with Ritchie was coming to an end. He could feel the storm just over the horizon. It made his joints ache, like he had old battle wounds. But there was nothing he could do to head it off.

Because he knew in his heart what Ritchie had only half said in the shuttle.

*I wish I could believe you.*

But she couldn't. He already knew it. How much longer before she knew it, too? How much longer could he keep her in the dark?

Fitz threw the towel around his neck and headed for the showers. At least he and Ritchie still had one thing in common. They both hated everything but each other. That was all he had to hold into. And he would hold on tight, for as long as he could.

For as long as she would hold on to it with him.

# CHECK OUT BOOK FOUR

The Ritchie and Fitz Sci-Fi Murder Mysteries will continue with Book Four, Death on the Summit.

The cadets of the Oymyakon Foreign Service Academy know more than most about challenging environments. They experience one every day just while crossing their campus. Their planet barely ranks as habitable on the best of days. But now the third and fourth year cadets face even harsher conditions, climbing to heights nearly at the edge of space and totally within the heart of Oymyakon's ever-present storms.

Murdina Ritchie relishes the opportunity to test her mettle in ways she never could back home in the stable, comfortable environment of a space station. Shackleton Fitz IV delights in freedom from campus life and distance from the growing rumors of political turmoil in the Union of Free Worlds, if only for a few days.

Then a fellow cadet falls to her death. No one in the camp thinks this an accident. But with no way down off the mountain until the storm passes, they all live with the knowledge that a murderer lurks among them, possibly planning to kill again.

Ritchie and Fitz face death all the time. But if a human killer fails to end them, the planet itself just might finish the job. Staying alive calls on them to apply everything they've learned at the academy. But will it be enough?

Death on the Summit, book four in the Ritchie and Fitz Sci-Fi Murder Mystery series.

# NEW SERIES: THE FORGOTTEN PLANET

Coming soon from Ratatoskr Press Books, the new YA sci-fi series *The Forgotten Planet* starts with book 1: *Raiding the Forgotten Derelict*.

**History sleeps beneath them all, but only she sees it.**

Lafayette Eloi always knew her parents thought differently from others. They kept their books buried beneath her mother's house. They spoke an old language in the dead of night, whispering behind closed doors and bolted shutters. She grew up in a village where no one was related to her, and she never knew why.

Then, after her mother died, her father came to fetch her. Now she and her mother's dog assist her father in his work. The work discussed in whispers in the dark. The work that had cost Lafayette so much all her young life.

But now she learns just how much her father's work means to their entire world. Only no one knows anything about it. Only her father. And only Lafayette.

Because the work that consumed her father's entire life and her mother's too now nibbles at the fringe's of Lafayette's own life. And she cannot refuse its call.

*Raiding the Forgotten Derelict,* first book in the new YA sci-fu series *The Forgotten Planet,* available in September 2024 from Ratatoskr Press Books.

# COMPLETE SERIES: THE RITCHIE AND FITZ SCI-FI MURDER MYSTERIES

*The Ritchie and Fitz Sci-Fi Murder Mysteries* starts with *Murder on the Intergalactic Railway*.

For Murdina Ritchie, acceptance at the Oymyakon Foreign Service Academy means one last chance at her dream of becoming a diplomat for the Union of Free Worlds. For Shackleton Fitz IV, it represents his last chance not to fail out of military service entirely.

Strange that fate should throw them together now, among the last group of students admitted after the start of the semester. They had once shared the strongest of friendships. But that all ended a long time ago.

But when an insufferable but politically important woman turns up murdered, the two agree to put their differences aside and work together to solve the case.

Because the murderer might strike again. But more importantly, solving a murder would just have to impress the dour colonel who clearly thinks neither of them belong at his academy.

*Murder on the Intergalactic Railway*, the first book in *The Ritchie and Fitz Sci-Fi Murder Mysteries*.

# COMPLETE SERIES: THE TRAVELS OF SCOUT SHANNON

The complete six-book series *The Travels of Scout Shannon* begin with book one, *Under Falling Skies*.

Scout Shannon's whole family died the day the Space Farers dropped an asteroid on their domed city. Now she lives alone, out in the wild with only her dogs for company. She prefers it that way.

But Scout finds herself at a crossroads. One road leads back to a quiet life snug under the protective dome of a city. The other road leads to a life in the rebellion, a life of adventure and excitement but also danger. Dare she try to find the rebels hiding in the hills?

Then a chance encounter with a stranger from the other side of the galaxy threatens to derail what remains of Scout's life. The entire galaxy awaits her, if she survives the next four days.

*Under Falling Skies*, a young adult science fiction novel, set on a remote planet with a distinctly Old West feel. For fans of gunslinging women and young girl assassins. And dogs.

*Under Falling Skies,* the first book in *The Travels of Scout Shannon,* available everywhere now.

# SCI-FI SERIAL PODCAST!

Check out my new monthly podcast of serialized science fiction: THE TALES OF THE CHAI MAKHANI TRIO!

Elyot loathes the massive Commonwealth ships that hover menacingly over his home world of Adghal. He hates the Commonwealth enforcers who harass the populace even more. But with his mother missing and presumed dead, Elyot keeps his head down and strives to avoid notice. And he succeeds until the day two strangers enter his life...

New episodes of this sci-fi serial drop every 1st of the month.

Now streaming on all major podcast platforms. Also available in eBook and print everywhere books or sold. For a complete episode listing, check out the page on my website.

# ALSO FROM KATE MACLEOD

Love heists and capers? Then check out my new series, *The Vic Harper Capers*. The action starts with the novella THE THIRD POLE JOB.

Vic Harper and her gang retired wealthy from their life of thievery and heists. Whether in a luxury condo overlooking the river in Minneapolis or in a modernist mansion built into the side of a mountain in Colorado, life comes easy now.

Perhaps too easy.

When an old friend asks for a favor his niece, Vic and her mentor Chase Woodward leap at the chance to relieve a little of the boredom. But a quick bit of B&E in a wealthy suburb of Chicago leads to an even greater challenge.

The prize? Nothing much. Just the opportunity to level a playing field for their friend's niece.

But the heist? May prove to be their toughest ever. Because to get to the prize, they'll have to climb a mountain.

And not just any mountain. Their prize waits on the summit of Mount Everest.

THE THIRD POLE JOB, the first novella in *The Vic Harper Capers*. For those who love capers, heists and other impossible missions.

# ALSO FROM RATATOSKR PRESS

Also from Ratatoskr Press, *The Witches Three Cozy Mystery Series* by Cate Martin, a mix of mystery and magic that begins with Book 1: *Charm School*.

Amanda Clarke thinks of herself as perfectly ordinary in every way. Just a small-town girl who serves breakfast all day in a little diner nestled next to the highway, nothing but dairy farms for miles around. She fits in there.

But then an old woman she never met dies, and Amanda was named in her will. Now Amanda packs a bag and heads to the big city, to Miss Zenobia Weekes' Charm School for Exceptional Young Ladies. And it's not in just any neighborhood. No, she finds herself on Summit Avenue in St. Paul, a street lined with gorgeous old houses, the former homes of lumber barons, railroad millionaires, even the writer F. Scott Fitzgerald. Why, Amanda can practically hear the jazz music still playing across the decades.

Scratch that. The music really, literally, still plays in the backyard of the charm school. Because the house stretches across time itself. Without a witch to protect this tear in the fabric of the world, anything can spill over. Like music.

Or like murder.

The complete series is out now, and it all starts with *Charm School*.

# FREE EBOOK!

Like exclusive, free content?

To get two prequel short stories to THE RITCHIE AND FITZ SCI-FI MURDER MYSTERIES as well as a bonus prequel novelette to the completed six-book series THE TRAVELS OF SCOUT SHANNON, signup for my monthly newsletter at KateMacLeodWrites.com.

Thank you!

# ABOUT THE AUTHOR

Photograph © 2016 Jonathan Conklin

Kate MacLeod has written stories which have appeared in *Analog, Strange Horizons* and *Mythic Delirium*, among other places. She is also the author of two young adult science fictions series: *The Travels of Scout Shannon*, and *The Ritchie and Fitz Sci-Fi Murder Mysteries*. She also contributes to a serialized science fiction podcast called *The Tales of the Chai Makhani Trio*. She currently lives in Minneapolis, Minnesota.

Find out more about the author and sign up for her newsletter at KateMacLeodWrites.com.

# ALSO BY KATE MACLEOD

**Novels**

**The Slums of the Solar System:**

Mitwa

The Mars of Malcontents

The Whole World for Each

Books 1-3 Box Set

**The Travels of Scout Shannon:**

Under Falling Skies

In Quaking Hills

Among Treacherous Stars

Against Impassable Barriers

Over Freezing Altitudes

At Galactic Central

The Travels of Scout Shannon Books 1-3

The Travels of Scout Shannon Books 4-6

The Travels of Scout Shannon Books 1-6

**The Ritchie and Fitz Sci-Fi Murder Mysteries:**

Murder on the Intergalactic Railway

Murder in the Skies

Body in the Catacombs

Death on the Summit

An Undiplomatic Murder

A Lethal Betrayal

**The Forgotten Planet**

Raiding the Forgotten Derelict (Forthcoming September 2024)

**Sci-Fi Novellas**

The Intergenerational Tree

I Rise into a Daybreak

**Caper Novellas**

The Third Pole Job

The Twelve Days of Christmas Job

**10-Story Collections**

Tales of Blood and Ink

Tales of Old Gods and New

**5-Story Collections**

Tales from Heian-Kyo and Others

Tales from the Edges and Ends

Tales from Forgotten Days

Tales from Ancient and Future Times

Tales from Across Space